THE MEMORY OF US

A Novel

SCARLETT VALE

Content Note

This novel contains depictions of emotional abuse and controlling behavior (past), references to intimate partner violence, panic responses, emotional flashbacks, and scenes of sensuality. Reader discretion is advised.

For everyone who believes in love worth waiting for.

Author's Foreword

Every story begins with a spark — a moment of inspiration that refuses to let go. *The Memory of Us* was born from my fascination with the way memory shapes love, and how the people we hold in our hearts can become more vivid than reality itself.

Writing this novel has been a labor of love, and I could not have done it without the incredible people in my life who believed in this story — and in me.

To my wonderful, brilliant, and handsome husband — thank you for being my anchor, my sounding board, and my greatest champion. Your unwavering support and love made this book possible. You are my own love story come to life.

To my amazing son Gunner — you inspire me every day with your curiosity, your laughter, and your boundless heart. Being your mom is the greatest adventure of my life.

To my friends and family — thank you for your encouragement, your patience during my writing marathons, and for always asking how the book was coming along. Your support means the world to me.

And to you, dear reader — thank you for choosing to spend your time with Lucian and Elena. Stories only truly come alive when they find their way into someone's heart. I hope this one finds a home in yours.

With gratitude and love,

Scarlett Vale

PART ONE

THE AWAKENING

"We do not remember days, we remember moments."
— Cesare Pavese

CHAPTER ONE

ELENA

THE OCEAN LOOKED NOTHING like she remembered. Which was strange, Elena Ward thought, given that she had never been here before.

She stood at the edge of the weathered boardwalk, hands tucked deep into the pockets of her wool coat, watching the Atlantic fold itself over and over against the shore in shades of pewter and slate. The morning light was thin and reluctant. A salt-laced wind pushed against her, insistent and biting. She told herself it was just the wind. Not nerves. Not fear.

Fear was what she had left behind in Boston.

Camden's Rise was supposed to be a fresh start. Clean lines. New palette. Distance from everything she had fled six months ago — the apartment that had never quite felt like hers, the job that had bled the art out of her, and the man who had spent three years teaching her to apologize before anyone asked her to.

She had, before all of that, been the kind of woman who read poetry on her lunch breaks and stole hours in old libraries because she liked the smell. Who laughed loudly at her own bad jokes. Who could not pass a secondhand bookshop without going in. She was still looking, six months out, for where that woman had gone.

Adam. Even thinking his name sent a ripple through her chest. She pushed it down the way her therapist had taught her — acknowledge, observe, let it pass. She was seven hundred miles from Boston. She was free.

So why did she feel, standing here, as if she were returning to something rather than running from it?

Déjà vu, she told herself firmly. The brain's way of misfiring.

"Okay," she murmured, watching a gull wheel against the pewter sky. "Let's not have an existential crisis before coffee. We have standards."

To her right, rising above the harbor with the bearing of something that had once been grand and hadn't forgotten it, stood the hotel.

The Rowan. Four stories of native stone and weathered cedar, scaffolding clinging to its eastern facade. Tall arched windows staring out at the harbor with the patient gaze of a building that had seen everything. Wide verandas. Balusters carved with maritime motifs.

Elena loved it immediately.

She pulled her phone from her pocket. 8:03 a.m. The email from the hotel's owner had read: *We like to start early around here. Brains are fresher before the tourists wake up and start demanding lobster rolls.* Elena had liked her immediately, sight unseen. Anyone who held opinions about lobster rolls was her kind of person.

Her own brain, however, was not fresh. She had driven up from Boston the night before — four hours on the coastal highway — and slept badly in the rental above the bakery.

Just a job, she told herself, squaring her shoulders against the wind. A big one. A desperately needed one. But still — just a job.

The problem was that fresh starts always came with a silent question attached. *What if I fail at this too?*

The wind gusted, snapping a loose piece of caution tape on the hotel's perimeter fence. Elena turned away from the sea and started walking.

Camden's Rise smelled like wet wood, fresh coffee, and the particular brine of a harbor that had been welcoming fishing boats for two hundred years. People moved slowly here, even in the cold — or perhaps especially in the cold, as if hurrying might offend the deliberate pace of a town that measured time in tides rather than traffic lights. A woman in a cherry-red knit hat nodded at her as she passed. The bell over the café door jingled every few seconds, releasing steam and laughter into the gray morning air.

Up close, The Rowan showed its bones — the original 1882 stonework, the carved balusters worn soft by generations of hands, the tall windows with their graceful arched tops. Someone had loved this building once. Someone was trying to love it again.

Elena stepped around a stack of weathered lumber, ducked under the caution tape, and headed for the open front doors. Inside, the cold thickened into damp chill — old plaster, sawdust, something older seeping from the walls. The foyer was a work in progress: plastic sheeting, ladders, the skeleton of what would be a grand reception desk. Workers' voices echoed down the hall. But even in the disarray, Elena could see what the space wanted to become. The grand staircase swept upward with the kind of generous curve made for descent in a silk gown. Light fell through grimy windows in long golden bars.

Wake up, Elena thought at the building. *I'm here to wake you up.*

"Elena?"

She looked up. A petite woman in her late sixties was hurrying down the staircase, one hand on the padded railing. Short silver hair, sea-glass eyes, a pencil tucked behind one ear. Her face was lined with the kind of wrinkles that came from a lifetime of smiling.

"Mrs. Holloway?"

"Oh, for heaven's sake, call me June." The woman reached the bottom step and opened her arms wide, as if they had known each other for decades rather than only exchanging emails for the past month. "You must be absolutely frozen. Do you need coffee? The contractors drink it like their lives depend on it, which they might, given the hours they keep — but I'm sure I can wrestle a cup away for you."

"I'm okay, thank you." Elena stepped into the hug anyway, surprising herself. June smelled like lemon soap and sawdust and lavender — an unexpectedly comforting combination. "The walk from town warmed me up."

June pulled back and looked at her with the frank, assessing gaze of someone who had lived long enough to recognize deflection when she saw it, and liked you better for attempting it.

"You're younger than I expected."

"I get that a lot." Elena had learned to say it lightly, before anyone else could fill the silence with doubt. Thirty-two was not young, not really — but she had always had one of those faces. The kind that made clients ask for her supervisor. The kind that had let Adam call her lucky to have someone who would take care of her.

Stop thinking about Adam.

"Well, you came highly recommended." June linked her arm through Elena's and began steering her toward the back of the foyer with the comfortable authority of long practice. "And anyone who survived designing that architectural abomination on the Boston waterfront — what was it called? The Glass Hive?"

Elena laughed despite herself. "That was the nickname. The official name was the Meridian Complex, but nobody called it that."

"Dreadful building. All those angles and reflections. Made me seasick just looking at photographs." June patted her arm. "But everyone I spoke to said you fought for every decent design choice in that place. Stood up to the developers when they wanted to cut corners. That's what I need. Someone who will fight for my old girl here."

"Your old girl?"

"The Rowan." June gestured at the building around them with undisguised affection, the way another woman might gesture at a child. "She's been in my family for four generations. My great-great-grandfather built her in 1882.

Shipping money — back when Camden's Rise was a proper working port, not just a pretty place for tourists to buy lighthouse-themed souvenirs."

They passed through a set of double doors into a hallway lined with drop cloths and stacked with building materials. Elena's designer eye registered everything automatically: the original crown molding, mostly intact beneath decades of paint. Wainscoting that would need to be replaced in sections but was salvageable in others. Water damage on the ceiling that spoke of roof problems, hopefully now resolved.

"She was a private home first," June continued, her voice taking on the rhythm of a story told many times and loved with each telling. "Then a boarding house for sailors waiting on ships. Then a proper hotel when the railroad came through. Closed down in the eighties when the fishing industry collapsed and the town hit hard times. I used to sneak in as a girl, when my grandmother still had the keys. Pretend I was a princess in a castle, waiting for my prince to sail into the harbor."

"And now you're bringing her back."

"Trying to." June's voice softened, and for a moment Elena saw something flicker across her face — grief, maybe, or determination, or some complicated braiding of both. "My husband and I — we planned this together. Robert. He passed two years ago. Heart attack, no warning. Just there one moment and gone the next."

"I'm so sorry."

"Don't be. We had forty years of marriage, and he left me with a dream and the resources to make it real. Most people don't get that."

June stopped at another set of doors — taller, more ornate, carved with waves and ships and figures that might have been mermaids or might have been angels, the wood too worn to tell.

"Now. Let me show you why I really hired you."

She pushed the doors open.

Elena's breath stopped in her chest.

The ballroom stretched before her like a held breath. Sixty feet long. Cream-colored silk on the walls, faded and water-stained but still hinting at the hand-painted botanicals beneath — roses, lilies, twining vines. Tall arched windows flooding the space with gray morning light. And at the far end, flanking a marble fireplace, two matching chandeliers. Unlit. Dusty. Their crystal drops dim with decades of neglect.

And unmistakably magnificent.

"Oh," Elena breathed. It was inadequate — laughably, absurdly inadequate — but it was all she had.

"I know." June came to stand beside her. "She takes your breath away, doesn't she? Even like this."

Elena walked deeper into the room, her footsteps echoing. She could see it already — strip the damaged silk, refinish the floors, clean the chandeliers crystal by crystal until they blazed again. This was why she had become a designer. For rooms that held stories in their walls.

"This is where my great-great-grandparents held their wedding reception," June said, joining her in the center of the room. Her voice had gone soft, almost reverent. "And their children after them. And their children after that. My husband proposed to me under that chandelier." She pointed to the one on the right. "Got down on one knee right there, with the sunset coming through those windows and making everything look like it was on fire. I thought I would die of happiness."

Elena felt something shift in her chest — a loosening.

"It must have been beautiful."

"It was. It will be again." June's chin lifted with quiet determination. "I want to see couples dance here again. Make new memories in a room that's full of old ones. Prove that beautiful things can come back to life, if someone loves them enough to try."

Beautiful things can come back to life.

The words landed somewhere Elena had stopped letting words land six months ago.

"I can do this," she said, and meant it completely. "I can bring her back."

June smiled — the satisfied smile of a woman confirming something she already knew. "I know you can. That's why I —"

She stopped.

Elena followed her gaze toward the far doors, where a figure had just appeared.

A man. Tall, broad-shouldered, with the lean angular build of someone who spent more time in libraries than gyms. Gray wool coat over a dark sweater. Hair the color of aged oak, thick and slightly disheveled, as if he had been running his hands through it in thought. He stood in the doorway without moving, his attention fixed on her with a quiet that thinned the air.

His eyes were gray-blue. Storm-colored. They were looking at her the way a man looks at someone he had been told to expect and had not quite believed would arrive.

Her skin prickled. Attraction, yes. But she had known this man for three seconds, and after Adam she did not trust her first impression of any man who looked at her as if she mattered. She pushed the feeling down.

"Lucian!" June's voice broke whatever it was. "Perfect timing. Come meet our designer."

He crossed the ballroom with a stride that was neither hurried nor hesitant.

"Elena Ward," June said, "this is Lucian Calder. He's our historical consultant — makes sure we don't accidentally destroy anything priceless in the name of progress. Lucian, this is Elena. She's going to save my ballroom."

"Ms. Ward." His voice was low, slightly rough, as if he did not use it often. As if words cost him something.

He extended his hand. Elena took it.

The contact was brief — a handshake, professional and appropriate — but something passed through her palm and into the rest of her that she had no ready name for. She saw his breath catch. Saw his fingers tighten around hers for a fraction of a second before propriety made him let go.

"Mr. Calder."

"Lucian." He said it too quickly, the word escaping before he could stop it. "Please."

"Lucian."

They stood there, neither speaking, and June was looking between them with frank curiosity.

"Have you two met before?"

"No," Elena said.

"I don't — no," Lucian said at the same moment.

Something flickered in his eyes. Quickly suppressed.

"Strange," June said lightly. "You look at each other like old friends. Or something."

Lucian's jaw tightened. "I should go. I just came to drop off some documents — historical records June wanted for the restoration. I left them with Marcus."

"Stay for the tour," June said, in the tone of a woman not offering a choice. "You can bore Elena with the fascinating details about Victorian-era plasterwork. I know how much you love an audience."

Lucian took a breath. When he looked at Elena again, there was something almost braced in his expression, as if he were steeling himself. "Actually. Yes. I would like that."

They walked through the rest of the hotel together — June in the lead, chattering about square footage and building codes and her vision for the finished product; Lucian a half-step behind Elena, silent and watchful.

Every so often she felt his gaze on her. Every time she turned, he looked away. Not quite quickly enough.

After Adam, Elena thought, that kind of attention should have made her run. It didn't. The realization unsettled her more than it should have — because his attention did not feel like surveillance. It felt like something she did not yet have a word for.

They finished in the library on the second floor — dark wood and built-in shelves and a window seat overlooking the harbor. The smell of old books hung in the air. June's phone buzzed, and she excused herself to take the call.

The quiet between Elena and Lucian was not uncomfortable. It was the quiet of two people who had run out of small talk and were not afraid of what came after.

"You don't remember me." His voice was quiet. Almost gentle. "Do you."

It was not a question.

Elena turned to face him fully.

"Should I? Have we met before?"

Something flickered in his eyes — pain, maybe, or hope, or some combination she could not quite read.

"No," he said. "We have not."

But his voice cracked on the word, and Elena knew — with a certainty that made no rational sense, that her therapist would have a field day with — that he was not telling the whole truth.

She should have pressed. She didn't.

"I should go," she said. "Find my rental. Unpack. Try to locate my sanity somewhere amid the boxes."

She meant it as a joke. It came out shakier than she intended.

Lucian nodded slowly. "The apartment above the bakery. On Harborview Street."

Elena froze. "How did you know that?"

He blinked, and for a moment he looked almost as startled as she felt. "June mentioned it," he said. "Earlier. Before you arrived."

Had she? Elena could not remember. But then again, she could not remember much of anything clearly right now.

"Right," she said. "Of course."

She turned toward the door.

"Elena."

She stopped. Turned back.

10

Lucian was standing in a shaft of pale light from the window, and for a moment he did not say anything, and then he said:

"Welcome to Camden's Rise. I think you're going to like it here."

And despite everything — the strangeness, the uncertainty, the nagging sense that her carefully reconstructed life was about to be upended in ways she could not possibly predict — Elena found herself believing him.

"I think I am too," she said.

She left before she could say anything else. All the way back to her apartment she felt his gaze on her, though she did not turn to check.

She did not need to.

CHAPTER TWO

LUCIAN

HE ALMOST DIDN'T GO.

June had asked him twice — once in a voicemail, once in a text message that had the particular economy of a woman who did not waste words. *Come by the hotel tomorrow. Designer from Boston. I want you there.* Lucian had said yes both times and meant it neither time. His work on Theodore Rowan's correspondence was at a delicate stage, three boxes of unsorted documents fanned across his dining-room table in the order he had imposed on them, and interrupting the rhythm of a sort always cost him a day on the other end.

Also: he did not like meeting new people.

His condition, as Isabel called it — because Isabel was the only person in his life permitted to name it out loud — meant that meeting new people was never really meeting new people. It was taking in a complete stranger the way another man might take in a parking lot: every car, every dent, every license plate, filed forever. Most first encounters were ninety percent observation and ten percent conversation; the observation ran in the background and did not ask for permission to exist. It was exhausting. It was also, on his worst days, why he spent most of his time alone in a house that had belonged to his grandfather, with only Theodore Rowan's century-old handwriting for company.

Today was not one of his worst days. But it was not one of his best, either.

He made coffee he did not drink. He stood at the kitchen window and watched the harbor come up gray under a gray sky, the lighthouse beam sweeping across the water in the slow, patient rhythm he had grown up hearing in his sleep. Camden's Rise in November: a town half-asleep, gathering itself for the long cold months. The restaurants had cut their hours. The seasonal tourists had gone back to whatever their real lives were. The town belonged, for a little while, to the people who actually lived in it.

He liked November. He did not, he was aware, like much else.

At nine-fifteen he put on his coat and walked the seven blocks to the Rowan Hotel, hands in his pockets, breath fogging ahead of him. He had chosen the long way without noticing he had chosen it — past the harbor, past the bookstore where Mrs. Lindstrom was already arranging the morning's new arrivals in the window, past the bakery whose smell he had been avoiding successfully for three weeks because Marla had ruined croissants for him, though she did not know it. Marla Chen did not know she existed in his catalog. Neither did Elena Ward. Most of the people he had ever watched did not.

That was the shape of it. That had always been the shape of it.

He arrived at the Rowan at nine-twenty-three and stood for a moment on the sidewalk, looking up at the façade the way a man looks at something he has been entrusted with. Theodore Rowan had built this building in 1879 for a woman who had never lived to see it finished. The bones were good. The skin needed love. June had been pouring her inheritance into it for two years and was beginning — Lucian could see it in her face on Sundays, when she brought him letters she had found tucked inside walls and floorboards — to run out of faith. A designer from Boston was supposed to help. Lucian did not see how.

He went in.

The lobby smelled of sawdust and old plaster and something newer — the particular lacquer smell of fresh-stripped oak. A tarp covered the front desk. A man he vaguely knew, Marcus Chen, was kneeling on the staircase landing with a caulking gun and a look of concentrated despair. Marcus had begun working on the Rowan six months ago and had, Lucian thought, been quietly falling in love with June for about five of them. Neither of them knew. Everyone else in town did.

Lucian nodded at Marcus. Marcus nodded at Lucian. Men in New England said everything necessary with the tilt of a chin.

"She's in the ballroom," Marcus said. "With the designer."

"What's she like?"

Marcus considered this. "She's — careful."

"Careful how?"

"The way a person's careful when they've been handled wrong." Marcus shrugged. "Not my business. But watch your step with her, is what I mean."

Lucian thought about that as he crossed the lobby. It was a strange thing for Marcus to say about a stranger. Marcus was not given to character readings.

And then he walked into the ballroom and saw her.

He did not recognize her, at first, because his mind refused. His mind was a careful library, and the books in the library had subject headings, and the subject heading *Boston University Library, October 15, 2009, 3:47 p.m., second floor, literature section, table seven, hazel eyes and a poetry book* was not filed under *Camden's Rise, November, Rowan Hotel ballroom, designer from Boston.* The books did not want to be in the same room together. For a long second his mind simply refused the transaction, the way a register rejects a card.

Then it accepted. Everything he had ever known about her arrived at once — not the memories themselves, those were always there, but the fact that the woman standing twelve feet from him at the base of the ballroom's grand staircase was the woman from the library, and from Mount Washington, and from Brooklyn, and from D.C., and from the farmer's market in Portland, and from the train platform in

Boston, and from the beach in Rhode Island, and from all the other places he had catalogued her across fifteen years of accidents. The fact of it arrived like a wave arriving, all at once and everywhere.

June was introducing them.

He was saying, "Elena. It's a pleasure." He heard his own voice from a great distance. He extended his hand and watched his hand extend from the same distance. Her hand met his.

It was not a handshake that felt like a lightning strike, whatever she would tell her best friend later that night. It was a handshake that felt, to him, like putting his palm flat against a door he had been standing outside of for more than a decade, and discovering that the door was, after all, a door, and that doors opened.

She was saying something polite. He was saying something polite back. June was watching both of them with the benign, preoccupied attention of a woman running a restoration project in her head.

He could not remember afterward — which was funny, which was a joke his own brain had told him — exactly which polite thing he had said first. He remembered the rest. He remembered the dress she was wearing (charcoal wool, a collar he recognized as vintage, small silver earrings she kept touching). He remembered the way she stood (one hip cocked, weight on her left leg, the posture of a woman who had been taught to make herself smaller and had not yet unlearned it). He remembered that she had a bruise the size of a dime on the inside of her left wrist, faded to yellow, a week old or more. He remembered noticing that he was noticing, and looking away.

The tour lasted forty-seven minutes. June walked them through the ballroom, the library, the east wing guest rooms, the service staircase, the sad rooms where water had come through the roof in 2015 and nobody had ever quite fixed it. Elena touched things. She asked smart questions about the era of the fixtures and the provenance of the silk panels. She moved the way a woman moves in a building whose bones she can feel through her hands. He had watched her move this way once before, on Mount Washington, after she had twisted her ankle, when she had reached out and steadied herself against a tree and closed her eyes like she was listening to the bark.

Then June got a phone call and went to take it.

The library smelled of old books. Libraries always smelled of old books, and the smell always took him back, and he was always powerless against it.

"You're staring," Elena said.

She said it without turning around. She could feel the weight of his attention on her back.

"Sorry," he said. "Occupational hazard. Historians stare at things."

"Things. Not people."

"Sometimes people are things worth staring at." He heard what he had said and winced. "That came out wrong."

She turned to face him. The ghost of a smile. "It came out a little wrong, yes."

"I meant — you're looking at that window with the same expression I get when I find a document nobody's touched in a hundred years. Like you can see what it used to be."

"Can't you? This glass is original — 1882, if June's timeline is right. Look at the imperfections." She moved aside so he could see. "Each pane is different. Slightly wavy. You can't get glass like this anymore. Someone made it by hand, and their hands were in it — literally. Their breath was in it."

She was right. The glass was old enough to have warped subtly, turning the harbor beyond it into something impressionistic — Monet's water, not real water. Light caught in imperfection.

"You see things," Lucian said. "Things other people walk past."

"So do you. That's what historians do, isn't it? See what everyone else has forgotten?"

He looked at her. She looked at him. The light through the imperfect glass fell across them both, bending slightly, as if the present and the past were not as far apart as anyone supposed.

"Yes," he said. "That's exactly what we do."

His phone buzzed. He ignored it. Elena turned back to the window.

The moment dissolved.

When June returned, they finished the tour. Lucian offered informed commentary about the era of each room's fixtures. Elena asked smart questions about material provenance. They were professional. Courteous. Two strangers meeting for the first time in a hotel lobby.

At the door, Elena extended her hand again. "Thank you, Lucian. I think I'm going to love this building."

"It's easy to love," he said, taking her hand and releasing it in the same motion. Quick. Clean. No lingering. "The hard part is doing it justice."

She held his gaze for one beat longer than necessary. "I'm good at hard things."

Then she was gone, walking toward the harbor with her coat pulled tight against the November wind, and Lucian stood in the doorway of the Rowan Hotel and watched her go. He did not say goodbye to June. He did not remember, afterward, walking home. He remembered arriving at his front door. He remembered letting himself in and hanging his coat on the hook.

He remembered standing in his front hall for a long time without moving.

She had a bruise the size of a dime on the inside of her left wrist.

She had stood with her weight on her left leg, as if something hurt on the right.

Her laugh had a caught quality that he recognized from the Brooklyn café, that rainy afternoon in 2016 when a man twice her size had leaned across the table and laid a proprietary hand on hers.

Six years ago. Seven. He had watched her walk out of that café with the man who was doing it to her, and he had watched and he had done nothing.

He went to the study and opened the bottom drawer of his desk. Inside, beneath a stack of file folders and a leather journal he had not written in for years, was a book. Small. Worn. The spine cracked from use. On the inside cover, in faded blue ink, someone had written: *For Elena, who feels things deeply. Love always, Grandma Rose.*

He touched the inscription with his fingertip.

June had mentioned that the designer from Boston was a woman recovering from a bad relationship. *Take it easy on her, Lucian. She's having a hard year.* June had said that last week. He had nodded absently. He had not known, then, who June meant.

He knew now.

He closed the book. He closed the drawer. He sat for a long time in the darkening room, listening to the wind move through the old house.

He was not going to approach her. He was going to do, this time, what he had failed to do in Brooklyn: he was going to respect the shape of her life. If she wanted to know him, she would come to know him. He was not going to bring her his catalog and place it in her hands like an offering. He was not going to make her responsible for a decade of his quiet, private longing.

He had survived a very long time without being known by her. He could survive a little longer.

The decision, once he had made it, should have felt like discipline.

It felt like grief.

He stood at the study window and watched the lighthouse sweep its beam across the harbor, steady and patient, and he understood, for the first time, what Theodore Rowan had meant in the last letter he had read that morning, the one he had copied carefully into his notes:

I have found, to my astonishment, that one can love a person entirely from the inside of one's own head. That one can build a life around such a love, and have it be a real life, and a real love, and want for nothing. The only thing one cannot do is let the loved person know. To let her know would be to place the burden of my long devotion on her shoulders, and she has burdens enough.

Lucian had read that letter a dozen times. He had always found it beautiful.

Tonight, for the first time, he found it instructive — and, if he was honest with himself, which he was trying, these past few years, to be more often than not — he found it a thing he did not want to be true anymore. Theodore had loved Clara all his life and she had never known. That was not wisdom. That was not restraint. That was a man who had never learned to do the thing he had not yet had to do: to tell a woman who she had been to him, and to let her decide what she wanted to do with the information. Theodore had not been able to. Theodore had died not having been able to.

Lucian was not, he understood, as patient as Theodore had been. Or as honorable, maybe. Or — maybe — as cowardly. There were words for it in both directions.

He would not drive past her apartment. That much he could promise himself.

But he was not sure, standing at the window, watching the lighthouse, how long he would be able to promise the rest.

Theodore's letters were not going to sort themselves. He went back to the dining room and put on his cotton gloves and began, again, to lay the documents out in the order he had imposed on them. The work steadied his hands.

19

He kept only some of the promises he made himself, as it would turn out.

But he kept that one, for a while. That was a start.

CHAPTER THREE

❖

ELENA

THE CALL CAME AT 6:47 a.m. which meant Marla had been awake for at least an hour, pacing her Brooklyn apartment in her worn terrycloth robe and waiting for what she considered a socially acceptable time to demand answers. Elena was already awake. She had barely slept — too many dreams of storm-colored eyes, too many sensations of coming home to a place she had never been — and had given up around five. She made herself coffee in the tiny kitchen of her rental apartment, the old percolator gurgling and spitting like something from her grandmother's era, and watched the sunrise paint the harbor in shades of rose and amber and gold. The view almost made up for the sleepless night. Almost.

"Okay," Marla said without preamble when Elena answered, her voice carrying the caffeine-and-determination of a proper interrogation.

"First day. New town. Gorgeous historic hotel. Tell me everything and spare no details, especially if any of them involve attractive single men with tragic backstories and excellent bone structure." Elena laughed despite herself, the tension in her shoulders easing at the familiar sound of her best friend's voice.

Marla Chen had been her anchor since NYU. Marla had become a literary agent championing stories about complicated women; Elena had become a designer resurrecting spaces others had given up on. Neither had conquered the world yet. They were working on it.

"The hotel is incredible," Elena said, curling deeper into the window seat with her coffee, pulling her grandmother's quilt around her shoulders.

"You should see the ballroom, Mar. Original silk wall panels, hand-painted botanicals that look like something out of a Victorian fever dream, these massive crystal chandeliers that would make a Gilded Age heiress weep with envy. It's going to be spectacular when we're done."

"Uh-huh. And the attractive single men with excellent bone structure?"

"I didn't say anything about —"

"Elena Marie Ward." Marla's voice took on the particular tone she used when she was about to be insufferable — which was to say, right about everything and determined to prove it.

"I have known you for twelve years. I can hear it in your voice when something has happened. So spill, or I'll get on a train and make you spill in person." Elena closed her eyes and saw Lucian Calder in the ballroom doorway, the gray morning light falling across his angular features, looking at her like he had been searching for her across years and distances and found her.

"There's a historical consultant," she said carefully, choosing each word like stepping stones across a rushing river.

"Working on the restoration. His name is Lucian."

"Lucian." Marla drew out the syllables, savoring them.

"That's a romance novel name if I ever heard one. Please tell me he looked like his name. Please tell me he has haunted eyes and possibly a brooding disposition and at least one tragic secret."

"He's —" Elena searched for words that wouldn't betray too much, that wouldn't make her sound as unmoored as she felt.

"Tall. Bookish. Gray eyes — the color of the ocean in winter, if the ocean were holding a secret it was afraid to tell. The kind of face that looks like it belongs in an old

22

photograph. Or a library. Or standing on a cliff somewhere, staring at the horizon and thinking about lost love."

"Oh my God." Marla's delight was audible even through the phone, bright and sharp as champagne bubbles.

"You're already gone. One day in this town and you're already gone for some history nerd with cheekbones and a romantic name and — what did you say?— ocean eyes?"

"I'm not gone," Elena protested, but even she could hear how unconvincing it sounded.

Like someone insisting they weren't drunk while reaching for the bar to steady themselves.

"It's just — there was this moment. When we shook hands. And I felt —" She stopped.

How could she explain what she had felt? The a charge that had raced up her arm and pooled in her chest. The recognition that had no right to exist. The overwhelming sense that something important was happening, something she didn't understand but couldn't ignore, like hearing the first notes of a song you know you've heard before but can't quite name.

"Felt what?" Marla prompted, her voice softer now, the teasing edge giving way to genuine curiosity.

"Like I knew him." The words came out before Elena could stop them, before she could dress them up in qualifications and caveats and the protective armor of irony.

"Like we'd met before, even though I'm absolutely certain we haven't. And the way he looked at me, Mar — it was like he knew me too. Like he'd been waiting for me. Like —" She paused, struggling to articulate something that defied articulation.

"Like there you are." There was a pause on the other end of the line.

"That's either the most romantic thing I've ever heard," Marla said slowly, "or the opening scene of a true crime podcast. I need more data before I decide which." Elena laughed, but there was an edge to it — a tremor of something that wasn't quite humor.

"That's what worries me."

"Because of Adam." It wasn't a question.

Marla had been there through all of it — the slow unraveling of Elena's relationship with Adam Blackwell, the gradual realization that his attentiveness was actually surveillance, his devotion actually control. She had been the one who first named what was happening, gently and then less gently as Elena kept making excuses. She had been the one Elena called at 2 a.m. when she finally found the courage to leave, shaking so hard she could barely dial the phone. She had been the one waiting with a spare key and a bottle of wine and exactly zero judgment when Elena showed up on her doorstep with nothing but a suitcase and a shattered sense of self.

"Because of Adam," Elena confirmed, the name still leaving a bitter taste in her mouth even after all these months.

"I don't trust my judgment anymore. What if I'm just — what if I'm drawn to men who are too intense? What if there's something broken in me that mistakes obsession for love? What if the way I felt yesterday, that something vivid, that recognition — what if it's just my screwed-up radar pointing me toward another man who wants to own me?"

"Stop." Marla's voice was firm, brooking no argument.

"First of all, you are not broken. You were in a relationship with a manipulative, controlling asshole who spent three years systematically convincing you that you couldn't trust your own perceptions, and you got out. You recognized what he was doing and you left him. That takes strength, Elena. Not brokenness."

"But —"

"Second of all," Marla continued, steamrolling over Elena's objection with the practiced ease of a woman who had learned long ago that Elena needed to be interrupted when she was spiraling, "there's a difference between intensity and danger. Adam was dangerous because he wanted to own you. He collected information about you so he could use it against you. He monitored your phone and your email and your friendships, not because he loved you, but because he needed to control you. He made you smaller so he could feel bigger." She paused.

"Did this Lucian person do any of that?" Elena thought about it.

Really thought, instead of just reacting from the place of fear that Adam had carved out inside her. Lucian had been intense, yes. He had looked at her with an almost painful focus, like she was a work of art he was trying to memorize. But he had also been... gentle. Careful. Hesitant, even. Like he was the one who was scared.

"No," she admitted.

"He was actually kind of... nervous. Like he was afraid of saying the wrong thing. Like he was worried about scaring me away."

"Okay, see, that's adorable. That's the opposite of Adam." Marla's voice softened, losing its fierce edge and settling into the warm, steady tone she used when she was trying to reach past Elena's defenses.

"Elena, honey, you're allowed to be attracted to someone. You're allowed to feel things. You're allowed to shake hands with a handsome historian and feel like the earth moved. Just because Adam turned out to be a monster doesn't mean every intense connection is going to destroy you."

"I know." Elena took a deep breath, letting the cool morning air from the cracked window fill her lungs.

"I know that intellectually. I'm just — I'm still figuring out how to trust again. How to trust myself, especially. Adam spent three years teaching me that my instincts were wrong, that my feelings were overreactions, that I couldn't rely on my own perception of reality. It's hard to unlearn that."

"I know, sweetheart. And that's why you're in therapy, and that's why you're doing the work, and that's why I'm so goddamn proud of you." Marla's voice caught on something that might have been tears, quickly swallowed.

"But don't let Adam take this from you too, okay? Don't let him make you afraid to ever feel anything again. That would be letting him win, even now that you're seven hundred miles away from him." They talked for another twenty minutes — about Marla's latest manuscript acquisition (a dark academia romance that was going to make them both rich, she insisted), about Elena's plans for the ballroom (historically accurate but with modern touches, a bridge between eras), about the ridiculous price of rent in Brooklyn versus the even more ridiculous lack of good bagels in Maine.

By the time they hung up, the sun was fully up and Elena felt steadier. Grounded. Ready to face another day. Even if that day involved seeing Lucian Calder again. Especially if it did.

She found the problem in the east wing staircase. The balusters were wrong. Not damaged — wrong. Someone, decades ago, had replaced the original hand-carved spindles with machine-turned reproductions, and the difference was subtle enough that most people would never notice. But Elena noticed. Elena always noticed.

"These aren't original," she said, running her fingers along the turned wood.

Her voice had gone flat — the voice Marla called her "designer death tone." The one that preceded hours of fixation.

"They were replaced in the seventies," June said.

"The originals rotted. Water damage from a —"

"I can see that. But these are wrong. The profile is off — the original pattern would have been a barley twist with a lamb's tongue detail. These are generic Victorian. They look like something from a catalog."

"They've been here for fifty years. No one's ever —"

"I notice." Elena crouched, examining the joint where baluster met handrail.

"This is the kind of thing that separates a restoration from a renovation. If we leave these, the whole staircase will read as inauthentic, even if people can't articulate why. It'll feel wrong. They'll walk up these stairs and something in the back of their mind will say 'fake' and they won't know what triggered it, but they'll feel it." June was quiet for a moment.

"Elena. These are forty balusters. Custom-carved reproductions would cost —"

"I know what they'd cost."

"More than our entire fixtures budget."

"I know." Elena stood, brushed dust from her knees, and felt the familiar tightness — the one that came when the gap between what something was and what it should be felt unbridgeable.

"I know it's impractical. I know it doesn't matter to anyone but me. But this is what I do, June. I see what's wrong and I can't unsee it. Every time I walk up these stairs, I'll know." June studied her with those sea-glass eyes.

"You're a perfectionist."

"I prefer 'relentlessly detail-oriented.'"

"Those are the same thing, dear. One just sounds better on a résumé." June touched her arm.

"It's a gift. It's also, if you'll forgive me, a prison. Knowing the difference between those two things — that's the real skill." Elena looked at the balusters and said nothing.

Because June was right, and because the honest answer — that she'd spent most of her life unable to tell the difference, that Adam had exploited exactly this tendency, had learned that if he pointed out a flaw in her she would obsess over fixing it until she'd reshaped herself into whatever he wanted — was not something she was ready to say out loud.

"We'll keep the reproductions," she said finally.

"For now. But I'm ordering samples of the original profile. Just in case." June smiled.

"Just in case." It would take Elena three weeks to stop checking the balusters every time she passed them.

She never stopped noticing they were wrong.

Dorothy Hale ran the post office, which in Camden's Rise was less a government service and more an intelligence operation. Dorothy knew everyone's business because everyone's business passed through her hands — letters, packages, the occasional suspicious envelope from a law firm that meant someone was getting divorced. She was seventy-one years old, had lived in Camden's Rise her entire life, and regarded newcomers with the warmth of a border collie guarding a flock.

"You're the designer," Dorothy said when Elena came in to rent a P.O. box.

It was not a question.

"Elena Ward. Nice to meet you."

"Mmm." Dorothy processed the paperwork with the efficiency of a woman who had been doing this job since before Elena was born.

"You're staying at the apartment above Margaret's bookshop."

"Yes."

"How long?"

"I'm not sure yet. The hotel restoration —"

"Could take years. Could take forever. June's been saying she'd fix that place since Robert died, and that was five years ago. Before you, she hired a firm from Portland. They lasted three months." Dorothy looked at her over her reading glasses.

"What makes you different?"

"I don't know yet. I just got here."

"That's an honest answer. I don't hear many of those from people who come here to 'start over.'" She made air quotes with her fingers, a gesture that conveyed decades of watching people arrive in Camden's Rise fleeing something, fall in love with the quaintness, and leave when they realized quaintness included slow internet, no good sushi, and winters that lasted until May.

"The last 'start over' person opened a yoga studio. Lasted eight months. Before that, someone tried to turn the old cannery into an art gallery. Six months."

"I'm not opening a yoga studio."

"Good. We don't need one." Dorothy stamped the form with unnecessary force and handed over a key.

"Box 47. Mail comes at eleven. Don't leave packages sitting — we don't have the room." It wasn't hostile, exactly.

It was the careful appraisal of a woman who had learned that enthusiasm was a renewable resource but trust was not. Elena recognized it because she lived by the same principle now.

"Thank you, Dorothy."

"Mmm." Dorothy was already turning to the next task.

"We'll see." Three months later, when Elena dropped off a Christmas card for Dorothy with a hand-drawn sketch of the post office on the front — every detail correct, down to the crack in the front step and the flag that hung crooked — Dorothy put it on the wall behind the counter and left it there for the next two years.

She never said thank you. But the card stayed.

The silk panel she was examining blurred before her eyes. Adam. The memory surfaced unbidden, the way they always did — not when she expected them, but when her guard was down, when she was tired or distracted or standing in a beautiful room thinking about love. June 2019. A gallery opening in Boston. She had been standing in front of a Rothko, lost in the colors, when he appeared beside her. Tall. Golden-haired. Smiling with such warmth that she felt it like sunlight.

"You're looking at it wrong," he said.

She bristled.

"Excuse me?"

"The painting. You're trying to understand it." His voice was rich, confident — the voice of a man who had never questioned his welcome anywhere.

"Rothko doesn't want you to understand. He wants you to feel."

"And how would you know what Rothko wants?" He turned to face her fully, and she felt the full force of his attention — the blue eyes, the practiced smile, the way he looked at her like she was the most interesting thing in the room.

"I don't," he admitted.

"But I know what I feel, looking at this painting. And I know what I felt when I saw you standing here, absorbed. Like you were having a private conversation with the canvas that no one else was invited to."

"That's... actually a lovely thing to say."

"I'm actually a lovely person." He extended his hand.

"Adam Blackwell." She took it.

"Elena Ward."

"Elena." He said her name like he was tasting it, savoring it.

"That's beautiful. It suits you." And she had felt it — that flutter of warmth, that sense of being seen.

After years of feeling invisible in corporate design firms, here was a man who looked at her like she mattered. She hadn't known, then, that the warmth would turn to ice the first time she disappointed him. That disappointing him would become increasingly easy as time went on. The silk panel came back into focus. Elena realized her hands were shaking.

"Elena?" She turned.

Lucian was standing in the doorway, his expression shifting from curiosity to concern in the space of a heartbeat.

"You're shaking," he said quietly.

She looked at her hands. Unsteady. She hadn't noticed.

"Bad memory," she said.

"Just — a bad memory." He didn't move toward her.

Didn't crowd her space. Just stood there, solid and patient, his gray-blue eyes full of something that looked like understanding.

"Do you want to talk about it?"

"No." She wiped her face with the back of her hand.

"I want to talk about these silk panels. I think we can salvage more than I originally thought." He nodded slowly.

Accepted the change of subject without pressing. But she saw him hold onto it — saw the way his expression registered her trembling hands, the shadow that had crossed her face. She was learning that Lucian noticed everything. Unlike Adam, who had used her vulnerabilities as weapons, Lucian seemed to hold them carefully. *He's not Adam,* she told herself firmly. But the part of her Adam had damaged — the part that flinched from kindness because kindness had been the first step toward cruelty — that part was not ready to believe it yet. The Rowan was louder today. Elena arrived to find the restoration in full, glorious chaos: workers swarming the scaffolding on the east facade like industrious bees, the whine of power saws cutting through the morning air, pickup trucks unloading supplies in the gravel lot with a symphony of slamming doors and shouted instructions. It was the sound of a building coming back to life, and Elena felt her heart lift at the noise. This was what she loved. This was why she did this work. Taking something broken and making it whole again. Taking something forgotten and reminding it that it was worth remembering. June met her at the front door with a hard hat and a smile that suggested she was barely containing some kind of secret.

"Sleep well?"

"Well enough," Elena lied.

"Where do you want me to start?"

"Marcus is waiting for you in the east wing. He's found something he thinks you should see." June's eyes sparkled with barely contained excitement, the way a child's might on Christmas morning.

"I won't spoil it. Just trust me — it's worth the walk." The east wing was the oldest part of the hotel, dating back to the original 1882 construction.

The bones of the building were more visible here — exposed beams and original stonework, the handprints of craftsmen who had been dead for over a century still visible in the texture of the walls. Elena picked her way through the construction zone, stepping over cables and around ladders, breathing in the smell of old wood and fresh plaster and possibility. She found Marcus Chen supervising the removal of a section of damaged wall, his broad frame silhouetted against the dusty light from a boarded window. He was a solidly built man in his forties, with the weathered hands and permanently sunburned face of someone who had spent his life working outdoors.

"You must be the designer." He extended a dusty hand, his grip firm and callused.

"Marcus Chen. June's been talking about you nonstop."

"Elena Ward. And I hope it was all good things."

"Mostly about how you're going to turn her money pit into a showpiece." Marcus grinned, his face creasing with the kind of good humor that came from a life spent solving problems and taking satisfaction in a job well done.

"Come on. I've got something to show you." He led her deeper into the wing, to a room that had once been a parlor and was now a skeleton of exposed beams and crumbling plaster.

Weak light filtered through the gaps in the boarded windows, casting everything in shades of amber and dust. Three workers stood around a section of wall that had been partially removed, their expressions caught between confusion and wonder.

"We were taking down this panel to check for water damage," Marcus explained.

"And we found a cavity behind it. Someone had sealed off about two feet of space between the walls."

"That's not unusual in old buildings," Elena said.

"They often modified the floorplan over time —"

"Yeah, but look what was inside." Marcus stepped aside, gesturing for her to look.

Elena moved closer, peering into the gap where the wall had been opened, and felt her breath catch in her throat. There, resting on a narrow ledge that had once been part of a window frame, was a metal box. Old, by the look of it — tin, maybe, with a hinged lid and a clasp that had long since rusted shut. Someone had wrapped it in oilcloth, now brittle and yellowed with age, but still intact enough to have protected whatever was inside from the moisture and decay that would have destroyed it otherwise. Someone had hidden this deliberately. Someone had wanted it to survive.

"May I?" Elena asked, her voice coming out softer than she intended.

Marcus nodded.

"Careful. The metal's fragile." Elena reached into the cavity and lifted the box out, cradling it in her hands like something precious.

Like something that had been waiting over a hundred years for exactly this moment, for exactly these hands. It was lighter than she expected, and something shifted inside as she moved it — a soft rustling, like paper, like secrets. She carried it to a makeshift worktable and set it down gently. The clasp gave way with a little pressure, crumbling into rust flakes that drifted down like red snow, and the lid opened with a groan of protest. Inside, preserved by the oilcloth and the dry cavity of the wall, were letters. Dozens of them. Folded with careful precision and tied with ribbon that had once been cornflower blue and was now the color of old bone. The paper was thick and cream-colored, the kind made for correspondence between people who valued the written word, and the ink, where Elena could see it through the folds, was a faded sepia brown.

"Holy shit," one of the workers breathed, echoing Elena's thoughts exactly.

With trembling fingers, Elena untied the ribbon on the topmost bundle. The silk was so fragile it nearly disintegrated at her touch, releasing the letters. She carefully unfolded the first one, holding it by the edges, treating it with the reverence it deserved. The handwriting was elegant, slanted, unmistakably Victorian — the penmanship of a man who had been taught to write as an art form. At the top of the page, a date: March 15, 1883. Elena began to read.

My dearest Clara,

I know you will never read these words. I know that you are lost to me now, as surely as if the sea had taken you. But I find that I cannot stop writing to you. Perhaps because writing to you is the only way I can still speak to you. Perhaps because setting down these words is the only way I know to prove that what we had was real. Perhaps because I am simply a fool who cannot accept what is.

The hotel opens next month. Do you remember how we planned it together? How you chose the colors for the ballroom, the pattern for the china, the flowers for the garden? How you stood in the empty ballroom and spun in a circle, laughing, saying you could hear the music already?

Everywhere I look, I see your touch.
Everywhere I walk, I feel your absence.

They say time heals all wounds. I am beginning to suspect they are liars.

Forever yours,
Theodore

Elena's throat tightened. She reached for another letter, unfolding it with the same careful reverence, as if the paper might crumble to dust if she handled it too roughly. As if Theodore's grief might shatter in her hands.

June 2, 1883

My Clara,

A woman came to the hotel today who wore her hair the way you used to — pinned up with those tortoiseshell combs I brought you from Boston. For a moment, just a moment, I thought — but no. It was not you. It is never you.

I wonder sometimes if you think of me at all. If you remember the promises we made. If you regret, as I do, the circumstances that tore us apart.

The ballroom is finished now. The chandeliers are hung, just as you designed them. I stood beneath them last night, alone in the darkness, and I could almost hear your laughter echoing off the walls.

Almost is the cruelest word in the English language.

Eternally,
T.

Elena set the letter down and pressed her palms together, where something had begun to ache — a sharp, sweet pain, like a key turning in a lock she hadn't known was there. Theodore Rowan. It had to be — June's great-great-grandfather, the shipping magnate who had built the hotel.

And Clara... whoever Clara was, she had been the love of his life. A love that had clearly ended in tragedy, in loss, in letters hidden in walls because there was no one left to receive them.

"What is it?" Marcus asked, moving closer, his voice hushed as if he were in a church.

"What do they say?"

"Love letters," Elena said.

"From the man who built this hotel. Letters to a woman named Clara." She looked up at him, and she took a steadying breath.

"We need to get June."

June went quiet when she read them. She sat at the worktable, carefully turning pages that her ancestor had written more than a century ago. The morning light had shifted, streaming through the gaps in the boarded windows and illuminating the letters like manuscript pages in a medieval library.

"I knew there was a story," June said, her voice thick with emotion.

"Family legend, you know? Theodore built the hotel for a woman he loved, but she died before they could marry. That was all anyone ever said. Just — she died." June touched the edge of a letter with trembling fingers, she could feel Theodore's grief through the paper.

"But she didn't die, did she? She left. Or was taken. Or something."

"The letters don't say exactly what happened," Elena said, pulling up a chair beside her.

"Not the ones I've read so far. But there are dozens here. Maybe the later ones explain more."

"And he hid them in the wall." June shook her head in wonder, wiping her cheeks with the back of her hand.

"All these years. More than a hundred years, just waiting to be found. Waiting for someone to come along and —" She stopped, her voice catching.

"And what?" Elena prompted.

"And remember them." June looked up, her sea-glass eyes fierce with something that might have been hope.

"Isn't that what we all want, in the end? To be remembered? To know that our love meant something, that it left a mark on the world?" Elena thought of Adam, and the three years she had spent trying to disappear into someone else's idea of who she should be.

She thought of her grandmother, who had given her the Neruda book and told her that love should make you more, not less. She thought of Lucian Calder, looking at her across the ballroom like he had been waiting for her his entire life.

"Yes," she said.

"I think that's what we all want." Marcus cleared his throat, breaking the spell.

"He must have wanted them preserved," he offered.

"That oilcloth, the tin box — he was protecting them. But from what? Or from whom?" No one had an answer.

Elena's mind was spinning. A man who built a hotel for a woman he loved. A woman who disappeared. Letters hidden in walls, preserved for over a century. And now here she was, a designer hired to bring the building back to life, and she had stumbled upon the love story at its heart. It was like fate. Or coincidence. Or the kind of narrative symmetry that only happened in novels — the sort of thing Marla would say was too on-the-nose for fiction.

"We should have Lucian look at these," June said, carefully gathering the letters back into their box.

Her hands were still trembling, but her voice was steadier now, her practical nature reasserting itself.

"He'll know how to preserve them properly. And he might be able to help us find out more about Clara — who she was, what happened to her." Elena's heart skipped at the mention of his name.

"Lucian?"

"He's a historian, dear. This is exactly his wheelhouse." June looked up with a knowing smile, her face creasing with gentle mischief.

"I'll call him. He can come by this afternoon." Elena opened her mouth to say — what?

That she wasn't ready to see him again? That she needed more time to process whatever had happened between them yesterday? That she was simultaneously desperate to be in his presence and terrified of what that desperation meant?

"That sounds perfect," she said instead.

Because it did. Because despite everything — the confusion, the fear, the nagging sense that her carefully reconstructed life was about to change in ways she couldn't predict — she wanted to see him again. She wanted to understand why looking at him was like recognizing her own reflection in a mirror she didn't know existed. She wanted to know if the awareness she had felt was real, or if she was just a lonely woman imagining connections where none existed. Most of all, she wanted to know why Lucian Calder had looked at her like he had been waiting for her his entire life. And whether he had answers she hadn't even known she was seeking. As she helped June carry the box of letters to a secure location in the hotel's makeshift office, Elena glanced out the window at the gray harbor beyond. Somewhere out there, Lucian was going about his day, doing whatever historians did when they weren't making designers question their sanity. In a few hours, she would see him again. In a few hours, she might start getting some answers. Or, watching a gull wheel against the clouds like a benediction, she would only find more questions. Either way, she was beginning to suspect that Camden's Rise had plans for her. And that Theodore Rowan's letters were only the beginning.

CHAPTER FOUR

❖

LUCIAN

THE LETTERS WERE A gift and a curse, like most things in Lucian's life. He sat at June's dining room table, cotton gloves on his hands and a magnifying glass beside him, reading Theodore Rowan's words with the reverent attention of a man who understood, perhaps better than anyone alive, the weight of preserved memory. The paper was fragile but intact, the ink faded but legible. More than a century old, and still speaking. Still aching. Still reaching across time for a woman who would never answer. Elena sat across from him, close enough that he could smell her perfume. She was watching him read, her hazel eyes tracking his expression with focused attention, and the awareness of her gaze made his hands unsteady. He had dreamed of being in a room with her like this. The reality was too much. Every breath she took felt significant.

"What do you think?" June asked from the doorway.

She had been hovering for the past hour, unable to sit still, her excitement and sorrow braided together in equal measure.

"Can they be preserved? Are they authentic?"

"I think your great-great-grandfather was a remarkable writer." Lucian set down the letter he had been examining — dated September 1884, more than a year into Theodore's correspondence with a woman who would never read his words.

"The paper, the ink, the handwriting style — everything is consistent with the late Victorian period. And the content..." He paused, choosing his words carefully.

"The content is extraordinary. I think he was in tremendous pain, and he transformed that pain into art."

"The letters span almost twenty years," Elena said.

She had been helping him sort them chronologically, her quick mind immediately picking up on the dating system Theodore had used. Her fingers moved carefully across the aged paper, treating each letter like the precious artifact it was.

"The last one is from 1902. He was still writing to her two decades after she left." "Some loves don't fade," Lucian said quietly, and immediately wished he hadn't.

The words hung in the air, weighted with a meaning he hadn't intended to reveal. Elena's eyes met his. Something flickered — curiosity, maybe. Or recognition. He looked away before he could do something stupid, like tell her the truth.

"What happened to Clara?" June asked, moving closer to peer at the letters spread across the table.

"Do they ever say? Why did she leave him?"

"Not explicitly. But there are hints." Lucian reached for one of the later letters, handling it with the care it deserved.

"In this one, from 1886, he writes about 'the family that took you from me' and 'the cage they call a marriage.' It sounds like Clara was forced into an arranged marriage — perhaps to someone of higher social standing, or to settle a family debt."

"That was common in that era," Elena murmured.

"Women didn't have many choices."

"No," Lucian agreed, and he heard the echo of anger in his own voice — anger at a century of injustice, at the systems that had treated women as property to be traded.

"They didn't." He picked up another letter — one of his favorites, though he would never admit to having favorites.

The words had struck him when he first read them, and they struck him still.

"Listen to this. September 12, 1889." He began to read aloud, and his voice, trained by years of lectures and presentations, filled the quiet room.

My Clara,

I saw you today. Not truly — I know that. You are hundreds of miles away, trapped in a life we never chose. But a woman walked through the hotel lobby this afternoon, and for one breathless moment, I thought —

It does not matter what I thought. It was not you. It is never you.

I have been told that I should marry. That it is unseemly for a man of my position to remain alone. That the hotel needs a hostess, a woman's touch, a presence to soften its empty halls.

I cannot. How can I promise myself to another when my heart remains with you? How can I stand before God and make vows I do not mean? It would be a lie. It would be a betrayal — not of you, for you owe me nothing, but of myself. Of what I know to be true.

I would rather be alone with the memory of you than married to the reality of someone else.

Is that devotion? Or madness? Some days I cannot tell the difference.

Yours, in whatever way I am allowed to be,
Theodore

The room was silent when he finished. June had tears on her cheeks again, silvery tracks catching the afternoon light. Elena was staring at the table, her expression unreadable, her fingers pressed against her lips as if holding back words — or perhaps holding back the same sob that was threatening to rise in Lucian's own throat. He had his own letters, in a sense. Not written on paper, but stored in the Archive of his mind — every encounter with Elena catalogued and preserved, every moment a love letter she had never received. I would rather be alone with the memory of you than married to the reality of someone else. Yes. Theodore had understood.

"This is incredible," Elena said finally.

Her voice was husky, thick with emotion that surprised him.

"These should be preserved properly. Donated to a historical society, or —"

"They're staying here," June said.

"This is where Theodore wanted them. This is where they belong." She looked at Lucian with determination in her pale eyes.

"But you're right that they need to be preserved. Can you help with that?"

"Of course." He was already mentally absorbing what would be needed: acid-free folders, archival boxes, climate control, perhaps digitization for backup.

"I'll put together a comprehensive plan. In the meantime, they should be kept somewhere cool and dry, away from direct light."

"My study," June decided.

"I'll clear out a drawer." She gathered herself with visible effort, wiping her cheeks with the back of her hand.

"I need to make some calls. Let the family know what we've found. Lucian, Elena — thank you. Both of you." She hurried out, leaving them alone.

The silence that followed was different from before. Charged. Expectant. Like the moment before a thunderstorm, when the air goes still and everything seems to hold its breath.

"That letter," Elena said slowly.

"The one about devotion and madness. You read it like you understood it." Lucian's heart stuttered against his ribs.

"I'm a historian. Understanding old documents is my job."

"That's not what I meant." She was looking at him now, really looking, and being seen was both terrifying and exhilarating.

As if she had peeled back his skin and was examining the machinery of his heart.

"You read it like you'd written it yourself." He should deflect.

Change the subject. Make a joke about the occupational hazard of spending too much time with dead people's correspondence. Instead, he said: "Maybe I have." Elena's eyes searched his. He paused.

"What does that mean?" It means I've been in love with you for over a decade.

It means I have a room full of objects from our encounters, catalogued and preserved like Theodore's letters. It means I understand his madness because I share it.

"It means I should show you the lighthouse," he said instead.

"Before we lose the light."

His phone rang while he was cataloging Theodore's letters. The screen showed a name he hadn't seen in weeks: Tom Whitaker.

"Calder. You alive up there?" Tom's voice was loud and cheerful, the voice of a man who had spent thirty years lecturing undergraduates and never learned to modulate.

"I haven't heard from you since you vanished into the Maine wilderness. The department is starting a rumor you've joined a cult."

"It's not a cult. It's a hotel restoration."

"Same thing. Both involve blind devotion and questionable plumbing." Tom laughed at his own joke, as he always did.

"Listen, I'm presenting at the New England Historical Conference in Portland next month. Colonial shipping records — the riveting stuff. Come down, buy me a beer, tell me what you've found in that hotel. Word is there are letters?"

"Victorian correspondence. Unsent love letters from the hotel's founder. Twenty years' worth."

"Christ. That's a paper. That's three papers. You writing it up?"

"I'm thinking about it."

"Don't think. Write. You've been on sabbatical for two years, Lucian. The university likes you, but they like publications more. Publish or —"

"Perish. Yes. I've heard the phrase."

"Come to Portland. Present something. Even a preliminary finding. Keep your name in circulation." A pause.

"And bring that dog of yours. Helen misses him." Lucian glanced at the corner of the study where a graying Labrador named Keats was sprawled across an armchair, snoring with the commitment of someone who had given up all pretense of dignity.

Keats was eleven, arthritic, and devoted to exactly three things: his food bowl, his armchair, and the particular spot behind his left ear that, when scratched, made his back leg kick involuntarily.

"Keats doesn't travel well. He threw up in the car last time."

"He threw up on MY car. There's a difference. Helen still found pieces of kibble in the back seat three months later." But Tom's voice was warm.

"Seriously. Portland. Next month. I'll buy the first round."

"I'll think about it."

"That means yes. I've known you fifteen years, Calder. 'I'll think about it' is your version of 'absolutely.'" After they hung up, Lucian scratched Keats behind the left ear and watched the back leg kick.

The dog opened one eye, confirmed that attention was being paid, and returned to sleep. Tom was right. He'd been hiding in Camden's Rise, and while the hotel research was legitimate, the sabbatical had stretched long enough to raise questions. He needed to present something. He needed to remain a person with a career and a professional identity, not just a man who lived in a coastal town and thought about a woman. He picked up the phone and texted Tom: Portland. I'll be there. But I'm not bringing the dog. Tom's reply: Coward.

The lighthouse stood on a promontory half a mile from the hotel, its white tower stark against the gray November sky. Lucian had suggested the walk impulsively, desperate to escape the intimacy of June's dining room before he said something he couldn't take back. But now, picking their way along the coastal path with Elena beside him, he wasn't sure this was any better. The wind pushed them together, insistent and cold. The narrow trail forced them to walk close, their shoulders brushing with every other step. Every accidental touch sent a jolt crackling through his nervous system, a reminder of all that he wanted and couldn't have.

"It's beautiful here," Elena said, pausing to look out at the sea.

The wind whipped her hair across her face, and she pushed it back with one hand, the gesture so familiar it made his chest ache.

"I can see why Theodore built the hotel in this spot."

"The lighthouse was here first," Lucian said, grateful for the neutral topic.

"Built in 1847. Theodore bought the surrounding land in 1880, specifically because of the views. He wanted guests to wake up to the sound of the sea."

"You know a lot about him."

"I've been researching the hotel's history for two years." He paused, watching a gull wheel against the clouds.

"I never found any mention of Clara in the official records. She's been erased. Like she never existed."

"But Theodore remembered her." Elena's voice was soft.

"He kept her alive in those letters."

"Yes." Lucian swallowed hard.

"Memory is powerful that way. It can preserve what the world tries to erase." They reached the lighthouse and climbed the rocky path to its base.

The door was padlocked, but there was a viewing platform that wrapped around the tower, offering a panoramic view of the harbor and the open ocean beyond. The wind was stronger here, carrying the salt spray of the sea, and Elena gripped the railing as she gazed out at the horizon. In the fading afternoon light, she looked almost otherworldly — a figure from a painting, frozen in a moment of quiet contemplation. The setting sun gilded her hair, turning it to honey and amber, and he could see the pulse beating in her throat, quick and vital. And just like that, Lucian was pulled back into a different moment. A different view. A different almost. July 19, 2013. Mount Washington, New Hampshire. He had not planned to hike Mount Washington that day. He was in New Hampshire for a conference — some academic gathering about colonial trade routes that he no longer remembered — and had decided to take an extra day for himself. The mountain had seemed like a good idea at the time. Fresh air. Exercise. A chance to clear his head of footnotes and primary sources and the persistent ache of a love that had no outlet. He was halfway up the Tuckerman Ravine Trail when he saw her. She was sitting on a boulder beside the trail, her hiking boots unlaced, massaging her ankle with a grimace. Her hair was pulled back in a ponytail, and she wore a light blue windbreaker that made her hazel eyes look almost green in the mountain light. She was twenty-one years old, and she was even more beautiful than she had been the first time he had seen her — in the library, four years before, with the October light falling across the table and her lips moving as she read. Elena. His Elena. Four years after the library, and here she was — alone on a mountain, nursing what looked like a twisted ankle.

"Are you okay?" The words came out before he could stop them.

She looked up, and for one heart-stopping moment, he thought she recognized him. Her brow furrowed slightly, her head tilted in that particular way of hers, and something flickered in her expression — confusion, maybe, or the ghost of a memory she couldn't quite catch.

"I think I twisted it," she said, gesturing at her ankle.

"Stupid. I wasn't watching where I was stepping."

"May I?" He crouched beside her, medical training from a long-ago first aid course surfacing.

"I'm not a doctor, but I can check if it's serious." She hesitated for only a moment before nodding.

He took her ankle in his hands, gently, so gently, and probed the joint for signs of serious injury. Her skin was warm from the hike, and he could feel her pulse fluttering against his fingertips like a captured bird.

"Doesn't feel broken," he said, his voice steadier than he felt.

"Probably just a minor sprain. But you shouldn't keep hiking on it."

"I was almost to the summit." She sounded disappointed.

"Another mile, maybe."

"I could help you. If you wanted." He didn't know where the words came from — some brave part of himself he barely recognized.

"I'm heading that direction anyway." She looked at him then — really looked, the way she had looked at him in the library all those years ago.

Her hazel eyes searched his face, and he saw curiosity there, and uncertainty, and something that might have been the beginning of trust.

"I don't even know your name," she said.

"Lucian. Lucian Calder."

"Elena Ward." She smiled, and something shifted in him.

"I guess it would be stupid to turn down help from a Good Samaritan." He helped her to her feet, letting her lean on him as they continued up the trail.

They talked as they walked — about her job (she was a junior designer at a firm in Boston, already frustrated with the politics), about his work (he was a historian, specializing in colonial trade), about the mountain and the weather and a dozen other safe, neutral topics. But beneath the words was something else. A current. A connection. The sense that they were not strangers at all, but old friends meeting again after a long absence. At the summit, they found a bench with a view of the Presidential Range and sat together, catching their breath. The wind was cold at this altitude, and Elena shivered. Without thinking, Lucian took off his jacket and draped it around her shoulders.

"Thank you," she said, pulling it close.

"You're very kind."

"I'm not, usually." The admission surprised them both.

"I'm actually kind of awkward. I spend too much time with books."

"I like books." She was smiling at him — that warm, curious smile that had haunted him since the library.

"And I like kind. Kind is underrated." They sat in silence for a moment, looking out at the mountains.

And then, without quite meaning to, Lucian turned to face her. She was so close. Close enough that he could see the gold flecks in her eyes, the light dusting of freckles across her nose. Close enough that if he leaned forward, just a few inches — Her phone rang. The sound shattered the moment. Elena's expression changed instantly — the warmth draining away, replaced by something tight and careful. She fumbled for the phone in her pocket, glanced at the screen, and answered with a tone he didn't recognize.

"Yes. I'm fine. I'm on the mountain. I'll be back soon." A pause.

"No, I'm alone. I just — I twisted my ankle and had to rest." Another pause, longer this time.

"I'm sorry. I didn't mean to worry you. I'll be back by dinner. I promise." She hung up and sat there for a moment, staring at the phone in her hand.

"Everything okay?" Lucian asked.

"Fine." The word was too sharp, too bright.

"My — my boyfriend. He worries." Boyfriend.

The word landed like a blow.

"I should go," Elena said, rising carefully, testing her ankle.

"He's expecting me."

"Will you be able to make it down okay?"

"I'll be fine." She was already pulling away — not just physically, but emotionally, the walls going up, the connection they had built dissolving like morning mist.

"Thank you. For everything." She left him there on the summit, his jacket still around her shoulders.

He never got it back. But he remembered all of it. The way she laughed when he told her about a particularly absurd academic feud. The way she tilted her head when she was listening. The way she had looked at him in that moment before the phone rang, when the world had narrowed to just the two of them and anything had seemed possible. He remembered. And he never stopped wondering what might have happened if that phone hadn't rung.

"Lucian?" Elena's voice pulled him back to the present.

She was looking at him with concern, one hand on his arm, when had she touched him?, her brow furrowed.

"You went somewhere," she said.

"Just now. Where did you go?" To a mountain in New Hampshire.

To a bench with a view. To a moment that almost changed the shape of things.

"Nowhere," he said.

"Just thinking."

"About Theodore?"

"In a way." He took a breath, steadied himself.

"About love. About memory. About how some moments stay with us forever, while others fade." She was still touching his arm.

He could feel the warmth of her hand through his coat, and it took every ounce of control he had not to cover her fingers with his own.

"You speak like you've experienced that," she said.

"Like you're carrying memories that won't let go."

"I have." The words came out before he could stop them.

"I am." The wind pushed a strand of hair across her face.

Without thinking, without letting himself think, Lucian reached out to brush it back. His fingers grazed her cheek. Soft. Warm. Real. She inhaled sharply but didn't pull away.

"Lucian." Her voice was a whisper.

"What's happening here?"

"I don't know." It was the truest thing he had said all day.

"I've been asking myself the same question for over a decade." Her eyes widened.

"More than a decade?" He should stop.

He should pull back, change the subject, pretend he hadn't just revealed too much. But she was so close, and the lighthouse was glowing gold in the setting sun, and for one wild moment, he was back on that mountain bench, about to kiss her.

"Elena," he said, and her name was a prayer on his lips.

She leaned toward him. Fraction of an inch at a time. Her eyes dropped to his mouth. And his phone rang. The sound shattered the moment like glass. Lucian stepped back, his chest tightened, his hands shaking as he fumbled for his phone. Isabel. Of course it was Isabel.

"I'm sorry," he said, declining the call with trembling fingers.

50

"I should — we should get back. It's getting dark." Elena nodded, but she looked as shaken as he felt.

"Right. Yes. Dark." They walked back to the hotel in silence, the almost-kiss hanging between them like an unanswered question.

Lucian replayed the moment over and over — her eyes on his mouth, she had leaned toward him, the word *more than a decade* echoing in the space between them. He had said too much. Given too much away. And yet, she hadn't run. At the hotel's back entrance, they stopped. The windows were warm with light, and he could hear June laughing somewhere inside, talking on the phone with whoever she had called about the letters.

"Lucian," Elena said, and he turned to face her.

She was looking at him with something that might have been determination. Or fear. Or both.

"I don't understand what's happening," she said.

"I don't understand you, or this place, or why I feel like I'm waking up from a dream I've been having my whole life." She paused, took a breath.

"But I want to understand. So please. Don't shut me out."

"I'm not sure you're ready for the truth," he said quietly.

"Ready or not." She lifted her chin, and there it was again — that spark of fire he had first seen in a library all those years ago. "I'd rather know and be overwhelmed than stay in the dark and wonder." She went inside without waiting for his response, leaving him alone in the gathering dusk.

Lucian stood there for a long moment, watching the last light fade over the harbor. Then he pulled out his phone and texted Isabel: She's asking questions. I don't know how much longer I can keep this secret. Her reply came almost immediately: Then maybe it's time to stop trying. Perhaps. It was.

That night, after Elena had gone back to her apartment, Lucian sat alone with Theodore's letters and let another memory surface. September 8, 2014. Philadelphia Convention Center. He was presenting a paper on colonial shipping records — dry material that he managed to make interesting, or so his colleagues told him. The conference room was half-full, academics scattered across the seats like autumn leaves. He saw her during the Q&A. She was sitting in the back row, taking notes. Not an academic — he could tell by her clothes, her bearing, the way she looked at the presentation slides with practical rather than theoretical interest. She was wearing a tailored blazer and her hair was pulled back in a sleek ponytail. An interior designer, he learned later, researching historical details for a restoration project. She had wandered into his session by accident, drawn by the word "colonial" in the title.

She asked a question about period-appropriate color palettes. It was the first time he had ever heard her voice directed at him, even if she didn't know who he was. He answered carefully, professionally, trying to keep his voice steady. Trying not to stare. After the session, she approached the podium.

"Thank you," she said.

"That was actually incredibly helpful. I'm working on a Georgian townhouse in Boston, and the client wants everything authentic."

"I'm glad I could help." His mouth was dry.

His heart was pounding. She was so close — close enough to touch, if he dared.

"If you need more specific information, I could —" But someone else had approached, another academic wanting to discuss shipping manifests, and by the time Lucian looked up again, she was gone.

He had kept the conference program. It was in the Archive now, her question circled in red ink: "What colors would have been available for interior walls in 1780s Boston?" Five years before Brooklyn.

Four years before the gallery. The day she spoke to him and didn't know she was speaking to the man who had loved her since she was seventeen. Lucian touched Theodore's letters, thinking about the parallel. Theodore had watched Clara from a distance too. Had loved her in silence. Had kept every scrap of evidence that she existed. The difference was: Lucian's story wasn't over yet. His story was just beginning.

PART TWO

THE REMEMBERING

"Memory is not what the heart desires. That is only a mirror."

— J.R.R.

CHAPTER FIVE

❖

ELENA

"FIFTEEN YEARS?" MARLA'S VOICE came through the phone sharp enough to cut glass.

"He said all those years?" Elena was pacing her small apartment, too wired to sit still.

The floorboards creaked beneath her feet. Outside, the harbor had gone dark, the beacon sweeping across the water in slow, hypnotic circles — three seconds of brilliance, then darkness, then brilliance again. She had been watching it for the past hour, replaying every moment at the lighthouse, trying to make sense of what had happened. What had almost happened. His fingers on her cheek. The way she had leaned toward him. The words hanging between them like a door waiting to be opened.

"He said he's been asking himself what's happening between us for over a decade," Elena clarified, pausing by the window.

"Which doesn't make any sense, because I've only known him for two days."

"Unless you haven't." Marla's voice had gone thoughtful, the sharp edge softening into something more analytical.

This was her agent voice — the one she used when she was untangling a complicated plot hole in a manuscript, when the pieces didn't quite fit and she was determined to make them.

"Elena, think. Is there any way you could have met him before and forgotten?"

"I don't —" Elena stopped pacing.

Stared at the beacon as it swept past her window, painting a brief stripe of light across the ceiling.

"I don't know. I mean, I meet a lot of people. At events, conferences, through work. But if he first saw me all those years ago — fifteen years ago? I was seventeen. Still in high school. I was in school, in the suburbs." Elena pressed her fingers to her temples, trying to summon memories that felt impossibly distant — soft and blurred, like photographs left too long in the sun.

"I was just a kid, Mar. Worried about SATs and which colleges to apply to and whether Tommy Winters was going to ask me to prom. I wasn't meeting historians at conferences."

"Did you ever visit Boston proper? Libraries, museums, anywhere a historian might hang out?" Libraries.

The word snagged on something in Elena's memory — a flash of sunlight through tall windows, the smell of old books and industrial carpet cleaner, a feeling of being watched that hadn't felt threatening. More like... being seen.

"I used to go to the BU library sometimes," she said slowly, the memory surfacing like something rising from deep water.

"Senior year. I was taking a college-level literature class, and our school library didn't have the books I needed. So I would go to Boston University and study in their reading room."

"And?"

"And nothing. I went, I studied, I left." But even as she said it, Elena wasn't sure it was true.

There were gaps in her memory from that time — soft spots where specific days blurred together into a general haze of adolescence. Afternoons that felt significant but whose details had faded.

"I don't remember anything special happening."

"But he might." Marla's voice was quiet.

"If he remembers you from half your life ago, and you don't remember him, maybe there's a reason."

"What kind of reason makes someone remember a stranger for over a decade?"

"I don't know. But I think you need to find out." Marla paused, and Elena heard the familiar sound of her friend settling deeper into her couch, preparing for a proper investigation.

"What do you know about him? Besides the fact that he's a historian with cheekbones and a fifteen-year crush on you?"

"Not much." Elena ran through their conversations, searching for details.

"His name is Lucian Calder. He lives here in Camden's Rise, or nearby. He's been researching the hotel for two years. He has a sister named Isabel who texts him a lot." She paused, remembering the way he had read Theodore's letters — the raw understanding in his voice, the way the words seemed to cost him something.

"He reads old letters like they're love poems. Like they're written about him, not just by someone he's studying."

"That's not a lot to go on." The sound of typing came through the phone — Marla's fingers flying across her laptop keyboard.

"Hold on. Let me do what I do best."

"Marla, you don't have to —"

"Shush. I'm working." More typing, faster now.

"Lucian Calder... historian... Maine..." A long pause.

"Oh." Elena's heart skipped.

"Oh? What does 'oh' mean?"

"It means I found him. And I found something very interesting." Marla's voice had taken on a strange quality — part curiosity, part concern, part the particular excitement she got when she discovered something unexpected in a manuscript.

"Elena, have you ever heard of HSAM?"

"No. What is it?"

"Highly Superior Autobiographical Memory. It's a neurological condition — extremely rare. People who have it remember every day of their lives in vivid detail. Every face they've ever seen. Every moment preserved." Elena felt the floor shift beneath her.

"And Lucian has this?"

"According to everything I can find, yes." More typing.

"There's an interview in Psychology Today from a few years back." Marla cleared her throat and began: "For most people, memory is a faded photograph — impressionistic, incomplete, subject to revision over time. For Lucian Calder, it's more like a film archive. Every moment of his life is stored in vivid detail, accessible at will."'It sounds like a gift,' Calder says, when I meet him at a café in Portland, Maine.

He's tall, soft-spoken, with the careful demeanor that suggests he's used to being misunderstood. 'And sometimes it is. I never forget a birthday. I can recall exactly what I was doing on any date you name.' He pauses, stirring his coffee with methodical precision. 'But it's also a curse. Every mistake I've ever made is just as vivid as every triumph. Every loss is as fresh as the day it happened. There's no softening with time. No forgetting.' "The condition has shaped his career as a historian. 'I'm drawn to preservation,' he explains. 'To the idea that the past matters. That the people who came before us deserve to be remembered.' He looks out the window at the gray Maine sky, and something shifts in his expression — something that looks like longing. 'because I know what it's like to carry the past with you. Every day. Whether you want to or not.'" Marla stopped reading.

The silence stretched between them, vast and full.

"Elena? Are you still there?"

"I'm here." Elena's voice sounded strange to her own ears — thin, distant, like it was coming from somewhere far away.

"He remembers everything. Every day of his life." She let the implication land.

"So if we crossed paths, even years ago, even in passing —"

"He would remember." Elena pressed her palms together, where her heart was beating too fast, too hard.

"He would remember all of it. What I was wearing. What I said. How I looked. Every single detail."

"Yes." The implications crashed over her like a wave — relentless, overwhelming, reshaping the landscape of everything she thought she understood.

If Lucian had HSAM, and he had known her for over a decade, then every encounter they'd had, every moment she had forgotten, was preserved in his mind like a film on endless loop. He knew things about her that she didn't even know about herself. He had been carrying her, carrying them, for more than a decade. The implications settled slowly, like sediment in water. If Lucian had HSAM, then every encounter they'd had, every moment she'd forgotten, was still vivid for him. He'd been carrying something for more than a decade that she hadn't known existed.

"This is insane," she whispered.

Marla was quiet for a moment. When she spoke again, her voice was different — careful in a way Elena rarely heard from her. Marla was not a careful person. She was bold and blunt and gloriously tactless. Hearing her choose her words was like watching a bull tiptoe.

"I need to say something, and I need you to hear it as love and not as judgment."

"Okay."

"That's a lot, Elena."

"I know."

"No. I mean — a man who can't forget you. Who has remembered you, perfectly, for fifteen years. Who knows what you were wearing, what you were reading, things about you that you've forgotten about yourself." A pause.

"That is a LOT for anyone to carry about another person. And it's a lot to discover someone's been carrying about you."

"You think it's creepy."

"I think it's complicated. I think the romantic version of this story is a man who loved you across time and distance and never stopped hoping. And I think the other version of this story is a man who fixated on a stranger and built a life around it." Her voice softened.

"I don't know which version is true. Both. But you just got out of a relationship with someone who paid too much attention to you, Elena. I'd be a bad friend if I didn't say: be careful. Make sure you're choosing this with your eyes open, not because it feels like a fairy tale."

"You're comparing him to Adam."

"I'm not. I'm saying your radar for this stuff was broken. Adam broke it. And until it's healed, every intense man who pays a lot of attention to you deserves a second look. Not because he's guilty. Because you deserve to be sure." Elena was quiet for a long time.

"I felt something when he shook my hand," she said finally.

"Something I've never felt before. Not with Adam, not with anyone."

"I know. And that might be real. It probably is real." Marla's voice was gentle now.

"But 'I've never felt this before' is also what you said about Adam. First year. Remember?" Elena did remember.

"I'm not trying to ruin this," Marla said.

"I'm trying to make sure you go in awake. You deserve a great love story, Elena. But you also deserve one you chose with your whole brain, not just your whole heart."

"I need to talk to him. I need to hear it from him, not from a magazine article."

"Yes. And Elena? Take your time. You don't owe anyone an answer on their schedule — no matter how long they've been waiting." After they hung up, Elena sat in the darkness for a long time, watching the lighthouse beam sweep across the harbor.

All those years. Somewhere in her past, there were moments she had lost — moments that Lucian had carried for her, preserved in the amber of his impossible memory. The thought should have been unsettling. Instead, it felt almost... safe. Like discovering that someone had been watching over her all along, keeping pieces of her story that she had dropped along the way.

She couldn't sleep. At midnight, Elena gave up trying and opened her laptop, pulling up search results for Lucian Calder. The magazine interview Marla had found was just the beginning. There were academic papers with his name attached — dense, footnote-heavy explorations of New England maritime history that she couldn't entirely follow but found oddly comforting in their thoroughness. There were conference presentations, university profiles, a handful of book reviews he had written for obscure historical journals. And there were more articles about HSAM. She read them all, hungry for understanding. She learned that the condition was first documented in 2006, when a woman named Jill Price contacted researchers at UC Irvine with what she called "the running movie" of her life playing constantly in her head.

She learned that people with HSAM could be given any date from their past and recall it in vivid detail — the weather, their meals, the conversations they'd had, the emotions they'd felt. She learned that it wasn't always a gift. One researcher described it as "the inability to forget." Another called it "living with the volume turned up to eleven, all the time." People with HSAM reported difficulty moving on from painful experiences, struggle with letting go of grudges, a tendency to become lost in the past at the expense of the present.

Elena considered Lucian's voice as he read Theodore's letters. The raw understanding in his tone. The way he had said, Some loves don't fade. He hadn't been talking about Theodore. Not really. She closed her laptop and stared at the ceiling, her mind churning. Fifteen years of watching. Fifteen years ago, it would have been 2009. She would have been seventeen, a senior in high school. And he would have been... she did the math... twenty-two. A graduate student, probably. Young enough to fall hard, old enough to know better. Had they talked? Had they touched? Had there been a moment, a single, crystalline moment, when their eyes met across some crowded room, and something sparked between them? She wished she could remember. She wished she had Lucian's gift, or curse, just for one night, so she could find that moment and understand what had happened. Instead, she had only fragments. The library at Boston University, warm with afternoon light. A feeling of being watched. A book she had been reading, what book? She couldn't remember, and someone's eyes on her, gray and intense and strangely familiar. Had that been him? Had she smiled at him, spoken to him, given him something to hold onto for the next fifteen years? The not-knowing was maddening. She got out of bed, pulled on her coat, and went to the window. The town was dark and quiet, the only movement the distant sweep of the lighthouse beam. Here, past and present overlapped. That was why Lucian lived here, she thought. It was easier to carry years of memory in a place where history was woven into every cobblestone. Elena thought about Adam — the way he had collected information about her like ammunition, storing it away until he could use it to hurt her. The screenshots he kept of her texts, the detailed logs of her schedule, how he always seemed to know where she was and who she was with. That had been surveillance. That had been invasion. That had been suffocation. Lucian's attention was different. She didn't fully understand why, but she trusted the difference. Adam's knowledge had been wielded like a weapon. Lucian's seemed more like a wound — something he carried not because he wanted to, but because he couldn't help it. Every mistake I've ever made is just as vivid as every triumph. Every loss is as fresh as the day it happened. If he had loved her for over a decade — if he had carried her in his perfect, unforgiving memory all that time — then the pain he must have felt, watching her from a distance, unable to approach, unable to forget... It broke her heart a little, thinking about it. She made a decision. Tomorrow, she would find him. She would look him in the eye and tell him what she had learned, and she would ask him to tell her the truth. All of it. Every moment he remembered, every encounter she had forgotten, every piece of their shared history that only he could see. She wanted to know. More than that — she wanted to understand him. This man who had apparently spent those years loving her from afar, carrying her in his memory like a flame he couldn't extinguish. She wanted to know who he was beyond the historian, beyond the HSAM, beyond the careful restraint he wore like armor. And if the truth was overwhelming, if it was too much, too intense, too strange to bear, then at least she would know. At least she would have made the choice with her eyes open, like Marla said. Elena climbed back into bed and pulled the covers up to her chin. Outside, the beacon swept past her window, steady and sure, guiding ships through the darkness. Or she was romanticizing a situation she didn't fully understand, weaving a love story out of fragments and hints and the desperate hope that her life could still hold something beautiful. Either way, she was done wondering. Tomorrow, she would get answers. She fell asleep with Lucian's words echoing in her mind: I've been asking myself the same question for over a decade. Tomorrow, they would find the answer together.

At some point before dawn, she picked up her phone and typed a message to Marla.

I think I'm falling for him.

The response came immediately.

Falling? Honey, you fell the moment he shook your hand. I've been waiting for you to figure it out.

Elena laughed despite herself, wetly, into her pillow.

What do I do?

What do you want to do?

She thought about it. About the Archive. About those years. About the man who had watched her from a distance and loved her in silence and never once crossed the line into demanding anything from her.

I want to see it. I want to know everything.

Then go see it. And Elena?

Yeah?

Be brave. You deserve this.

Elena set down the phone and looked out at the lighthouse, steady on its promontory. She had spent three years with a man who made her small.

It was time to try something bigger.

CHAPTER SIX

❖

LUCIAN

THE KNOCK CAME AT 7:43 in the morning. Lucian was already awake — he was always awake early, his mind too full of memories to allow for restful sleep — and had been standing at his kitchen window for the better part of an hour, watching the fog roll in off the harbor while his coffee grew cold in his hands. The lighthouse beam cut through the mist, a ghost of light sweeping through the gray. He had spent the night replaying the moment at the lighthouse. The way Elena had leaned toward him, her lips parting, her eyes dropping to his mouth. The question in her eyes. The fifteen years that had slipped from his lips like a confession he hadn't meant to make. He had ruined everything. He was certain of it. By now, she had probably Googled him, found the articles about his condition, and decided he was exactly the kind of man she should run from: intense, obsessive, carrying a torch that had burned for more than a decade without ever finding its proper home. The knock came again, more insistent. Lucian set down his cold coffee and walked to the door, steeling himself for whoever might be on the other side. June, perhaps, with questions about the letters. Isabel, checking up on him. A neighbor wanting to borrow something mundane. It was Elena. She stood on his doorstep in jeans and a cream-colored sweater — the same color she had worn in the library, all those years ago. Her hair was loose around her shoulders, her cheeks flushed from the cold, her breath making small clouds in the morning air. She looked like she hadn't slept, there were shadows under her eyes, a tension in her jaw, but her gaze was steady. Determined. Like a woman who had come for answers and would not leave without them.

"I know about your memory," she said.

Lucian's heart stopped. Started again. Kept beating, even as the world tilted beneath his feet.

"Elena —"

"HSAM." She said it like a challenge, like a door she was forcing open.

"Highly Superior Autobiographical Memory. You remember everything. Every day of your life, in vivid detail." She took a breath, and he could see the effort it cost her to stay calm.

"Including me. Including every time we've ever met. Which apparently has been more than once." He should have expected this.

He should have prepared a speech, a careful explanation, a way to frame the truth that wouldn't make him sound like a man who had been stalking her memories for over a decade. Instead, he said: In the corner of the living room, Keats raised his graying head from the armchair, studied the tension in the room, and lowered it again. Even the dog knew this was above his pay grade.

"Twelve times." She went still.

"What?"

"We've met twelve times." His voice sounded strange to his own ears — rough, unsteady, nothing like the careful academic tone he usually cultivated.

"Over fifteen years. The first time was October 15, 2009, in the Boston University library. You were reading Neruda. Twenty Love Poems and a Song of Despair. You were sitting three tables away from me, with your legs tucked under you, and you looked up and smiled at me, and I —" He stopped.

Swallowed.

"I fell in love with you before I even knew your name." Elena stared at him.

The color had drained from her face, leaving her pale against the gray morning fog.

"Can I come in?" she asked quietly.

He stepped aside without a word, and she walked past him into his house.

His house was exactly what she might have expected from a historian with extraordinary memory: books everywhere, stacked on shelves and piled on tables and lining the walls in towering columns that threatened to topple at any moment. But there were surprises too. A grand piano in the corner, its surface dusty but cared for, as if he played it only when no one was listening. Photographs on the mantle — a woman who must be Isabel, laughing at something off-camera; a couple who must be his parents, standing in front of a lighthouse; a dog with a graying muzzle, its eyes kind and knowing. A kitchen that smelled of coffee and something herbal, rosemary maybe, growing in small clay pots on the windowsill. It was like a home. Like a life. Not the lair of an obsessed man, but the refuge of a lonely one. Elena turned to face him. He was standing by the door, his hands shoved in his pockets, looking at her like she might disappear at any moment. Like she was a dream he was afraid of waking from.

"Twelve times," she said.

"Tell me about them."

"Are you sure you want to know?"

"I'm sure I need to." She sat down on his couch, tucking her legs beneath her — the same way she had sat in the library, all those years ago, though she didn't know that.

"Start from the beginning." Lucian moved to the armchair across from her, keeping the coffee table between them like a barrier. A safety measure.

For her or for him, he wasn't sure.

"The library," he began.

"October 2009. I was twenty-two, working on my dissertation. You were —"

"Seventeen," she said.

"I was visiting the BU library for a literature class."

"You were reading poetry. Your lips moved when you read, like you were tasting the words." He closed his eyes, letting the memory wash over him — the October sunlight, the smell of old books, the way his heart had stopped when she looked up.

"You looked up. Our eyes met. You smiled at me like you recognized me from somewhere, even though we'd never met. And then your phone rang, and you left, and I thought I'd never see you again."

"But you did."

"Four years later. July 2013. Mount Washington." He opened his eyes, finding her watching him with an expression he couldn't read.

"You'd twisted your ankle on the trail. I helped you back down the mountain. We talked for two hours. You told me about your design studies, your dreams, your love of old buildings with good bones." Elena's hand went to her mouth.

"I remember that," she whispered.

"I remember a man helping me. I remember talking for hours, feeling like I could tell him anything. But I didn't — I couldn't picture his face afterward. It was like the memory was foggy."

"That's normal." The words were gentle, despite the ache.

"Most people's memories work that way. Details fade. Faces blur. You forget the things that don't seem important at the time."

"But you don't."

"No." He met her eyes.

"I don't."

"Tell me more." So he did.

He told her about Brooklyn. March 8, 2016. Prospect Heights, Brooklyn. He was in New York for a conference on maritime trade records. The hotel was in Midtown, but he had ventured to Brooklyn for the afternoon, drawn by the promise of a bookstore that specialized in antique maps. The café was an accident. He had been walking back toward the subway when the rain started — sudden, drenching, the kind of March downpour that turned sidewalks into rivers. He ducked into the first open door he saw: a small coffee shop with mismatched furniture and a chalkboard menu and the smell of fresh-baked scones. She was already there. Sitting at a corner table with a laptop open in front of her, her brow furrowed in concentration. She had cut her hair since Mount Washington — it fell just past her shoulders now, layered and professional. She wore a gray blazer over a soft blue blouse, and there was a half-eaten croissant on a plate beside her coffee. Lucian's heart stopped. Started. Kept going, even as his legs threatened to give out beneath him. Three years since Mount Washington. Seven years since the library. And here she was, like a mirage made flesh, close enough to touch. He should approach her. He should. Three encounters now, three moments of connection that she wouldn't remember but he couldn't forget. This was his chance to introduce himself properly, to become a real person in her life instead of a ghost passing through it. He ordered a coffee. Took a seat at a table near the window, where he could watch her without being obvious about it. Rehearsed opening lines in his head: Hi, I don't know if you remember me, but we met on Mount Washington a few years ago. Or: Excuse me, I couldn't help noticing — no, that was creepy. Or simply: Hello, I'm Lucian. Hello, I'm Lucian, and I've been in love with you for seven years. The rain drummed against the windows. Steam rose from his untouched coffee. Elena typed something on her laptop, paused, typed again. She bit her lower lip when she was thinking — the same habit she'd had in the library, all those years ago. He was gathering his courage, preparing to stand, when the door opened and a man walked in. Tall. Blond. Handsome in the polished, practiced way of men who knew their own worth and expected others to recognize it. He scanned the café until his eyes landed on Elena, and something in his expression shifted — a tightening, a possessiveness that made Lucian's stomach turn.

"There you are." The man crossed to Elena's table, not asking permission before pulling out a chair and sitting down.

"I've been calling you for an hour."

"I know. I was working." Elena's voice was different than Lucian remembered — quieter, more careful.

The spark he had seen on the mountain seemed dimmed, like a flame with too little oxygen.

"I told you I had a deadline."

"And I told you I needed you home by four. We have dinner with my partners tonight, remember?" The man — Adam, Lucian would later learn, though he didn't know it then — leaned across the table, his voice dropping to a murmur that Lucian could barely hear.

"You're embarrassing me, Elena. Running off to coffee shops, ignoring my calls. People are starting to talk."

"I just needed some space to work —"

"You have an office at home. You have everything you need at home." Adam's hand closed over Elena's wrist — not violent, not aggressive, but firm.

Controlling.

"Come on. We're going." Elena closed her laptop.

Gathered her things. She moved like someone who had learned to make herself small, to take up as little space as possible. When she stood, her eyes swept the café — and for one heart-stopping moment, they landed on Lucian. Recognition flickered in her gaze. That same almost-knowing look she had given him in the library, on the mountain. Like she could sense something familiar about him, even if she couldn't name it. And then Adam's hand was on her back, guiding her toward the door, and she was gone. Lucian sat in the café for another hour, his coffee growing cold, aching with a helplessness he had never felt before. He had found her again. And he had watched her walk away with a man who dimmed her light. He had done nothing. The guilt of that inaction would haunt him for years.

Elena was crying. Silent tears tracking down her cheeks, her hands pressed flat against her thighs like she was holding herself together by force of will. Lucian wanted to go to her, to gather her in his arms, to tell her that it was over now, that Adam couldn't hurt her anymore. But that wasn't his place. Not yet. Not ever.

"I remember that day," she said, her voice thick.

"March 2016. I was working on a presentation for a client, and Adam showed up at the café because I hadn't answered my phone. He was —" She stopped.

Took a shuddering breath.

"He was always showing up. Always finding me. I thought it meant he loved me. That he couldn't stand to be apart from me."

"Elena —"

"I didn't know it was control until later. Until Marla helped me see it." She wiped her cheeks with the back of her hand.

"But you saw it. That day in the café. You saw what he was doing to me."

"I should have done something." The words came out ragged, torn from somewhere deep inside him.

"I should have spoken up. Intervened. Something."

"What could you have done? You were a stranger. I wouldn't have listened." Elena looked at him, and despite the tears, there was something steady in her gaze.

"I wasn't ready to see it then. I wouldn't have believed you if you'd tried to tell me."

"That doesn't make it easier."

"No." She was quiet for a moment.

"What happened after? The other encounters?" So he told her.

The gallery in Washington, D.C. where he had seen her studying a Hopper painting with tears in her eyes — Nighthawks, the lonely figures in their pools of light. The bookstore in Cambridge where she had been buying architecture texts, her ring finger conspicuously bare. The farmer's market in Portland where she had been laughing with a woman he now knew was Marla, her smile brighter than he had seen it in years. He told her about the train platform in Boston, and the conference in Philadelphia, and the beach in Rhode Island where he had walked past her without stopping because she had been reading, lost in a book, and he hadn't wanted to disturb her peace. He stopped talking. The room was quiet.

"Why?" she asked when he finished.

"Why didn't you ever approach me? Introduce yourself?"

"Because what would I have said?" Lucian stood, moving to the window, unable to sit still any longer.

"Hi, you don't remember me, but we've met before, multiple times, and I've been carrying feelings for you for years even though we've never actually had a real conversation?" He laughed, but there was no humor in it.

"I would have sounded insane. I am insane, probably. What kind of person falls in love with someone they've barely spoken to?"

"The kind who can't forget." He turned.

Elena had stood too, and she was closer than he expected — close enough that he could see the gold flecks in her hazel eyes, the slight tremble in her lower lip.

"You didn't choose this," she said.

"You didn't choose to remember me. Your brain did that on its own."

"That doesn't excuse —"

"I need time to think about what this means," she said.

She took a step closer but stopped short of touching him.

"I'm not running. But I'm not ready to say it's fine, either. I need to sit with it."

"Lucian, you never approached me. You never stalked me, or manipulated me, or tried to insert yourself into my life. You just... remembered. And waited. And hoped."

"I have a room." The confession spilled out before he could stop it.

"In my basement. I call it the Archive. It has... things. Objects from our encounters. The book you left in the library. A napkin from the café. A ticket stub from the gallery." He could feel the shame burning in his cheeks.

"I kept them. Like evidence. Like proof that you were real, that our moments together weren't just something I imagined." He expected her to recoil.

To see the Archive for what it probably was — a shrine to an obsession, a monument to his inability to let go. Instead, she said: "Can I see it?" Lucian stared at her.

"What?"

"The Archive." Her voice was steady, her gaze unwavering.

"I want to see it. I want to see... us. The parts of us that I forgot."

"Elena, I don't think —"

"You've been carrying this alone for over a decade." She reached out and touched his arm, and the contact sent electricity singing through his veins.

"Let me carry it with you. Let me see what you've seen. Please." He should say no.

He should protect her from the full weight of his devotion, the strange and possibly unhealthy way he had loved her all these years. But she was asking. She was choosing to know. And he had never been able to deny her anything.

"Not today," he said quietly.

"It's... a lot. And my sister is coming to dinner tonight. She's been wanting to meet you."

"Isabel?"

"She knows everything. About you, about the encounters, about..." He gestured vaguely, encompassing a lifetime of love and longing.

"She's been telling me for years that I needed to either let you go or find a way to actually meet you. She was the one who encouraged me to take the consulting job with June."

"She sounds like Marla."

"They would probably get along terrifyingly well." A smile tugged at the corner of his mouth — the first real smile he had felt in days.

"Have dinner with us tonight. Meet Isabel. Let her tell you all the embarrassing stories about me that I'll conveniently forget to mention."

"You don't forget anything."

"Exactly." He held her gaze.

"So you'll have to trust Isabel to give you the unvarnished truth." Elena was quiet for a long moment.

The fog had begun to lift outside, pale sunlight filtering through the clouds, and it caught the gold in her hair, the warmth in her eyes.

"Okay," she said finally.

"Dinner tonight. Meet Isabel. And then..."

"And then we'll see," he finished.

She nodded. Turned toward the door. Then stopped, her hand on the frame.

"Lucian?"

"Yes?"

"The book I left in the library. The Neruda." She looked back at him over her shoulder.

"It was a gift from my grandmother. She died three months before that day. I was reading it because it made me feel close to her." His throat tightened.

"I didn't know."

"No. You couldn't have." She smiled — small, fragile, but real.

"But you kept it safe. All those years, you kept a piece of her safe, without even knowing what it meant to me." She left before he could respond.

Lucian stood in his living room, surrounded by books and memories and the fading scent of her perfume, and felt something shift in his chest. For years, he had been the keeper of their story — the only one who remembered, the only one who knew. Now, finally, he wasn't alone. Now, finally, they could write the next chapter together.

That night, after Elena left, Lucian sat alone in his living room and called Isabel.

"She knows," he said.

"She found out about HSAM. She came to my door this morning and asked me to tell her the truth."

"And did you?"

"I told her about the library. The mountain. The café in Brooklyn." He paused.

"She didn't run."

"Good. That's good." But Isabel's voice had an edge he recognized — Doctor Isabel, not Sister Isabel.

"Can I say something uncomfortable?"

"When have you ever not?"

"The Elena in your head — the one you've been carrying since you first saw her, all those years ago. Is she a person or a photograph?" He didn't answer immediately.

"Because here's what worries me," Isabel continued.

"You've told me about Elena for over a decade. How she tilts her head. How she reads with her lips moving. How she laughed on that mountain. Beautiful details, observed with love. But they're all exterior. You've never once told me what makes her angry. What she's afraid of. What her bad days look like."

"I haven't had the chance —"

"That's my point. You've had over a decade. Twelve encounters. And you don't know her. You know her surface — her at her best, reading poetry, laughing in good light. That's not a person. That's an ideal." The word settled into him like cold water.

"I'm not saying don't pursue this. The chemistry sounds genuine. But please — go into this knowing the difference between the Elena you've imagined and the Elena who exists. Because if she discovers you've built a shrine to a version of her that isn't real, that's not romantic. That's pressure."

"You think I'm obsessed."

"I think you're in love. And I think that for a person with HSAM, love and obsession share a border that other people don't have to navigate." Her voice softened.

"I love you. I want this for you. But I want it to be real — the actual, messy, imperfect thing. Not a fifteen-year fantasy."

"What if the actual, messy, imperfect thing isn't as good as the story?"

"Then you grieve the story and fall in love with the mess. That's what the rest of us do. Welcome to normal human romance — it's terrible and wonderful and nothing like a fantasy, and I promise you it's better." After they hung up, Lucian sat in his study for a long time, thinking about the difference between knowing someone and knowing about them.

That night, after Elena left, Lucian sat alone in his living room and wondered if he had made a terrible mistake.

He had shown her the Neruda book. Told her about the Archive. Revealed the scope of his obsession — because that's what it was, wasn't it? Fifteen years of watching, waiting, collecting. Any rational person would run. But Elena hadn't run. She had looked at him with those dark eyes, and instead of fear or disgust, he had seen... understanding. Recognition. Something that looked almost like hope. Isabel had texted him three times in the past hour: How did it go? Lucian. LUCIAN. If you don't respond in the next five minutes I'm driving up there. He typed back: She knows. She's coming to see the Archive tomorrow. The response was immediate: And? And she didn't run. OH MY GOD. Then, a moment later: I'm so proud of you. And so scared for you. And so hopeful. Is that possible? To be all three at once? I feel the same way. Get some sleep. You're going to need it. But sleep seemed impossible. His mind was racing, replaying every moment of the past few days. Elena walking into the ballroom. How she had shaken his hand and something in her eyes had flickered — that same almost-recognition he had seen so many times before. She had said his name, like it was a word she was just learning but wanted to keep saying. He went to the Archive. The room was small — a converted study, really, with built-in bookshelves and a large desk. But every surface was covered with evidence. Years of memory made tangible. He ran his fingers across the spines of the books — the Neruda, of course, but also a novel she had been reading on the beach, a guidebook from Mount Washington, an architecture text from the Philadelphia conference. Each one a connection. A thread in the tapestry he had been weaving without knowing why. Tomorrow, she would see all of this. Tomorrow, she would understand the full weight of what he had been carrying. And then — He didn't know what came next. He had never let himself imagine beyond this moment, this threshold. For so many years, the fantasy had been enough. The dream of someday. But now someday was here, and he was terrified. What if she decided it was too much? What if she looked at the Archive, at the depth and breadth of his devotion, and couldn't love him back? He would survive. He had survived this long without her; he could survive a lifetime. The memories would sustain him, as they always had. But God, he didn't want to just survive anymore. He wanted to live. He wanted her. And for the first time, that want felt possible. Real. Close enough to touch. Lucian sat down at the desk, surrounded by a lifetime of love made visible, and let himself hope. Tomorrow, he would show her everything. And maybe, just maybe, everything would finally be enough.

CHAPTER SEVEN

ELENA

SHE CHANGED HER OUTFIT four times. Which was ridiculous. It was just dinner. With a man she had technically known for three days and his sister whom she had never met. There was no reason for the butterflies staging a full revolt in her stomach, no reason for the way her hands trembled as she applied mascara for the third time. Except that nothing about this situation was normal. Elena stared at her reflection in the small bathroom mirror of her rental apartment, the overhead light casting shadows that made her look older, more tired than she felt. She had settled on a deep green dress that Marla always said brought out her eyes — a wrap style that hugged her curves without being too obvious about it — paired with ankle boots and a cream cardigan in case Lucian's house was cold. Her hair was down, falling in waves past her shoulders, he seemed to like it — She caught herself, lipstick hovering midway to her mouth. How he seemed to like it. How would she know what he liked? They had barely spoken before this week. Except they had. Twelve times over the years, according to him. And he remembered every detail of every encounter with vivid clarity. He knew what she looked like with her hair down because he had seen it that way before. On a mountain trail where autumn was turning the trees to fire. In a café where she had been too absorbed in her work to notice the man watching her from across the room. In a library when she was seventeen and reading poetry and had no idea that a stranger three tables away was falling in love with her. The thought should have been unsettling. Instead, it made her feel... seen. Known in a way that transcended the normal getting-to-know-you rituals of new relationships — the careful revelations, the curated vulnerability, the slow peeling back of layers. Lucian already knew her layers. He had been studying them for over a decade. Not that this was a relationship. Not yet. Not ever. But as she looked at herself in the mirror — really looked, she imagined Lucian had looked at her all those times — she saw something she hadn't seen in years. A woman who might be worth remembering. She grabbed her coat and headed out before she could change her mind.

Lucian's house looked different in the evening light. Warmer, More alive. The windows glowed golden against the deepening dusk, and she could see movement inside — two figures in the kitchen, one tall and angular, one smaller and animated. The smell of something savory drifted through the cold November air as she approached the door: herbs and roasting meat and something else, something that smelled like home. The fog had rolled back in, softening the edges of everything, and the light. The lighthouse visible in the distance, sweeping its patient arc across the water. Elena paused on the walkway, her breath making small clouds in the chill, and let herself feel the moment. The anticipation. The fear. The strange, impossible hope that had been growing since she first shook Lucian's hand and felt the world tilt on its axis. Before she could knock, the door swung open. The woman standing there was immediately recognizable as Lucian's sister. She had the same gray-blue eyes, the same sharp cheekbones, the same way of tilting her head when she was studying something — or someone. But where Lucian was all restrained intensity, carefully contained, Isabel Calder practically vibrated with energy. Her dark hair was cut in a stylish bob that framed her face, her smile was wide and welcoming, and she was wearing an apron that said "Kiss the Psychologist" in bright pink letters.

"You must be Elena." Isabel didn't wait for confirmation before pulling her into a hug that smelled of wine and expensive perfume.

"I've heard so much about you. And by 'so much,' I mean everything. Every single detail. For fifteen years. Do you know how hard it is to compete with a woman your brother has been obsessing over since grad school?"

"Isabel." Lucian's voice came from somewhere behind his sister, mortified.

"We talked about this."

"We talked about me being 'appropriate and not overwhelming.'" Isabel released Elena from the hug but kept hold of her shoulders, examining her face with frank curiosity that somehow didn't feel invasive.

"I never agreed to any of that. Now come in, come in. Lucian made his famous chicken, which is the only thing he knows how to cook, so you're in for a treat." Elena found herself swept into the house on a wave of Isabel's enthusiasm.

The interior was exactly as she remembered from that morning — books everywhere, photographs on the mantle, the grand piano gleaming in the corner — but the candlelight transformed it into something softer, more intimate. The scent of rosemary and thyme hung in the air, and somewhere soft music was playing, something classical she couldn't quite identify. Lucian was standing by the kitchen island, looking like he wanted the floor to swallow him whole. He had changed since that morning — wearing a soft gray sweater now that brought out the blue in his eyes, his hair still damp from a shower. He looked nervous. Human. Achingly beautiful in a way that caught her off guard.

"I'm sorry," he said.

"I tried to warn you."

"Don't apologize for me." Isabel was already pouring wine into three glasses — crystal, catching the candlelight and throwing tiny rainbows across the counter.

"I'm delightful. Elena, red or white? Actually, don't answer that — Lucian, what does she prefer?" Lucian's cheeks flushed, the color rising from his collar to his cheekbones.

"That's not, I don't,"

"Red," Elena said, surprising herself with how steady her voice came out.

"I usually prefer red." Isabel turned to her brother with a triumphant expression.

"See? Half a lifetime of paying attention, and you can't even tell the woman what wine she likes. Some memory you've got."

"That's because I've never seen her drink wine." Lucian accepted the glass Isabel handed him with a long-suffering expression that suggested this was a familiar dynamic.

"Memory only works if there's something to remember."

"Convenient excuse." Isabel handed Elena her glass — the wine was a deep garnet, swirling like captured sunset — and raised her own in a toast.

"To finally meeting you, Elena. You have no idea how long I've been waiting for this." They drank.

The wine was excellent — rich and smooth, with notes of dark cherry and something that might have been chocolate — and Elena felt some of the tension in her shoulders begin to ease. Isabel was overwhelming, yes, but in a warm way. Like being caught in a very enthusiastic tide that was determined to carry you somewhere wonderful whether you liked it or not.

"So," Isabel said, settling onto one of the kitchen stools and patting the one beside her for Elena, "how are you processing all of this? Finding out my brother has been carrying a torch for you since the Bush administration?"

"It was 2009," Lucian muttered, turning back to the stove where something was sizzling gently in a pan.

"Obama had already been inaugurated."

"Details." Isabel waved a hand dismissively.

"The point stands. Elena, honestly — how are you doing with this?" Elena considered the question, rolling the stem of her wine glass between her fingers.

She had been asked versions of it by Marla, by herself, by the anxious voice in her head that still sometimes sounded like Adam, telling her that her feelings were wrong, that she should be afraid, that anyone who paid this much attention to her must want something dangerous. But coming from Isabel, a psychologist, someone who dealt in feelings for a living, it felt different. More permission to be honest.

"I'm not sure," she admitted.

"It's a lot to take in. Finding out someone has known you, remembered you, for over a decade when you had no idea they existed..." She shook her head, watching the wine swirl in her glass.

"Part of me wants to be freaked out. Part of me thinks I should be running for the hills."

"And the other parts?" Elena glanced at Lucian, who was studiously attending to something on the stove, his back to them.

She could see the tension in his shoulders, the careful stillness of his posture, he was clearly listening to every word while pretending he wasn't.

"The other parts feel like I've been missing something my whole life," she said quietly, "and I just found it." Lucian's shoulders relaxed, just slightly.

Just enough for her to notice. Isabel's expression softened, the playful energy giving way to something more serious.

"Can I tell you something? As his sister, and as a psychologist who has watched him navigate this condition his whole life?"

"Please."

"HSAM is... complicated." Isabel swirled her wine, choosing her words with the careful precision of someone who had thought about this many times.

"People think it sounds amazing — extraordinary memory, never forgetting anything. Like a superpower. But it's also a burden. Every embarrassing moment, every failure, every heartbreak — it's all right there, as vivid as the day it happened. Lucian can't move on from things the way the rest of us do. Time doesn't heal his wounds because time doesn't dim his memories."

"I've read about that," Elena said.

"The articles called it 'the inability to forget.'"

"Exactly." Isabel nodded.

"And that's why what he felt for you is... remarkable. Not creepy, not obsessive — remarkable. Because he could have let those early encounters become painful. Every time he saw you and couldn't speak to you, every time he watched you with someone else, every time he came close and then had to let you go — he could have let those memories become wounds that never healed. Instead, he chose to let them be something beautiful. Something to hope for." Lucian turned around, leaning against the counter with his wine glass cradled in his hands.

His expression was vulnerable in a way Elena had never seen — stripped of its usual careful composure, open and raw and terrified.

"Isabel," he said quietly.

"You don't have to —"

"Yes, I do." Isabel's voice was firm, the voice of a woman who had clearly had this argument before and was not going to lose it now.

"Because you won't. You'll stand there being stoic and noble and refusing to advocate for yourself, and Elena deserves to know who she's dealing with." She turned back to Elena.

"My brother is the most decent person I know. When he saw you with that man — Adam — in Brooklyn, he wanted to intervene. He wanted to say something, do something. But he didn't, because It wasn't his place. Because he respected your autonomy even when it was killing him to watch." Elena thought about the café.

About Adam's hand on her wrist, his fingers pressing just hard enough to leave marks she would notice later. His voice in her ear, low and controlled, making threats that sounded like concern. How she had made herself small to accommodate his anger, had packed up her laptop and her dreams and followed him out the door like a dog that had been trained to heel. And somewhere in that same room, three tables away, Lucian had been watching. Hurting. Doing nothing because doing something would have overstepped. Would have made him no better than the man he was watching.

"He told me he felt guilty about that," Elena said.

"Of course he did. He feels guilty about everything." Isabel rolled her eyes affectionately.

"He feels guilty that he remembers you when you don't remember him. He feels guilty that he kept objects from your encounters. He feels guilty that he's been in love with you for over a decade without your knowledge or consent, as if feelings were something that required a permission slip."

"They're not," Elena said, surprising herself with the firmness in her voice.

"Feelings aren't a crime. And neither is memory." Isabel smiled — a real smile, warm and pleased, the smile of a woman who had just confirmed something she had hoped was true.

"I like you. I knew I would, but it's nice to have it confirmed."

"The chicken is ready," Lucian said abruptly, his voice too loud, a little too bright.

"Can we please stop psychoanalyzing my emotional landscape and eat?"

Dinner was delicious, as promised.

The chicken was herb-roasted and perfectly seasoned, the skin golden and crispy, the meat so tender it practically fell off the bone. It was served with roasted vegetables — carrots and parsnips and Brussels sprouts caramelized to perfection — and a crusty bread that Lucian admitted, with some embarrassment, he had bought from the bakery in town. They ate at his small dining table, surrounded by towers of books and the soft glow of candles that Isabel had insisted on lighting "for ambiance." The conversation flowed more easily than Elena had expected.

Isabel told stories about their childhood in Connecticut — about Lucian's early struggles with HSAM, the way teachers had accused him of cheating because he could recall textbook pages verbatim, the time he had won a state history competition by reciting dates that even the judges had to look up.

"He was insufferable," Isabel said, grinning over her wine glass.

"But also kind of amazing. Do you know he can tell you what day of the week any date fell on? Go ahead, test him."

"That's just a parlor trick," Lucian protested, but there was a small smile tugging at the corner of his mouth.

"March 15, 1991," Elena said.

Lucian didn't even pause.

"Friday."

"That's my birthday." A flutter in her chest, something warm and unexpected.

"My parents always told me I was born on the Ides of March, like it was some kind of omen."

"It was." Lucian's their gazes connected hers across the table, gray-blue and intense and soft.

"Just not the kind they expected." The moment stretched, warm and electric, the air between them humming with something unspoken.

Isabel cleared her throat.

"Well," she said, standing and gathering plates with pointed efficiency, "I'm going to do the dishes. No, don't argue, it's the least I can do after you cooked. Elena, there's more wine in the kitchen if you want it. Lucian —" She fixed her brother with a meaningful look that communicated entire volumes.

"show her the piano?" She disappeared into the kitchen before either of them could respond.

"The piano?" Elena asked.

Lucian's cheeks flushed, the color visible even in the candlelight.

"I play. A little. Nothing special."

"He's being modest," Isabel called from the kitchen, her voice carrying easily through the open doorway.

"He plays beautifully. Our mother was a concert pianist before she had us. He got her talent."

"And Isabel got her inability to mind her own business," Lucian muttered, but there was no heat in it.

Only the resignation of a man who had long ago accepted that his sister would always be impossible. Elena stood and walked to the grand piano in the corner. It was a beautiful instrument — old but well-maintained, its black surface gleaming in the candlelight like still water. She ran her fingers along the closed lid, feeling the smooth wood beneath her touch.

"Will you play something for me?" Lucian hesitated.

She could see him weighing the request, the risk of it — opening himself up in a way that went beyond words, beyond memory, into something more vulnerable still. Then he crossed the room and sat down on the bench beside her. Their shoulders brushed, sending a jolt of awareness through her body, and she inhaled the scent of him — clean soap and something warm, something that made her want to lean closer.

"Any requests?"

"Something you love." He was quiet for a moment, his fingers hovering over the keys.

Then his hands found their positions, and music began to fill the room. It was Chopin — Elena recognized it from somewhere, a nocturne maybe, something slow and achingly beautiful. The notes fell slowly, like something being let go of. Lucian played with his eyes half-closed, his hands moving over the keys with easy mastery that came from years of practice, years of solitude, years of channeling all that he felt into something that could be heard but not spoken. The music swelled and fell like breathing. Like the ocean outside the window. Elena watched his face as he played. The furrow of concentration between his brows. The way his lips parted slightly, as if the music required air. The absolute stillness of the rest of him, all his usual tension channeled into his hands, into the keys, into the sound that filled the room like light. This was who he was, she realized. Beneath the careful composure and the impossible memory and the years of waiting. A man who felt things deeply and expressed them through beauty. A man who had taken his curse and turned it into something that could create moments like this. The music ended softly, the last notes hanging in the air like a question that didn't require an answer.

"That was beautiful," Elena said quietly.

"My mother used to play it for us when we couldn't sleep." Lucian's hands rested on the keys, not playing, just touching, as if drawing comfort from the instrument.

"She said Chopin understood that sadness and beauty were the same thing, sometimes."

"Is that what you feel? Sad?" He turned to look at her.

They were so close on the narrow bench — close enough that she could see the flecks of silver in storm-colored eyes, the slight stubble on his jaw, the way his breath caught when she found his eyes. Close enough to kiss, if either of them were brave enough.

"Not anymore," he said.

"Not since you walked into the ballroom." From the kitchen, the sound of running water and Isabel's deliberate humming provided a thin curtain of privacy.

"Lucian," Elena said, and she wasn't sure what she was going to say next — thank you, or I'm scared, or I think I'm falling for you too.

"You don't have to decide anything," he said, as if reading her thoughts.

"I've waited so long. I can wait longer. I can wait as long as you need."

"What if I don't want to wait?" The question hung between them, heavy with possibility.

Lucian's hand lifted from the keys, hovering in the space between them like he wanted to touch her but didn't dare.

"Then tell me," he said, his voice rough.

"Tell me what you want, and I'll give it to you. Whatever it is. Whatever you need." Elena thought about Adam — about the way he had demanded things from her, taken things, made her feel like her wants were inconvenient obstacles to be managed.

The years she had spent making herself small, dimming her own light, forgetting who she was in order to become who he needed her to be. And Lucian — who had waited so long without ever asking for anything. Who had watched from a distance and hoped and never pushed. Who was sitting here now, his heart in his eyes, offering to wait even longer if that was what she needed. The difference was as clear as the difference between a cage and an open door.

"I want to see the Archive," she said.

"Tomorrow. I want to see everything." Something flickered in his eyes — surprise, maybe, or fear, or hope.

All three at once.

"Are you sure?"

"No." She smiled, and it was like the first real smile she had given anyone in a very long time.

"But I'm done being sure about things. Sure hasn't gotten me anywhere good. I'd rather be brave." Lucian's hand finally bridged the gap between them, his fingers brushing her cheek with a tenderness that made her breath catch.

His touch was warm, gentle, reverent — like she was something precious, something worth protecting.

"Tomorrow," he agreed.

"I'll show you everything." From the kitchen, Isabel's humming grew louder and more pointed.

Elena laughed — actually laughed, the sound bubbling up from somewhere deep inside her, somewhere she had forgotten existed — and Lucian smiled, and the candles flickered, and somewhere outside the beacon swept across the harbor like it was keeping watch over all of them. She said goodnight and walked home through the cold, her mind full of Chopin and candlelight and a man who couldn't forget.

CHAPTER EIGHT

LUCIAN

BEFORE THE GALA, LUCIAN found Marcus on the hotel's back porch. Both holding coffee. Both watching the harbor the way men do when they have something to say and haven't found the way to say it.

"You're nervous about something," Marcus said.

"Is it that obvious?"

"You've been straightening the same picture frame for ten minutes. It was straight after the first one." Marcus took a sip of coffee.

"Woman trouble?"

"That's reductive."

"Most things are, when you boil them down." Marcus set his mug on the railing.

"I was married once. Marie. Seventeen years. Cancer got her — fast. Eight months from diagnosis to the end."

"I'm sorry."

"It was twelve years ago. But here's what I want to tell you — after she died, I held on to everything. Her clothes. Her shampoo. Same brand, same scent, for four years. I'd walk into the bathroom and smell her, and for half a second, she was still there." He flexed his calloused hands.

"People told me it was unhealthy. My sister said I was building a shrine."

"Were they right?"

"Probably. But those objects weren't about Marie. Not really. They were about who I was when she was alive. I was holding on to the version of myself that existed in her eyes." The words landed somewhere deep in Lucian's chest.

"When I finally packed up her things," Marcus continued, "I didn't feel like I was letting her go. I felt like I was letting me go — the me that needed her presence to feel real." He turned to look at Lucian.

"I'm not going to ask what you're carrying. But if you're holding on to something because it makes you feel like the person you want to be — make sure the thing is worth the weight." Lucian thought about the Archive.

About the Neruda book, the napkin, the ticket stubs.

"Would you keep it even if she never found out?" Marcus asked.

"If the only person who would ever look at it was you — would you still hold on?"

"Yes," Lucian said.

Marcus nodded.

"Then the reasons might be right. Or they might just be yours. Either way, that's something." He clapped Lucian on the shoulder and went back inside.

The ballroom had been transformed. Lucian stood in the doorway, transfixed. The chandeliers — cleaned and restored over the past weeks, every crystal drop polished until it gleamed — blazed with light, throwing rainbows across the walls in a kaleidoscope of color. The damaged silk panels had been temporarily concealed behind swaths of ivory fabric that Elena had sourced from somewhere in Boston, and every available surface had been covered with candles — hundreds of them, their flames dancing in the drafts from the old windows. Winter greenery wound around the columns and draped across the mantels: pine boughs and holly, their scent mingling with the beeswax candles and the subtle perfume of the women who had begun to fill the room. A string quartet played in the corner, their music weaving through the crowd like a silk ribbon, something by Vivaldi that Lucian's mother used to play on Sunday mornings. June's fundraiser. The first event the Rowan had hosted in nearly forty years. The restoration was nowhere near complete — the chandeliers worked but the electrical system was still a patchwork of old and new, half the guest rooms were still gutted, and the kitchen was being run out of a temporary setup that Marcus had rigged together with creative use of extension cords — but June had insisted.

"The town needs to see what we're building," she had said, her clear eyes steady with determination.

"They need to remember what this place used to mean. What it can mean again." So here they were — half of Camden's Rise, it seemed, dressed in their finest and milling about the ballroom like they had stepped back in time.

The mayor was holding court by the fireplace, his wife's diamonds catching the candlelight. The owner of the bookstore was arguing amiably with the librarian about something — first editions, probably, or the merits of hardcovers versus paperbacks. Marcus Chen, looking uncomfortable in a suit that was clearly borrowed, was nursing a drink near the windows and trying not to stare at June. Lucian noticed that last detail with some amusement. The contractor had been finding increasingly flimsy excuses to stay late at the hotel — double-checking wiring that had already been checked, inspecting plasterwork that needed no inspection — and June had been bringing him coffee with suspicious frequency. Neither of them seemed willing to acknowledge what everyone else could plainly see. But all of that faded to background noise when Elena walked in. She was wearing a dress the color of midnight — deep blue, almost black, that caught the light when she moved and threw off subtle hints of violet and indigo. It left her shoulders bare, the neckline skimming her collarbones, and fell in a graceful column to the floor. Her hair was swept up in an elegant twist that exposed the long line of her neck, and she was wearing small diamond earrings that caught the candlelight like stars. She looked like something out of a painting. Like something out of a dream. Like something out of his memory — except she had never looked quite like this in any of their twelve encounters. This was new. This was a version of Elena he was seeing . And she was looking directly at him. He caught her eye across the crowded room — just like the library, fifteen years ago, except now she was walking toward him instead of away. Now she was smiling, a small, private smile that seemed meant only for him, and his pulse was racing.

"You clean up well," she said when she reached him.

He had worn his best suit — charcoal gray, well-fitted, the one Isabel had forced him to buy for academic conferences. He had even managed to tame his hair into something respectable. But standing next to Elena, he felt like a shadow beside a flame.

"You're beautiful," he said, and then immediately wanted to kick himself for the inadequacy of the words.

Beautiful didn't begin to cover it. Every synonym he could think of fell short. But Elena's smile widened, a flush of color rising to her cheeks.

"You're not so bad yourself." She glanced around the ballroom, her designer's eye taking in the fabric, the candles, the light on the chandeliers.

"This is incredible. June must be over the moon."

"She's been floating six inches off the ground all week." Lucian followed her gaze, watching the candlelight play across the crystal drops above them.

"You did good work here. The fabric draping was your idea, wasn't it?"

"How did you —" She stopped.

Laughed, the sound like bells.

"Right. You remember everything. Including every conversation I've had with June about the restoration."

"I try not to be creepy about it."

"You're doing a terrible job." But she was still smiling, and she stepped closer to him, close enough that he could smell her perfume — that same light floral scent with vanilla beneath, warm and familiar and intoxicating.

"Dance with me?" The string quartet had shifted into something slower, a waltz that Lucian recognized from his mother's old recordings — Shostakovich, something romantic and slightly melancholy.

Couples were drifting onto the dance floor, swaying together in the golden light.

"I should warn you," he said, "I haven't danced in years."

"But you remember how."

"Remembering and executing are two different things."

"Then we'll figure it out together." She held out her hand, and he could no more have refused her than he could have stopped breathing.

He took her hand and led her onto the floor.

Dancing with Elena was nothing like he had imagined. It was better. In his fantasies — and he had fantasized, over the years, more times than he cared to admit — he had always been smooth, confident, leading her effortlessly across the floor like some kind of period drama hero. The reality was messier: a stumbled step here, a moment of confusion about which way to turn there. They were both rusty, both out of practice, both laughing quietly at their own awkwardness as they tried to remember how to waltz. And it was right. Her hand in his felt like it belonged there. The warmth of her through the silk of her dress, how she moved with him even when they stumbled, the sound of her quiet laughter when he stepped on her toe — all of it was right in its imperfection. This was real in a way his fantasies had never been.

"June and Marcus," Elena murmured, her chin tilted toward the edge of the dance floor.

"Tell me you see what I see." Lucian glanced over.

June was standing near the refreshment table, her silver hair gleaming in the candlelight, wearing a dress of deep green that made her look a decade younger. And Marcus had materialized beside her. They weren't touching, weren't even standing particularly close, but there was something in the way they leaned toward each other — like flowers turning toward the sun.

"I've been watching it develop for weeks," he admitted.

"He finds excuses to stay late. She finds excuses to bring him coffee."

"Do you think they know?"

"I think they're both terrified to acknowledge it." He guided Elena through a turn, his hand steady on her waist, marveling at the way her body responded to his guidance.

"June lost her husband two years ago. I don't think she expected to feel anything like this again."

"And Marcus?"

"Divorced. Five years. His ex-wife was —" Lucian stopped, realizing he was drawing on conversations he had overheard, details he had absorbed without meaning to.

"Sorry. That's not my story to tell."

"You really do remember everything, don't you?" Elena's voice was soft, curious rather than accusatory.

"Everything I hear. Everything I see. Everything I..." He swallowed.

"Feel." She was quiet for a moment, her hand warm in his, her body swaying with his to the music.

The quartet had shifted into something even slower, something that seemed designed specifically for moments like this.

"What do you feel right now?" The question was a precipice.

He could deflect, make a joke, retreat into the safety of casual conversation. That was what he had always done — kept his feelings hidden, protected himself from the vulnerability of honesty. But Elena had asked. And she deserved the truth.

"Terrified," he said quietly.

"And hopeful. And grateful. And like I'm standing on the edge of something that's going to change everything."

"That's a lot of feelings."

"I've been saving them up for over a decade." She laughed, and the sound was like music, like the quartet and the candlelight and the chandeliers all wrapped up in one beautiful note.

"You're ridiculous," she said.

"I know."

"And romantic. Annoyingly romantic."

"I've been told."

"And I'm not sure what to do with you." But she was smiling as she said it, and her hand tightened in his, and she moved a half-step closer so that their bodies were almost touching, her head tilting up to look at him.

The music swelled around them. The chandeliers blazed. And Lucian thought that if his memory preserved this moment forever — the weight of her hand in his, the warmth of her breath on his cheek, the impossible reality of holding her at last — then maybe his condition wasn't a curse after all. It was the only gift that mattered.

They danced three more songs before the quartet took a break. By then, Lucian's feet ached and his heart was so full he thought it might burst. They had talked as they danced — about the hotel, about Theodore's letters, about Isabel's increasingly pointed texts asking how the evening was going. Elena had laughed at his imitation of the mayor's pompous speech. He had marveled at her insights into the restoration, she saw not just what the ballroom was but what it could become. When the music stopped, they drifted to the edge of the room, neither quite ready to let go of the other.

"I need air," Elena said, her cheeks flushed from dancing.

"Come with me?" They slipped out through the side door, onto the veranda that wrapped around the hotel's first floor.

The night was cold and clear, the stars scattered like diamonds across the black velvet sky. The lighthouse light swept across the harbor in its steady rhythm, a heartbeat of light in the darkness. Elena shivered, and Lucian shrugged off his jacket, draping it around her shoulders before he could think better of it. She pulled it close, and the sight of her wrapped in his clothes did something complicated to his chest — something possessive and tender and utterly new.

"Thank you," she said quietly.

"You're welcome." They stood at the railing, looking out at the harbor.

Inside, the quartet had started up again, the music floating through the windows like a whisper. The cold air was sharp and clean, carrying the salt-smell of the sea.

"I've been thinking," Elena said, "about Theodore and Clara."

"What about them?"

"He wrote her letters for twenty years. Even after she was gone, even after there was no hope of her reading them, he kept writing." She turned to look at him, and in the starlight her eyes were luminous.

"That's what you've been doing, isn't it? Writing letters she would never read. Keeping a record of a love she didn't know existed." Lucian's throat tightened.

"I suppose that's one way to look at it."

"It's a beautiful way to look at it." She stepped closer, and he could feel the warmth of her through the cold night air.

"Theodore never got to give Clara his letters. He never got to tell her what she meant to him. He lived his whole life carrying that love alone."

"Elena —"

"But you're not Theodore." She reached up and touched his face, her fingers cool against his cheek.

"And I'm not Clara. I'm here. I'm real. And I'm asking you to stop carrying this alone." The world narrowed to this moment: her hand on his face, her eyes searching his, the sound of the waves and the distant music and his own pulse racing like a drum.

"I don't know how to do this," he admitted.

"I've imagined it so many times, but the reality is —"

"Scarier?"

"Realer." He covered her hand with his, holding it against his cheek.

"In my memories, you're perfect. Untouchable. Safe behind the glass of the past. But here, now, you're —"

"Complicated?" She smiled.

"Messy? A work in progress with trust issues and a complicated history and absolutely no idea what she's doing?"

"Human," he said.

"You're human. And that's terrifying because humans can leave. Humans can change their minds. Humans can —"

"Lucian." She cut him off, her voice gentle but firm.

"Stop. Stop trying to protect yourself from possibilities. Stop waiting for me to disappear." She moved even closer, her face inches from his.

"I'm right here. I'm not going anywhere. And if you don't kiss me in the next thirty seconds, I'm going to be very disappointed in both of us." He stared at her.

"Did you just —"

"Twenty-five seconds."

"Elena —"

"Twenty." He kissed her.

The moment their lips touched, all that waiting collapsed into a single, perfect point. She tasted like champagne and starlight, and her hands came up to grip his shoulders, and he pulled her close, closer, as close as physics would allow. The kiss was all that he had imagined and nothing like he had imagined. It was softer than his fantasies, more tentative at first — two people learning the shape of each other, finding the rhythm. And then it deepened, and Elena made a small sound against his mouth, and Lucian forgot how to think about anything except the miracle of holding her at last. When they finally broke apart, they were both breathing hard. Elena's lipstick was smudged — he would remember that detail forever, the exact shade of pink on her swollen lips — and her eyes were bright with something that looked like wonder.

"Well," she said.

"That was worth waiting for." He laughed — actually laughed, the sound startling in the quiet night.

"Half her life and you're giving it a 'well'?"

"I'm not grading on a curve." But she was smiling, that secret smile that seemed meant only for him.

"Though I might need more data before I can give a final assessment."

"More data?"

"Mm-hmm." She pulled him down for another kiss, and this one was less tentative, more certain.

This one was a promise. Behind them, through the windows, the music played on. The chandeliers blazed. The fundraiser continued, oblivious to the fact that the world had just shifted on its axis. And on the veranda, wrapped in starlight and possibility, Lucian Calder kissed Elena Ward and felt, for the first time in all that time, like he had finally come home.

They stayed on the veranda until the cold became unbearable. When they finally slipped back inside, flushed and slightly disheveled, June caught Lucian's eye from across the room. She raised an eyebrow, glanced at Elena, and smiled — a knowing, satisfied smile that suggested she had been hoping for exactly this outcome. Marcus was still beside her, Lucian noticed. Closer now than before. Their shoulders were touching.

"I think we might have started something," Elena murmured, following his gaze.

"What do you mean?"

"June and Marcus. They've been circling each other for weeks, but neither one wanted to make the first move." She squeezed his hand.

"seeing us together gave them permission." As if to prove her point, Marcus leaned down and said something to June that made her laugh — a real laugh, bright and surprised.

She touched his arm, just briefly, but it was enough.

"Theodore would be happy," Lucian said quietly.

"To see the ballroom full of love again." Elena looked up at him.

"You really believe that? That love leaves traces? That these walls remember?"

"I believe that everything leaves traces." He turned to face her fully, the crowd and the music fading to background noise.

"Every moment, every emotion, every connection — it all becomes part of a place. Part of its story." He touched her face, marveling that he was allowed to do this now, that she was letting him.

"Tonight became part of this ballroom's story. We became part of it."

"The historian in you is showing."

"The historian in me is always showing. It's part of my charm."

"Is that what we're calling it?" But she was smiling, and she rose on her toes to kiss him again — quick and soft, a stolen moment in the crowded room.

"Tomorrow," she said when she pulled back.

"The Archive. You promised."

"I remember."

"Of course you do." She took his hand, threading her fingers through his.

"Walk me home?" They said their goodbyes to June, who hugged them both and whispered something in Elena's ear that made her blush.

They nodded to Marcus, who was clearly working up the courage to ask June for a dance. They slipped out the front door, into the cold night, the sound of music and laughter following them into the darkness. The walk to Elena's apartment was short — fifteen minutes along the harbor, past closed shops and sleeping houses and the eternal sweep of the lighthouse beam. They walked not talking much, letting the silence speak for them. At her door, they stopped.

"Thank you," Elena said.

"For tonight. For all of it."

"Thank you for giving me a chance." He lifted their joined hands and pressed a kiss to her knuckles.

"I know this isn't... normal. I know I'm not easy to love."

"You're easy to love." She said it like a fact, like something obvious and inarguable.

"You're difficult to understand, maybe. Complicated. Intense. But easy to love? Lucian, I've known you for less than a week, and I already —" She stopped.

Shook her head.

"Never mind. It's too soon. I shouldn't —"

"It's not too soon for me," he said quietly.

"It's been more than a decade. Nothing about this is too soon for me." their eyes found each other.

The light swept past the window. Somewhere in the harbor, a bell buoy rang.

"Tomorrow," Elena said.

"Show me the Archive. Show me everything. And then..."

"And then?" She smiled — that secret smile, the one that was becoming his favorite thing in the world.

"And then we start making new memories," she said.

"Together." She kissed him one last time, lingering, sweet, full of promise, and disappeared inside.

Lucian stood on her doorstep for a long moment, the cold forgotten, his heart so full it ached. Years of waiting. And tomorrow, finally, they would begin.

Later, lying tangled together in Elena's sheets, she asked him about the chandeliers.

"Tell me about them. Theodore had them made specially — I've seen the invoices. They cost more than some people's houses." Lucian was quiet for a moment, sorting through his mental archive.

"Clara loved light," he said finally.

"Theodore mentioned it in one of the letters — how she would stand by windows for hours, watching the way sunlight changed through the day. She said light was alive, that it told stories if you knew how to listen."

"So the chandeliers were for her."

"Everything was for her. The silk panels were designed to catch the light. The chandeliers were positioned to reflect it back. Even the ballroom's orientation — facing east and west — was calculated to capture the sunrise and sunset."

"He built her a room made of light."

"He built her a whole world made of light. And then she was gone, and all that light was just... beautiful, but empty." Elena traced patterns on his chest.

"When we light the chandeliers for the opening, it won't be empty anymore."

"The light will have somewhere to go. To June and Marcus. To us." He pressed a kiss to her temple.

"Theodore built the room for Clara, but we're the ones who get to fill it."

"Do you think he'd be happy? Knowing strangers will dance under his chandeliers?"

"I think he'd be relieved. I think he spent his whole life hoping someone would find the light again." Elena closed her eyes, letting his warmth sink into her.

"Tell me more," she said.

"Tell me about the silk panels. Tell me everything." And he did — his voice low and steady in the darkness, weaving together history and memory and love, until she fell asleep still listening.

CHAPTER NINE

❖

ELENA

THE MEMORY CAME TO her that afternoon without warning, the way they sometimes did now — less often than they had in the first year, but still, still, the body kept its own ledger and sometimes turned a page without asking.

She had been standing in the Rowan's kitchen, helping June with the china inventory, cataloguing pieces of a set that had not been used since 1987. A small thing. A Tuesday. June had handed her a dinner plate to examine for chips, and Elena had taken it, and the plate had been the exact shade of cream her mother's plates had been, with the same small gold ring around the edge, and Elena had been standing there holding the plate, and suddenly she was twenty-eight years old and in her and Adam's kitchen on a Sunday evening, setting the table for his colleagues, and Adam was behind her, and he was saying, in the voice he used when he was pretending to be patient —

Sweetheart. That's the wrong side.

She had been setting the forks on the right. Adam had explained, once, that forks went on the left, and she had known that — of course she had known that, she had set a dinner table since she was a child — but somewhere that evening, in the flurry of getting everything ready before his partners arrived, she had gotten confused, and put them on the right, and he had seen it, and he had come up behind her and laid a hand on her shoulder that was not unkind but was not nothing, and he had said it the way he said all the things he corrected — *sweetheart, that's the wrong side* — and she had felt her face flush hot, and she had gone around the table and moved every single fork, the eight of them, while Adam watched and did not help, and she had apologized three times, and he had said it was fine, he had said it was sweet, he had said he just wanted things to be right because his partners noticed things, and she had believed him.

She had believed him.

She had served dinner and laughed at his partners' jokes and poured the wine when the glasses got low. She had done everything right. She had been the kind of wife he had told her she was lucky to get to be. And that night, in bed, after the guests had left, Adam had turned to her in the dark and said, with real tenderness, *You were wonderful tonight, Elena. I'm proud of you.* And she had felt, for a full thirty seconds, the warmth of having been proud of.

Thirty seconds. She could still measure it. Thirty seconds of warmth against three hours of quietly moving forks.

She had not understood, then, what that ratio was. She had understood only that she wanted more of the warmth, and had noticed only that the warmth came when she had done something carefully. She had adjusted. For a long time she had adjusted without knowing she was adjusting, the way a person lost in the woods keeps choosing the path that looks most like a path, until she has walked so far from where she began that she can no longer remember what the beginning looked like.

She stood in the Rowan's kitchen, holding the cream-colored plate, and she understood now what the ratio had been. Understanding did not make it go away. But it made it small, and nameable, and hers — a thing that had happened to her, not a thing she was.

"Everything all right, dear?" June was looking at her. Gently. Not pressing.

"Yes." Elena set the plate down on the counter. "Just — just a memory. One of the old ones. It's gone now."

"Good ones or bad ones?"

"Bad ones."

"I'm sorry, honey."

"It's all right." Elena picked up the next plate. Her hands were steady. She was proud of that, in the small private way she had come to be proud of small private things. "I'm getting better at them. They come through and they go out again. They don't stay the way they used to."

June reached across and squeezed her wrist — the particular two-second squeeze of a woman who had lived a long time and was not going to make a big deal of a moment that did not need a big deal made of it — and Elena laughed, once, wetly, and they went back to the china.

She had gotten most of the way through the set when it occurred to her that she had been setting tables for three years with the forks on the left without thinking about it. And that the table she had set last week, at Lucian's house, when June and Marcus had come over for dinner, had been her table. Her forks. Her rules. Her choice of where they went.

She had put them on the left that night. Not because Adam had told her to.

Because they went there.

It was a small victory and she would not mention it to anyone. But she noticed it. She had gotten better, these past two years, at noticing her own small victories, because no one else was going to notice them for her, and that — the noticing — was the work.

The work, her therapist had said once, *is not the grand gesture. The work is putting the forks where they belong. Every day. Without asking anyone for permission.*

She set the last plate in the rack. She dried her hands. She looked, for a second, at her own reflection in the window over the sink, and she thought: *I put them on the left last night. Nobody told me to. That was mine.*

Something about the sentence, said inside her own head without apology, made the next moment — June coming in, asking if Elena wanted tea, the afternoon going on — feel like a moment she had walked into instead of a moment that had happened to her.

That was, she was beginning to understand, the difference. A life could happen to you, or you could walk into it. For three years she had let one happen to her. The work, now, was the walking in.

Marla Chen arrived in Camden's Rise like a hurricane in designer boots. Elena spotted her from the window of the hotel lobby, where she had been reviewing fabric samples with June. A sleek black rental car pulled up to the curb, and out stepped her best friend — five feet four inches of fierce energy wrapped in a cashmere coat, oversized sunglasses, and an expression that suggested she was ready to either hug someone or interrogate them, possibly both.

"That's her, isn't it?" June peered out the window with undisguised curiosity.

"Your friend from New York?"

"Brooklyn," Elena corrected automatically.

"And yes. That's Marla."

"She looks... formidable."

"That's one word for it." Elena was already moving toward the door, her heart lifting at the sight of her best friend.

They had talked on the phone nearly every day since Elena arrived in Camden's Rise, but it wasn't the same as having Marla here in person.

"She's also loyal, brilliant, and slightly terrifying when she thinks someone has wronged me."

"Should I be worried for your historian?" Elena thought about Lucian — about the kiss on the veranda, the way his hands had trembled when he touched her face, the vulnerability in his eyes when he talked about waiting all those years.

"He'll survive," she said.

"Probably." She pushed through the hotel's front door just as Marla reached the steps.

"Elena Ward." Marla pulled off her sunglasses and fixed Elena with a look that was half accusation, half relief.

"You kissed him. You kissed the memory man. I leave you alone for one week and you go full romance novel protagonist on me."

"How did you —"

"Your voice on the phone last night. You had that dreamy quality. The one you get when you've eaten really good chocolate or seen a particularly beautiful sunset." Marla climbed the steps and pulled Elena into a fierce hug.

"Also, you texted me seventeen exclamation points with zero context, which is basically a confession." Elena laughed into her friend's shoulder.

"I missed you."

"Of course you did. I'm delightful." Marla pulled back, her hands on Elena's shoulders, studying her face with the intensity of a doctor examining a patient.

"You look good. Better than good. You look like someone who's actually sleeping for once."

"The sea air."

"The sea air, my ass." Marla's eyes narrowed.

"This is the glow of a woman who's been kissed properly. And don't even try to deny it, because I have known you for twelve years and I can read you like a large-print edition."

"Fine." Elena was the smile that spread across her face.

"It was... it was really good, Mar. Like, embarrassingly good. Like, I may have forgotten how to breathe for a few seconds." Marla's expression softened into something genuine and warm.

"Good. You deserve breathlessness. You deserve someone who makes you forget how oxygen works." Then she straightened, her game face returning.

"But I'm still going to interrogate him. That's non-negotiable."

"I would expect nothing less."

They walked through town, Marla's designer boots clicking against the cobblestones as she took in Camden's Rise with the sharp-eyed assessment of someone who evaluated things for a living.

"It's charming," she admitted, eyeing the antique shops and the bakery and the bookstore with its hand-painted sign.

"In a 'small town where everyone knows your business' kind of way. How are you not climbing the walls?"

"I thought I would be." Elena steered them toward the coffee shop, where she had become a regular over the past week.

"But it's... peaceful. In a way I didn't know I needed."

"Peaceful is good. Peaceful is healing." Marla pushed open the coffee shop door, setting off a cheerful jingle.

"Peaceful is also where people go to hide from their problems, but we'll table that discussion for now." They ordered — Elena's usual latte, Marla's complicated concoction involving oat milk and lavender — and settled into a corner booth with a view of the harbor.

"Okay," Marla said, wrapping her hands around her cup.

"Start from the beginning. And I mean the beginning. Not the 'he kissed me and it was magical' beginning. The 'he has extraordinary memory and has apparently been in love with me since the Bush administration' beginning."

"Obama," Elena corrected.

"He's very insistent about that."

"Noted. Continue." So Elena did.

She told Marla everything — not just the highlights she had shared over the phone, but the details. The way Lucian had looked at her in the ballroom, like he was seeing a ghost made flesh. The lighthouse almost-kiss. Theodore's letters and the parallel to Lucian's own devotion. The dinner with Isabel, the piano music, the moment at the fundraiser when he had finally kissed her and the world had tilted on its axis. Marla listened without interrupting, which was unusual for her. Her expression cycled through various stages — skepticism, curiosity, concern, something that might have been wonder — but she let Elena tell the whole story before speaking.

"So," she said finally.

"He has an actual room in his basement. Called 'The Archive.' Full of objects from your encounters over the years."

"Yes."

"And you're... okay with that?" Elena considered the question.

It was the same one she had been asking herself for days.

"I think I am? I know it sounds strange. I know in any other context, a man keeping a collection of objects related to a woman he barely knows would be a major red flag."

"A red flag the size of a football field."

"But Lucian isn't any other man. He literally cannot forget. Everything that happens to him is preserved in vivid detail, forever. The Archive isn't about obsession — it's about... making sense of his own experience. Giving physical form to memories that never fade." Marla was quiet for a moment, tapping her fingers against her cup.

"You've really thought about this."

"I've had to. After Adam, I promised myself I would never ignore warning signs again. I would never let romance blind me to reality." Elena met her friend's eyes.

"But the thing is, Mar — I've looked for the warning signs with Lucian. I've looked hard. And what I keep finding instead is just... a man who loves deeply and doesn't know how to stop. A man who has spent those years waiting instead of pursuing. A man who, when he finally had the chance to tell me everything, led with his vulnerabilities instead of trying to impress me."

"That's very mature of you."

"I had a good therapist."

"You had a great therapist. I'm the one who found her." Marla smiled, but there was still a thread of concern in her eyes.

"Elena, I'm not trying to talk you out of this. If anyone deserves a sweeping romance with a tragic hero who's been pining for her across time, it's you. I just..." She trailed off, searching for words.

"You're worried."

"I'm always worried. It's my brand." Marla reached across the table and took Elena's hand.

"I watched Adam break you down, piece by piece, over four years. I watched you shrink yourself to fit into the space he allowed. And I was so goddamn relieved when you finally got out that I would have cheered if you'd sworn off men entirely."

"But?"

"But that's not what you want. And it's not what you deserve." Marla squeezed her hand.

"What you deserve is someone who sees you — really sees you — and loves what he sees. Someone who makes you feel bigger, not smaller. Someone who looks at you like you're the most fascinating thing in any room." Elena thought about the way Lucian looked at her.

The intensity of his attention, yes, but also the tenderness. The way he seemed to be drinking her in, not to possess her but to understand her.

"He does," she said quietly.

"He really does."

"Then I need to meet him." Marla released her hand and sat back, her expression shifting into something more businesslike.

"I need to look him in the eye and make sure he's worthy of my best friend. And also possibly threaten him with bodily harm if he hurts you, because I've been told I'm quite intimidating when I want to be."

"You're terrifying when you want to be."

"Same thing." Marla checked her phone.

"When can we do this? Today? I have a red-eye back to New York tomorrow, and I refuse to leave without putting the fear of God into your memory man."

"He's coming for dinner tonight. I was going to cook, but —"

"Perfect. I'll cook. You'll make moon eyes at each other. And I'll conduct a thorough investigation disguised as friendly conversation." Marla was already on her feet, gathering her coat.

"Where's the nearest grocery store? I need ingredients for my grandmother's dumplings. No one can resist my grandmother's dumplings, and if he's unmoved by them, he's clearly a sociopath." Elena laughed, warmth spreading through her chest.

"I love you, you know that?"

"Obviously. I'm extremely lovable." Marla pulled her into another hug.

"Now let's go buy groceries and grill your boyfriend about his intentions. It's going to be fun."

"He's not my —" Elena started, but Marla was already out the door.

Lucian arrived at seven, carrying a bottle of wine and looking like a man walking to his own execution.

"She's going to hate me," he said when Elena opened the door.

"Your best friend is going to take one look at me and decide I'm a creep who's been stalking you for over a decade."

"You're not a stalker."

"I have a room full of objects related to a woman I'd barely spoken to. The jury's still out." He ran a hand through his hair, a nervous gesture Elena was beginning to recognize.

"What if she convinces you this is insane? What if she's right?" Elena reached up and touched his face the way she had at the fundraiser — the way that seemed to calm him.

"Lucian. Marla has been my best friend for twelve years. She held my hand through the worst relationship of my life and never once said 'I told you so.' She's the one who found my therapist, my new apartment, and the courage I needed to leave Adam." She held his gaze.

"If anyone has earned the right to be protective of me, it's her. And if anyone is capable of seeing through bullshit, it's also her."

"That's not as reassuring as you think it is."

"It should be." She rose on her toes and kissed him, soft and quick.

"Because if Marla decides you're worthy, it means you actually are. And I think you are. I just need her to confirm it."

"No pressure, then."

"None at all." She took his hand and led him inside.

Marla was in the small kitchen of Elena's rental apartment, surrounded by chaos that somehow seemed intentional. Pots bubbled on the stove, vegetables lined the counter in neat piles, and the air smelled of ginger and garlic and something savory that made Elena's mouth water. She looked up as they entered, wiping her hands on a dish towel, and Elena watched her best friend's face as she took in Lucian for the first time. The sharp assessment. The absorbing of details. The moment of decision.

"So," Marla said.

"You're the one with the extraordinary memory."

"And you're the one who's going to decide if I'm worthy." Lucian's voice was steady, though Elena could feel the tension in his hand.

"I've heard a lot about you."

"All good, I hope."

"All true. Which is better." Something flickered in Marla's expression — surprise, maybe, or reluctant approval.

"Smooth answer. Did you practice that?"

"I've been practicing this entire conversation for the past six hours." Lucian offered the wine bottle.

"I brought a Burgundy. Elena mentioned you appreciated good wine."

"Elena mentioned that, did she?" Marla took the bottle, examined the label, and raised an eyebrow.

"This is a very good Burgundy. You're either trying to impress me or you have excellent taste."

"Both. Definitely both." Marla's lips twitched.

She glanced at Elena, then back at Lucian.

"Okay. You can stay. But I reserve the right to change my mind at any point during dinner."

"That's fair."

"It's not. But you're being gracious about it, which counts for something." She handed the bottle back to him.

"Open this. Make yourself useful. Elena, come help me with the dumplings." Elena squeezed Lucian's hand and followed Marla to the stove, leaving him to search for a corkscrew.

"He's nervous," Marla murmured, low enough that Lucian couldn't hear.

"Like, actually nervous. Not performing nervousness to seem endearing."

"I told you."

"You told me. I didn't believe you." Marla glanced over her shoulder at Lucian, who was methodically opening the wine with the focus of a man defusing a bomb.

"He looks at you the way I look at a really good manuscript. Like he can't quite believe you're real, and he's trying to memorize every detail before you disappear."

"He doesn't need to memorize anything. He already remembers everything."

"And somehow that makes it worse and better at the same time." Marla shook her head.

"This is going to end up in a book someday. You know that, right? Someone's going to write a novel about this."

"we'll write it ourselves."

"There's a thought." Marla turned back to the stove.

"Now help me fold these dumplings. And tell your memory man to pour the wine. It's going to be a long night."

The night was long, but in the best possible way. Marla's dumplings were, as promised, impossible to resist. They sat around Elena's tiny dining table, the Burgundy warming their throats, and talked for hours. Marla asked questions, dozens of them, about Lucian's work, his family, his experience with HSAM. She asked about the Archive, about the encounters he remembered that Elena had forgotten, about what it was like to carry all that time of unrequited love. And Lucian answered. Every question. Without deflection or evasion. He told Marla about the library, about Mount Washington, about Brooklyn. He told her about the guilt he had carried for not intervening when he saw Adam controlling Elena. He told her about Isabel, about his parents, about the loneliness of living with a mind that never let anything go. And somewhere in the middle of it all, Elena watched Marla's expression shift. The suspicion fading. The protectiveness softening into something that looked like respect.

"One more question," Marla said, when the dumplings were gone and the wine was running low.

She leaned forward, her dark eyes pinning Lucian in place.

"And I need you to answer honestly."

"I've been answering honestly all night."

"I know. That's what scares me." Marla's voice was quiet but intense.

"If Elena decides this isn't what she wants — if she wakes up tomorrow and realizes she's not ready for this, or next month realizes it's too much, or next year decides she needs something different — what would you do?" The question hung in the air.

Elena found herself holding her breath. Lucian was quiet for a long moment. When he spoke, his voice was rough.

"I would let her go."

"Just like that?"

"Not 'just like' anything." He met Marla's eyes, and Elena saw the pain there, the bone-deep understanding of what he was saying.

"It would break me. I won't pretend otherwise. So many years of hoping, and to have it end —" He swallowed.

"But I would let her go. Because her happiness matters more than my pain. Because I've already spent too long loving her from a distance, and if that's what she needs, I know how to do it." He paused.

"I just... hope I don't have to." Marla stared at him for a long moment.

Then she turned to Elena.

"I approve."

"Just like that?" Elena echoed.

"Adam would never have said that." Marla's voice was flat with certainty.

"Adam would have talked about fighting for you, not giving up, proving his love. He would have made it about him — about his feelings, his needs, his inability to let go." She looked at Lucian with something like wonder.

"But this one? This one just said he would let you go if that's what you needed, even though it would destroy him. That's not obsession. That's love."

"Marla —" Elena's voice caught.

"I'm not done." Marla stood up, walked around the table, and stopped in front of Lucian.

"If you hurt her, I will make your life a living hell. I know people in publishing, which means I know people who can destroy reputations with a single well-placed review. I will ruin your academic career. I will ensure no one ever takes your research seriously again. Are we clear?"

"Crystal."

"Good." She stuck out her hand.

"Welcome to the family. Such as it is." Lucian shook her hand, and something in his expression finally relaxed.

"Thank you. For looking out for her. For the past twelve years."

"That's what best friends are for." Marla released his hand and turned to Elena.

"Okay. I'm going to my hotel now, because you two clearly need some alone time, and I have a very early flight tomorrow." She pulled Elena into a hug.

"Be happy," she whispered.

"You deserve this. You deserve him."

"I love you."

"I know. It's my cross to bear." Marla pulled back, gathered her coat, and swept toward the door with all the dramatic flair Elena had come to expect.

"Lucian, don't forget what I said about ruining your career. I wasn't joking."

"I'll remember," he said.

"I remember everything." Marla laughed, a real laugh, surprised out of her, and disappeared into the night.

The door closed behind her. The apartment fell quiet. Elena turned to Lucian, who was standing in the middle of her living room looking slightly shell-shocked.

"You survived," she said.

"Barely." But he was smiling, and when he opened his arms, she stepped into them without hesitation.

"She's terrifying."

"I know."

"I like her."

"I know that too." Elena pressed her face into his chest, breathing in the scent of him — wool and wine and something warm underneath.

"Thank you. For being honest with her. For not trying to be charming or clever. For just... being you."

"I don't know how to be anything else."

"I know." She looked up at him.

"That's what I love about you." The word hung between them.

117

Love. She hadn't meant to say it. Not yet. Not like this. But Lucian's eyes went soft, and his arms tightened around her, and when he kissed her, it felt like an answer.

"Tomorrow," he murmured against her lips.

"The Archive. I promised."

"Tomorrow," she agreed.

But tonight, she thought, holding him close in the quiet apartment while the beacon swept past the window — tonight, this was enough. Tonight, they had each other. And that was more than she had ever dared to hope for.

After dinner, Elena and Marla walked back to Marla's hotel along the harbor. The moon was high and full, painting silver streaks across the dark water, and the lighthouse swept past them like a benediction.

"So," Marla said, linking her arm through Elena's, "on a scale of one to ten, how terrified are you?" Elena considered the question. A week ago, she would have said eleven.

The intensity of Lucian's devotion, the weight of years of memory — it should have been overwhelming. It should have sent her running. Instead, it felt like shelter.

"Three," she said.

"Maybe two and a half." Marla stopped walking.

"Seriously?"

"Seriously." Elena turned to face her friend, the cold wind whipping her hair across her face.

"I know it doesn't make sense. I know the whole situation is objectively insane. A man I barely know has been in love with me for over a decade, keeps a room full of objects from our encounters, remembers every detail of every moment we've ever shared — and instead of being terrified, I feel... safe."

"Elena —"

"Adam made me feel like I was crazy," Elena continued, the words coming faster now, things she hadn't said to anyone, not even her therapist.

"Every time I questioned something, every time I thought this wasn't normal, he convinced me I was overreacting. That I was too sensitive. That his attention was love, not control, and I should be grateful for it." She took a shaky breath.

"But Lucian's attention doesn't feel like that. It feels like being seen, not watched. Like being cherished, not owned. He remembers everything about me, but he's never used that knowledge as a weapon. He's just... held it. Like a gift he wasn't sure he was allowed to give." Marla was quiet for a long moment.

Then she pulled Elena into a fierce hug.

"God, I hate that you had to learn the difference," she whispered.

"I hate that Adam taught you what love isn't before you got to learn what it is."

"But I'm learning now." Elena hugged her back, pressing her lips together hard.

"That's what matters, right? That I'm finally learning?"

"Yeah," Marla said, pulling back and wiping at her own eyes.

"That's what matters." They stood there for a moment, two women on a moonlit harbor, the past and the future spreading out before them like the endless sea.

Then Marla straightened her shoulders and fixed Elena with a stern look.

"If he hurts you, I will absolutely destroy him."

"I know."

"Good." Marla linked her arm through Elena's again and resumed walking.

"Now tell me more about this Archive. Is it romantic or creepy? I need to know how worried I should be." Elena laughed, and the sound carried out across the water, mixing with the crash of the waves and the eternal sweep of the lighthouse beam.

"Definitely both."

"That tracks," Marla said.

"Romance is always a little creepy when you think about it too hard. The key is not thinking too hard."

"Sound advice from a woman who reads romance novels for a living."

"The soundest. Now come on — I want to see this hotel you've been going on about. Show me the ballroom where you had your Disney princess moment." They walked on together, arm in arm, as the moon rose higher and the stars wheeled overhead.

And Elena thought that maybe, just maybe, she was finally finding her way home.

CHAPTER TEN

ELENA

ISABEL ARRIVED ON A Wednesday, blowing into Camden's Rise like a small, opinionated hurricane.

"I had to see it with my own eyes," she announced, dropping her overnight bag in Lucian's foyer.

"My brother, the monk, finally talking to a woman like a normal human being. The apocalypse must be imminent."

"Isabel —"

"Where is she? Is she here? Did you finally tell her about the —" She lowered her voice dramatically. "— the Shrine?"

"It's not a shrine. And yes. She knows everything." Isabel's eyebrows shot up.

"Everything everything? The postcards? The coffee receipts? The disturbingly detailed floor plan of the library where you first saw her?"

"It's not disturbingly detailed. It's architecturally accurate."

"Lucian." Isabel took his face in her hands, examining him like a specimen.

"You're different. Your eyes are doing a thing."

"What thing?"

"A sparkly thing. Like you've discovered emotions and you're not sure what to do with them." She released him and spun toward the door.

"I need to meet this woman immediately. Where is she?"

"Working. At the hotel. And you can't just — Isabel!" But she was already out the door, leaving Lucian to follow in her wake with the resigned expression of a man who had been managing his sister's chaos for thirty-five years.

They found Elena on a ladder in the ballroom, examining the crystal drops of the chandelier with a magnifying glass.

"Oh my god," Isabel breathed.

"She's perfect. She's literally up a ladder examining historical crystal. It's like someone designed her in a lab to be your ideal woman."

"Isabel, please —"

"ELENA!" Elena startled, nearly dropping the magnifying glass.

She looked down to find a small, fierce-looking woman with Lucian's eyes beaming up at her.

"You must be Isabel," Elena said, climbing down carefully. "Lucian's told me about you."

"Everything good, I hope?"

"He said you once put hot sauce in his coffee because he forgot to call on your birthday." Isabel's grin widened.

"I love that he told you that. It means he's being honest about the family dysfunction." She grabbed Elena's hands and squeezed.

"Okay, let me look at you. Yes. Good bones. Kind eyes. That slightly terrified expression that suggests my brother has already overwhelmed you with his intensity. Perfect."

"Isabel." Lucian's voice carried a warning.

"What? I'm being supportive!" She linked her arm through Elena's.

"Come. We're going to have lunch and you're going to tell me everything. Including how you reacted to the Shrine, because Lucian is constitutionally incapable of describing emotional conversations."

"It's not a —"

"It's a shrine, Lucian. Accept it. Embrace it. Own your romantic lunacy." Elena was laughing, actually laughing, and something in Lucian's chest loosened.

Isabel was chaos, but she was also warmth. And watching her fold Elena into the family with her particular brand of aggressive affection made him feel like maybe, finally, things were falling into place.

"I like her," Elena said, as Isabel dragged her toward the door.

"Everyone likes me," Isabel called back.

"I'm delightful. Now hurry up, I need to know if you've seen the postcards. The postcards are my favorite part."

Over lunch at the café, Isabel told stories that made Lucian want to sink through the floor.

"— and then there was the time he memorized the entire bus schedule for the route you took to work. 'Just in case,' he said. In case of what, Lucian? In case you needed to stage an elaborate coincidental encounter?"

"I never actually used it —"

"The point is that you could have. The point is that my brother has been planning your romance for over a decade, and I have been listening to him not talk about it for just as long." Isabel reached across the table and squeezed Elena's hand.

"He's a weird man. But he's the best weird man I know."

"I'm sitting right here," Lucian pointed out.

"Yes, and I'm publicly embarrassing you in front of your girlfriend because I love you. That's what siblings do." Isabel's expression softened.

"Seriously, Elena. I've never seen him like this. Happy. Present. Actually engaged with the world instead of hiding in his memories. Whatever you're doing, keep doing it." Elena looked at Lucian across the table. Something passed between them — gratitude, maybe, or recognition.

"I'm trying," she said.

"We're both trying."

"That's all anyone can do." Isabel raised her coffee cup.

"To trying. And to my brother finally getting out of his own way long enough to have a life." They clinked cups.

Lucian found himself smiling despite the embarrassment. His sister was chaos. But she was right. He was happy. For the first time in years, he was truly, incandescently happy. And it felt like coming home.

When Lucian went to settle the check, Isabel turned to Elena with an expression that had dropped all of its theater.

"I need you to know something about my brother," she said quietly. "And I'm going to say it once, and then we'll go back to making fun of him together, because he deserves that too."

Elena set down her coffee.

"My brother has been faithful to a memory for more than a decade. Most people couldn't stay faithful to a person they saw every day. Do you understand what I'm telling you?"

"I think so."

"I hope you do. Because whatever this is between you — whatever you decide to do with it — you need to know that he will never forget a single thing about you. Not one. Not ever." Isabel's eyes held hers, steady. "That's a gift. It's also a responsibility. Please be careful with it."

"I will."

"I know you will." Isabel softened. "I can tell. I saw your face when he walked over to the table. You were already scared of hurting him. That's why I feel safe leaving him with you."

She reached across the table and squeezed Elena's hand. Then Lucian was back, and Isabel was announcing too loudly that the café's pastries were a crime against French patisserie, and the moment passed.

But Elena held onto it. All afternoon, as she went back to the hotel and climbed the ladder and resumed her slow inventory of the chandelier's crystals, Isabel's voice stayed with her.

He will never forget a single thing about you.

It was — as Isabel had said — a responsibility.

It was also, she realized, a kind of love she had never been offered before.

The final journal had a different feel than the others.

It was late. June and Marcus had gone home for the night. The contractors had finished for the day. Elena was alone in the library, working by the light of a single desk lamp, because Theodore Rowan's correspondence was more than a century old and did not deserve to be hurried.

She had promised Lucian she would stop by nine. It was already well past.

Elena held the last journal carefully, aware that she was touching something precious. The leather was softer than the others, the pages more fragile. She opened it, expecting more letters, more entries, more of the same careful handwriting she had grown to know. Instead, tucked between the front cover and the first page, was a photograph, sepia-toned and faded, of a young woman in a high-collared dress.

"Clara," she breathed.

But as she lifted the photograph into the lamplight, something strange happened. Her hands began to shake. It wasn't recognition, exactly. She had never seen this photograph before, had never known Clara existed until a few weeks ago. But something in the woman's face — the set of her jaw, the slight upturn at the corners of her mouth, how she held herself with quiet dignity even in stillness — felt unbearably familiar. Like looking into a mirror that showed not her reflection, but her essence.

"Elena?" Lucian's voice seemed to come from very far away.

"You've gone pale."

"Her eyes." Elena's voice came out strange, thick.

"Lucian, look at her eyes." He moved closer, looking over her shoulder at the photograph.

She felt him go still.

"They're your eyes," he said quietly.

"That's impossible. That's — we're not —" But even as she said it, she was turning the photograph over with trembling fingers.

And there, in Clara's elegant hand, was an inscription: For my cousin Evangeline, on the occasion of her engagement. May your marriage be filled with the joy that mine was denied. With all my love, Clara Ashford, 1897. The room tilted.

"Evangeline," Elena whispered.

"That's my great-grandmother's name. Evangeline Ward. But her maiden name was..." She couldn't finish.

Couldn't breathe. The photograph was shaking in her hands — no, she was shaking, her whole body trembling with something that felt like recognition and grief and homecoming all tangled together.

"Ashford," Lucian finished for her.

"Clara's maiden name was Ashford." Elena looked up at him, and her expression had changed — open, unguarded, the walls down for the first time since he'd known her.

"I'm related to her. I'm —" She pressed the photograph against her chest, as if she could somehow absorb Clara through her skin.

"That's why the hotel felt familiar. That's why I dreamed about this place before I ever saw it. That's why —" She broke off, overwhelmed.

Lucian knelt beside her chair, his hands covering hers where they clutched the photograph.

"You came home," he said.

"You didn't know it, but you arrived."

"She never got her happy ending." Elena's voice cracked.

"Theodore loved her for twenty years and she died before he could tell her. She never knew —"

"But you do." Lucian lifted her chin, making her meet his eyes.

"You know, Elena. Everything Theodore couldn't give Clara, everything they lost — you and I have the chance to live it. To finish the story they started." She stared at him — this man who had loved her for over a decade, who had waited and hoped and never given up.

And behind him, in the photograph pressed against her heart, her ancestor stared back — the woman who had inspired a twenty-year devotion and never lived to see it fulfilled.

"We have Clara's eyes," she said.

"Both of us."

"What do you mean?"

"You and Theodore. You both see something worth waiting for." She pulled him close, burying her face in his shoulder, holding on.

"And you were both right. We were both worth it." They held each other in the lamplight, surrounded by a century of letters, while the lighthouse beam swept past the window and the old story finally found its way toward peace.

CHAPTER ELEVEN

LUCIAN

THE STORM ARRIVED AT noon, and it brought Elena with it. Lucian had been watching the sky darken all morning, the clouds rolling in from the Atlantic like an invading army. By the time she knocked on his door, the first fat drops of rain were already falling, and the wind had begun to howl around the corners of his old Victorian house. She stood on his porch, slightly damp, her hair curling from the humidity. She wore jeans and a soft gray sweater, and she looked at him with an expression that was part anticipation, part fear, part something else he couldn't quite name.

"I'm ready," she said.

He wasn't sure he was. But he had promised.

"Come in," he said, stepping aside.

"Before the storm gets worse." As if on cue, lightning split the sky, followed by a crack of thunder that rattled the windows.

The lights flickered once, twice, then held.

"Dramatic timing," Elena said, shaking rain from her hair.

"The universe has a flair for theatrical."

"It's been practicing for over a decade. It wants to make sure we get this right." She laughed, but there was a nervous edge to it.

He understood. He felt it too — the weight of what was about to happen, the significance of what he was about to show her.

"Do you want coffee first?" he asked.

"Tea? Something stronger?"

"No." She met his eyes, her chin lifting with that determination he had come to love.

"I don't want to stall. I want to see it. I want to see everything." So he led her to the basement.

The door to the Archive was plain oak, unremarkable, the same as any other door in the house. Lucian paused with his hand on the knob, his heart hammering against his ribs. Behind this door was all that he had kept hidden for fifteen years. Every object, every memory, every piece of evidence that proved the depth of his devotion — or, perhaps, the extent of his madness.

"I need you to know," he said quietly, "that I've never shown this to anyone. Isabel knows it exists, but even she hasn't been inside."

"Why not?"

"Because it's not about her." He turned to face Elena.

"It's about you. It's always been about you. And showing it to anyone else felt like... a betrayal. Like sharing something sacred without permission." Elena reached up and touched his face, her palm warm against his cheek.

"I'm giving you permission now." He took a breath.

Turned the knob. Opened the door. The Archive was small, perhaps ten feet by twelve, but it felt larger because of what it contained. The walls were lined with shelves, and on those shelves, arranged with the meticulous care of a museum exhibit, were the artifacts of years of chance encounters. A book with a worn spine and a faded cover: Twenty Love Poems and a Song of Despair. A napkin from a Brooklyn café, folded and pressed flat, with the establishment's logo barely visible. A ticket stub from the National Gallery. A trail map from Mount Washington, its folds softened by handling. A receipt from a Cambridge bookstore. A pressed flower from a farmer's market in Portland. Each object was labeled with a small card, written in Lucian's careful handwriting: the date, the location, a brief note about what had happened. October 15, 2009. Boston University Library. First encounter. July 19,

2013. Mount Washington, NH. Helped her with twisted ankle. Kissed her. March 8, 2016. Brooklyn café. Saw her with him. Couldn't intervene. Elena moved through the room slowly, her fingers hovering over each object without quite touching. Her face was unreadable, her breath coming in small, measured increments. Lucian stood by the door, watching her, his hands shoved in his pockets to hide their trembling. She stopped at the book.

"The Neruda," she whispered.

"You left it in the library. That first day." Lucian's voice was rough.

"I found it on the table after you ran out. There was a name inside — your name — and a phone number that was disconnected when I tried to call it."

"It was my grandmother's number." Elena picked up the book with reverent hands, cradling it like something precious.

"She died three months before. I was using her old address book as a bookmark." She looked up at him, her voice unsteady.

"I thought I'd lost this forever. I looked for days when I realized it was gone."

"I'm sorry. I should have found a way to return it —"

"No." She clutched the book to her chest.

"No, don't you see? You kept it safe. For years of watching, you kept a piece of her safe, and you didn't even know what it meant." She pressed her fingers to her mouth.

"That's not creepy, Lucian. That's providence." He didn't know what to say.

He had imagined this moment a thousand times, had rehearsed explanations and apologies and defenses, but none of them fit the reality of Elena standing in his Archive, holding her grandmother's book, looking at him like he had given her something precious instead of revealing something shameful. She set the book back on its shelf with care, then moved to the next item. The napkin. The ticket stub. The trail map with its worn creases.

"Tell me about this one," she said, pointing to a photograph tucked into a small frame.

It showed a woman reading on a beach, her face turned away from the camera, her dark hair blowing in the wind.

"Rhode Island. August 2019." Lucian stepped closer, looking at the image he had studied so many times he could trace it from memory.

"You were at Narragansett Beach, reading under an umbrella. I was there for a conference at URI. I walked past you three times before I convinced myself not to approach."

"Why not?"

"You looked peaceful." He swallowed hard.

"You were smiling at whatever you were reading, and the sun was in your hair, and you just looked... free. Lighter than I'd seen you in years." He paused.

"I found out later that was the summer after you left Adam. You were just starting to find yourself again. And I thought... if I approached you then, with everything I felt, it would be too much. It would overwhelm you before you were ready."

"So you took a picture instead."

"I took a picture." Shame colored his voice.

"I know how that sounds. I know how this all sounds. A room full of objects, a photograph taken without permission —"

"It sounds like a man who didn't know how to love someone without keeping them at a distance." Elena's voice was gentle, not accusatory.

"It sounds like someone who was so afraid of overwhelming me that he never gave himself a chance to know me."

"Yes." The word came out broken.

"That's exactly what it is." She turned to face him fully.

Outside, the storm raged — rain lashing against the small basement windows, thunder rolling like the growl of some great beast — but inside the Archive, there was only the two of them and the weight of years finally laid bare.

131

"Do you know what I see when I look at this room?" Elena asked.

"A shrine to obsession? Evidence of a man who should have moved on years ago?"

"No." She stepped toward him, closing the distance between them.

"I see a love story. I see a man who crossed paths with a woman again and again, who fell for her before he knew her, and who spent those years keeping her memory alive because he couldn't bear to let it die." Another step.

"I see someone who collected these things not to possess me, but to prove to himself that the connection was real. That the moments we shared, however brief, actually happened."

"Elena —"

"I see Theodore Rowan," she continued, her voice cracking.

"Writing letters to a woman who would never read them, because the alternative was to stop loving her. And I see you, keeping these objects, cataloguing these memories, because the alternative was to forget." She was close enough to touch now, close enough that he could see the pulse in her throat.

"But you can't forget, can you? You've never been able to forget anything. So you made this room instead. You gave your love a physical form, because that was the only way you knew how to hold it."

"I don't deserve —"

"Don't." She reached up and pressed her fingers to his lips, silencing him.

"Don't tell me what you don't deserve. I spent four years with a man who told me I didn't deserve things — happiness, freedom, my own thoughts and feelings. I am done being told what I deserve." Her eyes blazed.

"I get to decide. And I have decided that you, Lucian Calder, are the most remarkable man I have ever met. You have loved me for over a decade without asking for anything in return. You have kept pieces of my history safe when I didn't even know they were lost. You have waited, and waited, and waited, and now —" Her voice broke.

"Now I'm here. I'm standing in your Archive, surrounded by the evidence of your devotion, and I'm telling you that I love you too." The world stopped.

Or maybe it was just Lucian's heart, stuttering to a halt in his chest before starting again with a force that left him breathless.

"You —" He couldn't form the words.

"Elena, you don't have to —"

"I know I don't have to." She was laughing now, breathless and disbelieving, and it was the most beautiful sound he had ever heard.

"That's the whole point. I don't have to love you. I want to. I choose to. I've spent so long having my choices made for me, and now I'm making this one myself." She cupped his face in her hands.

"I choose you. I choose this. I choose us." He kissed her.

Not the careful, tentative kiss of the veranda, or the sweet, exploratory kisses they had shared since. This was something else entirely — desperate and consuming, years of longing finally given permission to exist. He pulled her against him, and she melted into his arms, and the storm outside seemed to pale in comparison to the one raging between them. When they finally broke apart, both gasping for breath, the lights flickered and died. The basement plunged into darkness, lit only by the occasional flash of lightning through the small windows. Elena laughed — that bright, startled laugh that he wanted to hear for the rest of his life.

"The universe really does have a flair for drama," she said.

"There are candles upstairs." His voice was rough, unsteady.

"And a fireplace. And a very comfortable couch."

"Is that an invitation?"

"It's whatever you want it to be." She found his hand in the darkness, threading her fingers through his.

"Then take me upstairs, Lucian. Take me somewhere warm. And tell me more about the encounters I've forgotten." He led her up the stairs by memory alone, navigating the familiar path with ease.

The living room was cold, but he found candles by touch, lit them with steady hands that had finally stopped trembling. The fireplace caught on the third try, and within minutes, warmth was spreading through the room, casting dancing shadows on the walls. They settled on the couch, wrapped in a blanket he kept draped over the armrest. The storm howled outside, but inside there was only candlelight, firelight, and Elena pressed against his side like she had always belonged there.

"Tell me," she said.

"Tell me about the encounters I don't remember." So he did.

He told her about the gallery in Washington, where she had stood in front of Hopper's Nighthawks for twenty minutes, tears streaming down her face. He told her about the bookstore in Cambridge, where she had been so absorbed in the architecture section that she hadn't noticed him standing two aisles away, paralyzed by the sight of her. He told her about the train platform in Boston, where they had stood three feet apart for fifteen minutes, and he had spent the entire time rehearsing what he would say, only to watch her board a different car. He told her about every moment. Every near-miss. Every time fate had brought them together and his own fear had kept them apart. And Elena listened, her head on his shoulder, her hand in his, absorbing the history of a love story she hadn't known she was part of.

"I wish I remembered," she said quietly, when he fell silent.

"I wish I could see it the way you see it."

"You will." He pressed a kiss to her temple.

"Not the old memories. Those are mine to keep. But from now on, every moment we share, every kiss, every

134

conversation, we'll build those memories together. And this time, you'll remember them too." She turned in his arms, facing him.

The firelight painted her face in gold and shadow, and she had never looked more beautiful to him than in this moment — vulnerable and strong, cautious and brave, choosing him despite everything.

"I love you," she said again.

"I know it's fast. I know we've only really known each other for a week. But I love you, Lucian. I love your impossible memory and your careful hands and the way you look at me like I'm something precious." She leaned in close, her lips brushing his.

"I love that you waited. And I love that you finally stopped waiting."

"I love you," he breathed against her mouth.

"I've loved you for all those years. I'll love you for fifteen more, and fifteen after that, and every year I'm given until my memory finally fails and even then —" He kissed her, soft and deep.

"Even then, I think I'll still love you. Some things are written into the soul, not just the mind." The kiss deepened.

The blanket fell away. Hands explored, tentative at first, then bolder as permission was given and received in gasped words and murmured names. Outside, the storm raged on. Inside, two people who had circled each other for over a decade finally stopped circling. They had found each other at last.

Later, much later, they lay tangled together in front of the dying fire, the blanket pulled over them, the storm finally beginning to fade into a steady rain. Elena was tracing patterns on his chest, her touch light and wondering.

"What are you thinking about?"

"Everything." He captured her hand, pressed a kiss to her palm.

"This moment. The sound of the rain. The way your hair smells like vanilla and rain. The fact that you're here, in my arms, and it's not a dream." He smiled.

"I'm cataloguing it all. Building a new section of the Archive."

"A good section?"

"The best section." He pulled her closer, tucking her head under his chin.

"The section where you chose me. The section where we finally began." She was quiet for a moment, her breath warm against his skin.

"This scares me," she admitted.

"How fast this is. How much I feel. After Adam, I promised myself I would be careful. That I would take things slow, protect myself, not fall so hard."

"Are you regretting —"

"No." She pushed up on her elbow to look at him.

"That's what scares me. I should be more afraid, more cautious. But when I'm with you, I just feel..." She searched for the word.

"Safe. Like I can fall and you'll catch me. Like I don't have to protect myself from you."

"You don't." He touched her face, tracing the line of her cheekbone.

"I would never hurt you, Elena. I couldn't. Hurting you would be like hurting myself — unforgettable, unforgivable."

"I know." She turned her head to kiss his palm.

"That's what I'm saying. I know that, in my bones, in a way I've never known anything before. And it terrifies me, because what if I'm wrong? What if I'm missing something?"

"Then we'll figure it out together." He pulled her down for a kiss, soft and reassuring.

"I'm not asking you to trust blindly. I'm asking you to trust us — the process, the journey, the work of building something real. We'll take it one day at a time. One memory at a time.

And if you ever need to slow down, to step back, to catch your breath —"

"You'll wait."

"I'll wait." He smiled.

"I'm very good at waiting. I've had years of practice." She laughed, and the sound was light and free, nothing like the nervous laugh from earlier.

This was the laugh of a woman who was beginning to believe that happiness might be possible after all.

"No more waiting," she said.

"No more distance. From now on, we do this together. Partners. Equals. No more shrine-keeper and unknowing muse."

"Partners," he agreed.

"Equals. Co-authors of whatever story comes next." The fire had burned down to embers.

The rain had faded to a whisper. Somewhere in the distance, the lighthouse beam was sweeping across the harbor, steady and sure. Lucian held Elena close and let his mind do what it did best — preserve every detail of this moment, hold onto it in the most cherished corner of his memory. The weight of her in his arms. The sound of her breathing as she drifted toward sleep. The knowledge that after all this time of hoping, years of waiting, years of loving her from afar — She was finally, miraculously his. And he was hers. For as long as memory lasted. For as long as love endured.

They stood there for a long moment, surrounded by years of memory, while the storm raged outside and something new and fragile took root between them.

"Take me upstairs," Elena said.

Lucian's heart stopped.

"Elena —"

"I've spent the last hour looking at evidence that you loved me before you knew me. That you waited. That you hoped." She crossed to him, took his hands in hers.

"I spent three years with a man who claimed to love me and couldn't remember my birthday. Who made me feel like wanting things was a weakness. Who taught me that my body wasn't mine to give — it was his to take."

"Elena." Her name came out broken.

"I'm taking it back." She lifted his hands to her face, pressed his palms against her cheeks.

"I'm choosing. Do you understand? in years, I am choosing what I want, and who I want, and when I want it." Her eyes held his, steady and certain.

"I want you, Lucian. Tonight. Now. Take me upstairs." He couldn't speak.

Couldn't find words for what was crashing through him — hope and terror and desire so sharp it hurt to breathe. So he simply nodded. And led her up the stairs.

His bedroom was dark except for the moonlight spilling through the windows. Elena stood in the center of the room, watching him. He hadn't turned on the lights, hadn't even thought to, and now he was grateful. The darkness felt like a gift. A space between the world they had left behind and the one they were about to create.

"I don't know how to do this," he admitted.

The words surprised him — he hadn't meant to say them. But she deserved honesty, even when it made him look foolish.

"I've imagined it. God knows I've imagined it. But the reality of you, here, in my room —" He stopped.

Swallowed.

"I don't want to get it wrong." Elena crossed to him.

In the moonlight, her face was soft, unguarded in a way he had rarely seen.

"There's no wrong," she said quietly.

"There's just us. Figuring it out together."

"I'm not good at figuring things out. I'm good at remembering. At cataloging. At standing on the outside and watching." The confession felt like peeling off skin.

"I've never been good at being inside the moment."

"Then let me help you." She reached up and began unbuttoning his shirt.

Slowly. Deliberately. Her fingers brushed his chest as she worked, and each touch sent electricity sparking through his nervous system.

"You spent years watching me," she said, freeing another button.

"Waiting. Hoping. Never acting." Another button.

"That ends tonight." The last button fell free, and she pushed the fabric from his shoulders.

"Tonight, you get to touch what you've been looking at. You get to have what you've been wanting." Her hands flattened against his bare chest, and he shuddered.

"You get to be inside the moment, Lucian. Finally."

"I don't deserve —"

"Stop." Her voice was firm.

"You don't get to decide what you deserve. I do. And I say you deserve this." She rose on her toes and kissed him — not gently, not carefully, but with intention.

With demand.

"I say you deserve me." Something broke loose in his chest.

Not just arousal — permission. The permission he had never given himself. He pulled her against him, and this time he wasn't careful.

Later, he would remember everything. The way her dress fell away like water. The small sound she made when he lifted her onto the bed — surprise and want tangled together. She pulled him down to her with hands that knew exactly what they wanted. He would remember the moonlight on her skin, turning her into something luminous. The taste of her — salt and sweetness and something that was just Elena, that he would crave for the rest of his life. The way her fingers dug into his shoulders when he found the place that made her gasp. But in the moment itself, he was not cataloging. He was not filing away details for later examination. For once in his life, Lucian Calder was simply present — drowning in sensation, in her, in the impossible reality of a dream that had finally decided to come true.

"I wanted this," she breathed against his neck as they moved together.

"Before I knew what wanting was. Before I knew your name. Some part of me wanted this."

"I know." He kissed her temple, her cheek, the corner of her mouth.

"I felt it too. Every time we crossed paths. Like gravity."

"Like coming home."

"Yes." The word was a groan, pulled from somewhere deep in his chest.

"God, Elena. Yes." She arched against him, and he felt her begin to tremble — felt the tension building in her body, the way her breath came faster, she clung to him like he was the only solid thing in a dissolving world.

"Let go," he whispered.

"I've got you. I'll always have you." She came apart in his arms, gasping his name, and the sound of it, his name in her voice, breaking with pleasure, sent him tumbling after her into the abyss.

They lay tangled together afterward, her head on his chest, his hand stroking lazy patterns on her back.

"That was..." she started.

"I know."

"You don't know what I was going to say."

"You were going to say it was nothing like you expected. That it was better. That you didn't know it could feel like that." He pressed a kiss to the top of her head.

"Because that's what I was thinking." She laughed softly.

"I hate that you can do that."

"Read your mind?"

"Remember everything. Know everything." But she was smiling against his chest.

"It's going to be incredibly annoying, living with someone who never forgets." Living with.

The words hit him like a wave.

"Does that mean —"

"It means I'm not going anywhere." She lifted her head to look at him, and in the moonlight her eyes were bright.

"It means that whatever this is, wherever it goes, I want to find out. With you."

"Even after seeing the Archive?"

"Especially after seeing the Archive." She kissed him softly.

"You built a shrine to hope, Lucian. Most people can barely remember to send a birthday card. You spent those years believing in something you had no reason to believe in." Another kiss.

"That's not creepy. That's beautiful." He pulled her closer, burying his face in her hair.

He didn't trust himself to speak.

"Besides," she added, her voice lighter now, teasing, "now you'll have new memories to add. Better ones. Memories where I'm actually participating instead of just being watched from across a room."

"I liked watching you from across the room."

"Noted. But this —" She pressed herself against him, and heat stirred in his blood again, impossibly soon.

"This is better, isn't it?"

"This is everything." He rolled them over, settling above her, watching the way her he paused.

"this is what I wanted I never let myself hope for."

"Then stop talking," she said, pulling him down to her, "and hope a little more."

Much later, as Elena slept beside him, Lucian let another memory surface. One he hadn't shared yet. November 3,

2018. National Gallery of Art, Washington D.C. He had wandered into the gallery on his lunch break, seeking the quiet solace of art. The East Building was nearly empty on that gray Tuesday afternoon. He found her in front of Hopper's Nighthawks. She was standing still, her arms wrapped around herself, staring at the painting with an intensity that made his breath catch. The Hopper depicted figures hunched at a late-night diner counter, isolated even in proximity — the particular loneliness of people who share a space but not a connection. Elena was crying. Not distressed — just still. Absolutely still, the way people go still when something hurts too much to move. She was thinner than the last time he'd seen her. Paler. The spark he remembered from the mountain seemed dimmed to nothing. He should leave. He should let her have this moment of private grief. Instead, he moved closer — not to her, but close enough that if she turned, she would see him. Close enough that if she needed someone, he would be there. She stayed in front of the Hopper for twenty-three minutes. He counted every one. When she finally turned to leave, her eyes swept across the gallery and landed on him for just a moment. That same flicker of almost-recognition. And then she was gone. He had a postcard of that Hopper painting in the Archive. A reminder of the day he watched Elena cry and wished he could help her. Now, with her warm and real beside him, he finally could. He pressed a kiss to her hair, careful not to wake her, and closed his eyes. Tomorrow, they would start building new memories. Tonight, for the first time in so many years, the old ones felt like they belonged to him and Elena both.

The storm was still raging when they came back upstairs. Elena's hands were cold from the basement — the Archive had no heating, and she'd spent an hour holding paper and photographs and the worn spine of a Neruda book that felt, impossibly, like holding a piece of her own forgotten history. Lucian made tea. She sat on his couch wrapped in a blanket and watched him move through his kitchen with the careful precision of a man who did everything deliberately.

"You're shaking," he said, setting the mug in front of her.

"I'm cold."

"That's not why you're shaking." She looked at him.

He was standing by the kitchen doorway, half-lit by the lamp, his face more open and afraid than she had ever seen it. He had just shown her the most vulnerable thing he possessed — not the Archive, but the fact of it. The admission that he had organized his inner life around a woman who hadn't known he existed.

"Come here," she said.

He crossed the room and sat beside her. Not touching. Close enough that she could feel the warmth of him through the blanket, could smell the clean-soap scent of his skin, could see the pulse beating in his throat.

"I'm not going to run," she said.

"I need you to hear that."

"I hear it."

"Good." She set down the tea.

"Now I need you to hear something else."

"Okay."

"I don't want to be careful anymore." She turned to face him, and her voice was steady even though her hands were not.

"I've been careful for two years. Careful about who I let close, careful about what I let myself feel, careful about everything because careful felt safe. And it was. But safe isn't the same as alive." Lucian was very still.

"Elena —"

"I'm not finished." She reached out and touched his face — his jaw, the stubble there, the warmth of his skin under her fingertips.

He closed his eyes, and the sound he made — not a word, something quieter — told her everything she needed to know

143

about what this cost him. To be touched. To be chosen. To be allowed.

"I want to stay tonight," she said.

"Not because I'm scared, and not because of Adam, and not because the storm is bad. Because I want to. Because this is my choice, and I'm making it with my eyes open." He opened his eyes.

They were gray in the lamplight, and wet, and looking at her with a focus that would have been frightening from anyone else — the absolute, total attention of a man whose brain could not do anything by halves.

"Are you sure?" he asked.

"I've never been less sure of anything in my life." She smiled.

"That's how I know it's right." He kissed her.

Not the careful, questioning kiss from the gala — this was different. This was the kiss of a man who had been given permission to stop waiting. His hands found her waist, the curve of her hip, the small of her back, and she felt the restraint in him, all those years of restraint, begin to give way, and it was like watching a dam crack: slow at first, then all at once. They didn't make it to the bedroom. The couch was narrow and the blanket kept tangling around their legs and at one point Keats wandered in, assessed the situation, and retreated to the kitchen with the dignified horror of a dog who had seen quite enough, thank you. Elena laughed against Lucian's mouth.

"Your dog is scandalized."

"He's eleven. He's forgotten what this is."

"Have you?"

"I've never done this." The words came out raw. Honest.

"Not like this. Not with someone who —" He stopped.

"Not with you." She pulled him closer.

"Then let's make a memory worth keeping." Afterward, they lay on the narrow couch, Elena's back against his chest, the storm still hammering the windows.

His arm was around her, his thumb tracing slow circles on her wrist, and she could feel his breathing gradually steady against her spine.

"You're memorizing this," she said.

Not a question.

"I can't help it."

"I know." She turned her head to look at him.

"What will you remember?" He was quiet for a moment.

"The sound of the rain. The way you laughed when Keats left the room. The fact that you chose this, chose me, on a night when you had every reason not to." His voice dropped.

"The way you said 'let's make a memory worth keeping,' and meant it."

"That's a lot of detail."

"It always is. That's the curse."

"And the gift?"

"And the gift." He pressed his lips to her hair.

"Mostly the gift, tonight." She fell asleep listening to the storm, and to his heartbeat, and to the particular silence of a man who was doing what he always did, remembering, but doing it, with the person he was remembering lying in his arms, breathing, real, and choosing to stay.

PART THREE

THE RECKONING

"The real voyage of discovery consists not in seeking new landscapes, but in having new eyes."

— Marcel Proust

CHAPTER TWELVE

ELENA

IN THE EARLY DAYS, before the shape of it became clear, Adam had brought her coffee in bed on Saturday mornings.

He had made it the way she liked it — one sugar, a splash of the oat milk she preferred and he pretended to find ridiculous — and he had carried it in on a small wooden tray with a folded linen napkin and, sometimes, a flower from the window box. He would sit on the edge of the bed and watch her drink it with an expression of quiet contentment, and he would ask her about her day, and he would listen to her answer, and he would make her laugh at something he had read in the paper, and they would spend the morning in bed reading and talking, and those mornings had been, for almost a year, the happiest of her life.

She thought about those mornings, sometimes. Not often. Not often enough to worry Dr. Keane. But sometimes, walking in Camden's Rise in the early sunlight with the coffee cup from the bakery warming her hand, she would feel the old morning come up in her like a flavor on the back of her tongue, and she would have to stop walking for a second and wait for it to pass.

The truth, which she had taken a long time to learn, was that the mornings had been real. Adam had really loved her, in the particular way he was capable of loving. The coffee had not been a trick. The laughter had not been a performance. The trick was that the same hands that had carried the tray had also, eventually, gripped her wrist too hard when her phone rang at the wrong time. The performance was that the man who had asked her about her day in bed had also, eventually, wanted to know every other man whose day she had been asked about.

It was possible, she had come to understand, for a man to love you and to cost you too much at the same time. It was possible for the love to be real and for the damage to also be real. Dr. Keane had been particular on this point. *Nothing about accepting that he loved you,* Dr. Keane had said, *diminishes the fact that he should not have been allowed to keep loving you the way he loved you. Both things. Not one.*

Elena made her coffee the way she had learned to make it for herself after she left. One sugar. A splash of oat milk. No tray. No flower. Drunk standing up at the counter, in the soft light of her own window, in a town she had chosen for reasons that had belonged to her.

She was not sixteen in a parking lot. She was not twenty-four and new-married and hopeful. She was thirty-three and she had chosen this coffee and this window and this morning, and she was about to choose, in a way she would not have believed possible two years ago, a man who did not make coffee for anyone because he did not know how to make coffee, and who had therefore arranged for the bakery down the street to know his order and hers and to have them both ready by the time he walked in.

It was not a flower on a tray. It was something else.

She was going to find out what.

Three months of happiness. That was what Elena would think later, when the world came crashing down. Three months of waking in his arms. Three months of lazy breakfasts and stolen kisses when June pretended not to notice. Three months of learning his rhythms, his habits, the particular way he smiled when he was trying not to laugh. She should have known it couldn't last. The text came on a Tuesday, while she was reviewing fabric samples in the ballroom. The restoration was progressing beautifully — the damaged silk panels had been sent to a specialist in Boston, the chandeliers were fully restored, and Marcus's crew had finished the structural repairs to the east wing. In another month, the Rowan Hotel would be ready for its grand reopening. Elena's phone buzzed. She glanced at the screen, expecting Lucian or Marla or maybe June with another question about color palettes. The number was unfamiliar. The message was not. I know where you are, Elena. Did you really think you could run from me? The world tilted. She knew that voice, even in text. The cadence of it. The implicit threat wrapped in what looked like a simple question. Four years of her life had been spent learning to read Adam Blackwell's moods, to anticipate his anger, to make herself small enough to avoid his wrath. She had thought she was free. She had thought two years and five hundred miles would be enough distance. She had been wrong. Her hands were shaking as she lowered the phone. The fabric samples blurred in her vision, the beautiful ballroom suddenly feeling too large, too exposed. Anyone could be watching. Anyone could be — "Elena?" June's voice cut through the fog of panic.

Elena looked up to find the older woman standing in the doorway, her brow creased with concern.

"You've gone pale as a ghost, dear. What's wrong?"

"Nothing." The lie came automatically, a reflex from years of hiding Adam's behavior from the outside world.

"Just... a message I wasn't expecting." June's eyes narrowed.

She had the sharp perception of a woman who had lived long enough to recognize deflection when she saw it.

"Elena." Her voice was gentle but firm.

"I've known you for less than two months, but I like to think we've become friends. And friends don't lie to each other." She crossed the ballroom, her footsteps echoing on the newly refinished floor.

"What's really wrong?" Elena looked at the phone in her hand.

At the message that had shattered her peace with twelve words.

"My ex," she said quietly.

"The one I told you about. The one I left two years ago." She swallowed hard.

"He found me."

She called Lucian from June's office, her voice steadier than she felt. He arrived in twelve minutes. She knew because she counted every one of them, her eyes fixed on the door while June made tea neither of them would drink. When he walked in, his face was tight with worry, his hair windswept from the speed of his journey. His eyes found hers immediately, scanning her for signs of harm.

"What happened?" He crossed to her in three long strides, taking her hands in his.

"You sounded scared on the phone."

"I am scared." There was no point in pretending otherwise.

"Adam found me. He knows I'm here." She showed him the message.

Watched his jaw tighten as he read it, his hands curling into fists at his sides.

"How?" The word was clipped, controlled.

"How did he find you?"

"I don't know. I've been careful. I didn't tell anyone from my old life where I was going, except Marla, and she would never —" Elena's voice cracked.

"I don't know how he found me, Lucian. But he has. And if he's texting, that means he's planning something. He never just... reaches out. There's always a reason."

"What kind of reason?"

"Control." The word tasted bitter in her mouth.

"He wants me to know he can still reach me. That I'm not as free as I thought. It's a reminder that he's still there, still watching, still —" She took a shuddering breath.

"It's what he does. He makes you feel like you can never really escape." Lucian's expression was thunderous, but his touch remained gentle as he pulled her into his arms.

"He can't hurt you here. I won't let him."

"You don't know Adam." Elena pressed her face into his chest, drawing strength from the solid warmth of him.

"He's not violent — not physically. He's too smart for that. But he's relentless. He doesn't give up. When I left, he told me I would regret it. That no one else would ever want me. That I would come crawling back."

"He was wrong."

"Yes." She looked up at him, at this man who had loved her for fifteen years without ever demanding anything in return.

"He was wrong. But that doesn't mean he'll accept it." June, who had been sitting quietly at her desk, cleared her throat.

"I don't mean to interrupt, but I have a thought." She stood, moving to the window that overlooked the harbor.

"This man — Adam — he's looking for a reaction, yes? He wants Elena to be afraid, to feel powerless."

"That's his pattern," Elena confirmed.

"Then don't give him one." June turned back to face them, her sharp eyes sharp.

"Don't respond. Don't engage. Let him wonder if his message even reached you. Men like that feed on fear — starve him of it."

"And if he escalates?" Lucian's voice was tight.

"Then we deal with it. Together." June's voice was firm.

"Elena is not alone in this. She has you. She has me. She has this entire town, if it comes to that. Camden's Rise looks after its own." Elena's throat tightened.

"I'm not really one of yours. I've only been here two months."

"You're restoring my hotel. You're dating our most eligible historian. And you make the best latte at the coffee shop since you showed Sarah your secret for steaming milk." June smiled.

"That makes you family." Despite everything, Elena laughed.

It was watery and weak, but it was real.

"Okay," she said.

"Okay. I won't respond. I'll... I'll pretend I never got it."

"Good." Lucian pressed a kiss to her forehead.

"And tonight, you're staying with me. I don't want you alone in that apartment."

"I practically live at your house already."

"Then make it official." their gazes connected hers, steady and sure.

"Tonight, you're welcome here. If you want. No pressure, no timeline — just an open door. Whenever you need it." The words hung in the air.

June discreetly busied herself with papers on her desk, giving them a semblance of privacy.

"Lucian..." Elena's heart was racing.

"It's only been three weeks since —"

"It's been so many years." His voice was quiet but intense.

"I've been waiting for you for over a decade, Elena. I don't want to wait anymore. I don't want to be apart from you anymore." He touched her face, tilting it up to meet his gaze.

"Not because you're scared, and not because of Adam. Because you shouldn't have to be alone tonight if you don't want to be. That's all."

"Thank you," she said.

"I might take you up on that. Tonight, at least." It wasn't a declaration.

It wasn't a life change. It was one night, one open door, one woman choosing not to be alone with her fear. It was enough. His smile, that rare, unguarded smile that transformed his whole face, was worth every risk.

"Yes?"

"Yes." She kissed him, soft and certain.

"I'll move in with you. I'll stop splitting my time between two places. I'll —" She laughed against his mouth.

"I'll let you make me breakfast every morning."

"I make excellent breakfast."

"I know. I've been eating it for three weeks." From her desk, June cleared her throat again.

"I'm very happy for you both, truly. But perhaps we should also discuss practical matters? Like security? And whether we should alert the local police about this Adam person?" The joy dimmed, reality crashing back in.

"He hasn't done anything illegal," Elena said.

"Not technically. One text message isn't enough for the police to act on."

"But it's enough for them to know," June insisted.

"Chief Patterson is a friend. If there's someone potentially dangerous in town, she should be aware." Elena hesitated.

Part of her — the part that had spent four years minimizing Adam's behavior, making excuses, convincing herself it wasn't that bad — wanted to resist. To handle it quietly. To not make a fuss. But that was the old Elena. The Elena who had been so broken down she couldn't recognize abuse when it was standing right in front of her. The new Elena — the one who had chosen Lucian, chosen Camden's Rise, chosen to build a life worth living — knew better.

"Okay," she said.

"Call Chief Patterson. I'll tell her everything."

Patterson was a compact woman in her fifties with steel-gray hair and the kind of direct gaze that suggested she had seen everything and was prepared for anything. She listened to Elena's story without interruption, taking careful notes, asking clarifying questions only when necessary. When Elena finished — her voice hoarse from recounting four years of manipulation and control — the Chief sat back and studied her with something like respect.

"You're brave to tell me all this," she said.

"A lot of women wouldn't."

"I spent too long being quiet. It didn't protect me."

"No, it wouldn't have." Chief Patterson closed her notebook.

"Here's what I can do. One text message isn't enough for a restraining order — you're right about that. But I can make sure my officers know Adam Blackwell's name and face. If he shows up in Camden's Rise, we'll know about it. And if he contacts you again, in any way, I want you to document it and bring it to me. Patterns of behavior are what the courts care about."

"And if he does something... more?" Lucian's voice was tight.

"Then we act accordingly." The Chief's eyes were hard.

"I've dealt with men like this before, Mr. Calder. They think they're untouchable because they're smart enough not to leave bruises. But harassment, stalking, intimidation — those are crimes too. And I take them seriously." Elena felt something loosen in her chest.

She had expected dismissal, minimization, the usual response of authorities who didn't understand that abuse didn't always look like a black eye. Instead, she had found an ally.

"Thank you," she said.

"I... thank you."

"Don't thank me yet." Chief Patterson stood, extending her hand.

"Thank me when this is over and that man is out of your life for good." Elena shook her hand, drawing strength from the firm grip.

"I'll hold you to that."

"Please do." A hint of a smile crossed the Chief's stern face.

"Now go home. Both of you. Get some rest. And Elena?—" She paused.

"Don't let this man steal any more of your joy than he already has. You've built something good here. Don't give him the power to destroy it."

That night, Elena lay awake in Lucian's bed, listening to his steady breathing beside her. She had thought she was free. She had thought the hardest part was over — leaving Adam, rebuilding her life, learning to trust again. She had thought that falling in love with Lucian was the reward for all those years of suffering, the universe finally giving her something beautiful. And it was. But beautiful things attracted attention. And Adam, she had learned, could not stand to see someone else happy. She didn't know how he had found her. She didn't know what he wanted, beyond the obvious — control, submission, the satisfaction of knowing she was still afraid of him. She didn't know what he would do next. But she knew one thing with absolute certainty: she would not let him take this from her. Not Lucian. Not Camden's Rise. Not the life she was building, one restored ballroom and one morning kiss at a time. She had fought too hard. She had come too far. She had finally found someone who loved her how she deserved to be loved. Adam could send all the texts he wanted. He could show up in town, make threats, try to intimidate her. But she was not the same woman who had walked out of his apartment two years ago, broken and barely breathing. She was Elena Ward. She was loved. She was supported. She was surrounded by people who would fight for her. And she was done being afraid. She turned in Lucian's arms, pressing close to him. He stirred, murmuring something in his sleep, and his arm tightened around her instinctively.

"I love you," she whispered into the darkness.

"Love you too," he mumbled back, not quite awake.

"Always." Always.

She held onto that word as she finally drifted off to sleep. Whatever came next, whatever Adam tried to do, she had this.

She had always. And no one, not Adam, not fear, not the ghosts of her past, was going to take that away.

That night, after the discovery in the Archive, Elena couldn't sleep. She sat in her apartment with her laptop open, the documents Lucian had sent her spread across the screen. Clara Whitmore. The woman Theodore had loved, the woman who had been erased from history, the woman who had left behind nothing but a tin box full of letters and a mystery. The photograph they had found haunted her. Clara at perhaps twenty years old, standing in front of what must have been the Rowan in its earliest days. She was smiling — a private, knowing smile, as if she and the photographer shared a secret the camera couldn't capture. Elena understood that smile now. She had felt it on her own face, these past days with Lucian. The smile of a woman who was loved. The smile of a woman who had found someone who truly saw her. What had happened to Clara Whitmore? What had torn her away from the man who built a hotel in her honor, who wrote her letters for twenty years, who kept her memory alive long after the world had forgotten she existed? Elena pulled up the genealogical records they had accessed through June's family account. Clara Whitmore, born 1862 in Boston. Married to Harold Westbrook in 1884 — the same year Theodore's first letters began. Died 1923 in Newport, Rhode Island. Forty years. Clara had lived forty years after leaving Theodore. Had she been happy? Had she thought of him? Had she ever regretted the choice that had been made for her — because Elena was sure now that it had been made for her, not by her? the letters Theodore had written. The love that never faded. The hope that never quite died. I would rather be alone with the memory of you than married to the reality of someone else. Elena pressed her palms together, where something ached. She had been Clara. She had let Adam's family, Adam's expectations, Adam's version of her future become a cage she couldn't escape. She had lost herself in someone else's story. But she had gotten out. She had found her way here, to this coastal town, to this crumbling hotel, to a man who had loved her for over a decade without ever asking for anything in return. Theodore never got his happy ending. Clara never got to choose her own path. But Elena could. She could choose Lucian. She could choose this strange, impossible love that had somehow found her across the years of almost-meetings. She could choose to make the ending different. She picked up her phone and typed a message to Lucian: I've been thinking about Clara. About how she never got to make the choice herself. About how different things might have been if she had. His response came immediately, as if he had been awake too: I've been thinking about that too. About how Theodore spent his whole life wondering what if. We don't have to wonder, Elena typed back. We get to find out. There was a long pause. Then: Is that what you want? To find out? Elena smiled at her phone, at the uncertainty in his question, at the hope he was clearly trying not to feel. Yes, she typed. That's exactly what I want. Then come over tomorrow. Early. I have something I want to show you. Another artifact from the Archive? No. Something new. Something I've been working on. Elena's curiosity sparked, but she didn't push. Whatever Lucian was planning, she trusted him. I'll be there at eight, she typed. I'll have coffee ready. You're already learning. I've been paying attention for over a decade. I should hope I've learned something. She laughed, alone in her quiet apartment, and felt something ease. This was real. This was happening. After everything — after Adam, after running, after wondering if she would ever trust herself again — she was choosing love. Not love that controlled. Not the kind that diminished. But the kind that remembered. The kind that waited. The kind that built hotels and wrote letters and kept faith through the years of silence. She typed one more message: Goodnight, Lucian. Goodnight, Elena. Sleep well. You too. She set her phone aside and looked out the window at the lighthouse beam sweeping. Tomorrow, she would see what Lucian had been working on. Tomorrow, they would take another step forward. And somewhere in the past, she liked to think, Theodore Rowan was finally smiling.

The next evening, Elena asked him to tell her about the other encounters. The ones he hadn't shared yet. So he told her about the bookstore. April 22, 2019. Harvard Book Store, Cambridge. She looked different. Better. There was color in her cheeks again, and she was wearing jeans and a soft sweater instead of polished designer clothes. But the most significant change was her hands. Her ring finger was bare. She had left him. She had finally left Adam. He could have approached her. But she was healing, fragile. The last thing she needed was another man appearing out of nowhere, claiming to know her. So he watched from three aisles away as she selected four books on Victorian architecture. Watched her laugh at something the cashier said. Watched her step out into the rain with her purchases clutched to her chest, her face turned up to the sky like she was tasting freedom for the first time.

"You were there," Elena whispered.

"When I was just starting to put myself back together. You were there, and I didn't even know."

"I wanted to give you space. Time to heal."

"You've been giving me space for over a decade."

"I would have given you fifteen more if you needed them." She kissed him then, soft and fierce at once, and when she pulled back, her eyes were searching his face.

"Tell me about the beach," she said.

"The last time. Before Camden's Rise." So he told her about Narragansett.

About the pandemic summer. About watching her read on the beach, so peaceful, so free, and walking past without saying a word.

"You picked up a stone," Elena said.

"I remember — I remember feeling like someone was watching me that day. I thought I was being paranoid."

"You weren't. It was me." He pulled her closer.

"It was always me."

"I know." She rested her head on his chest.

"I know that now."

The morning after the Archive, Elena woke to sunlight and terror. For a moment, lying in Lucian's guest room where she'd fallen asleep after they talked until three a.m. she didn't understand the cold weight in her chest. The previous night had been beautiful. Overwhelming. She had seen the Archive, all devotion made tangible, and instead of running, she had chosen to stay. So why did she feel like she couldn't breathe? She found Lucian in the kitchen, making coffee with the careful precision of a man who had memorized the ideal water temperature and steep time. He looked up when she entered, and his face transformed with such hope, such joy, that it made her chest hurt.

"Good morning," he said.

"I made — are you okay?" She wasn't.

She could feel the panic building, the familiar tightness that preceded the worst episodes. Her therapist had a name for this. Trauma response. Hypervigilance. Your nervous system learned to expect pain after vulnerability, so now vulnerability triggers the same fear as actual danger.

"I need to go," she heard herself say.

Lucian's face shifted — not to anger, but to careful attention.

"Okay. Do you want to talk about —"

"No. I just need to go. I'm sorry. I'm so sorry." She was already moving toward the door, already fleeing, how she had learned to flee from Adam's rages.

Except Lucian wasn't raging. Lucian was standing very still in his kitchen, coffee pot in hand, watching her fall apart with an expression of devastating gentleness.

"Elena." His voice stopped her at the threshold.

"I'm not going to chase you. But I'll be here. When you're ready." She ran.

Three days passed. She did not return his texts. She threw herself into work, avoided the library, ate lunch in her apartment instead of the café where they had started meeting. Marla called, increasingly worried. Her therapist asked calm, probing questions. What are you actually afraid of? That he'll hurt me. Has he done anything to hurt you? No. He's been perfect. Then what are you afraid of? That I'll let him in. That I'll trust him. And then he'll change. The way Adam changed. On the fourth day, she found Lucian sitting on the steps of her apartment building. He looked exhausted. Stubble shadowed his jaw, and there were circles under his eyes that spoke of sleepless nights. He was holding a small box.

"I'm not here to pressure you," he said, before she could speak.

"I'm here to give you this." He held out the box.

She took it automatically, then opened it. Inside was a postcard. A Rothko painting — the same one she'd been standing in front of when she met Adam.

"How did you —"

"Washington D.C." Lucian said quietly.

"November 2018. National Gallery. You were crying in front of this painting. I was three rooms away. I saw you but didn't approach." She stared at the postcard, her blood rushed.

"I bought this from the gift shop after you left," he continued.

"I didn't know why you were crying. I didn't know about Adam yet — I wouldn't learn about him until later, from a mutual acquaintance's social media post. But I kept this postcard because it was part of your story, and I wanted to understand."

"You kept a postcard from a day you didn't even speak to me."

"I kept everything." He stood slowly, as if giving her time to adjust to his proximity.

"I know what it looks like, Elena. I know it seems obsessive. Maybe it is. But here's what I need you to understand." He stepped closer — not touching her, just close enough that she could see the sincerity in his gray-blue eyes.

"I am not Adam. I will never be Adam. And the difference between us isn't just that I would never hurt you — it's that I know what he took from you, and I am willing to spend the rest of my life proving that love doesn't have to feel like a trap."

"How?" Her voice came out broken.

"How can you prove that?"

"By not chasing you when you run. By being here when you come back. By never once making you feel crazy for protecting yourself." He took another breath.

"You asked me once what I felt. I said terrified and hopeful and grateful. I'm still all of those things. But I'm also patient, Elena. I have been patient for over a decade. I can be patient a little longer." She was quiet for a long time.

"I don't know if I can do this," she whispered.

"I want to. God, I want to. But every time I start to feel safe, something in me panics. Like my body is waiting for the trap to spring."

"Then we'll go slow." He reached out — slowly, telegraphing every movement — and took her hand.

"As slow as you need. We'll build trust one day at a time. And every time your brain tells you I'm going to become Adam, I'll prove it wrong. Over and over, until your nervous system learns that safety is real."

"That could take years."

"I have years." He smiled — that small, quiet smile that was becoming her favorite thing.

"I have a lifetime of years. And every single one of them is yours if you want them." She stood there, on the sidewalk in front of her apartment, holding a postcard from a day she'd been crying over her own captivity.

And for the first time since she'd fled his house three days ago, the panic began to ease.

"Okay," she said.

"Slow. One day at a time."

"One day at a time," he agreed.

He didn't kiss her. Didn't push for more. Just held her hand, solid and patient, while the fear slowly unclenched from around her heart. It would take months before she stopped waiting for the other shoe to drop. Months before she could accept his kindness without flinching. Months before her body learned what her mind already knew: that Lucian Calder was nothing like Adam Blackwell, and love didn't have to hurt. But this — this moment on the sidewalk, with the postcard in her hand and his patience wrapped around her like a blanket — this was where the healing really began.

Isabel came up from Portland the following Saturday without announcing herself.

She arrived on the noon train with a single overnight bag and an expression that informed Elena, before any words were exchanged, that this was not a social visit. Lucian picked her up at the station. Elena was in the kitchen of the old Victorian when they walked in — she had moved half her clothes into Lucian's closet at this point, and a toothbrush into his bathroom, and was in the slow process of discovering which corners of his life had space for her — and she was not, honestly, ready to be evaluated by Lucian's older sister. But

Isabel was the only family Lucian had left. Isabel had to be faced eventually.

"You must be Elena." Isabel set her bag down by the kitchen door and took Elena's hand in both of hers — the same two-handed clasp June used, which made Elena wonder, for a second, whether all women who had loved Lucian for a long time ended up holding hands the same way. "I have been hearing about you for three weeks and I am here to get a proper look at you. Lucian, take my bag upstairs, please, and give us the kitchen."

Lucian looked at Elena. Elena looked at Lucian.

"It's fine," Elena said.

Lucian took the bag upstairs.

Isabel sat down at the kitchen table and took off her coat. She was a smaller woman than Elena had expected — Lucian's description had made her sound physically formidable, and she was not, she was an ordinary-sized woman in her late forties with her brother's gray eyes and a very good wool cardigan. But there was a directness to her that took up the space her body didn't.

"I'm going to ask you some questions," Isabel said. "You don't have to answer them. I want you to know in advance that I am asking them because I love my brother and because I believe you probably love him too, and I want us to begin on that basis rather than on the basis of me pretending I dropped by to say hello. Is that acceptable?"

"Yes."

"Do you know what you're doing?"

Elena considered the question. It was a better question than she had expected. She had been braced for the usual — *How long have you known him, what are your intentions, where do you see this going* — and Isabel had cut past all of that in one sentence.

"I think I do," she said. "I know what I feel. I know I've been hurt before, and I've done the work to understand what that did to me, and I'm trying to be careful. I'm not fifteen years old and I'm not twenty-six and in love with the wrong man. I'm thirty-three and I know what it looks like when someone is good to you."

"Good answer." Isabel nodded once, the way a woman nods when she is crossing an item off an interior list. "Next question. Do you understand what it will be like to live with him?"

"I'm learning."

"Let me tell you the part you haven't learned yet." Isabel folded her hands on the table. Her voice dropped half a register. "I have lived with my brother and his condition since we were children. Our father had it too, though milder, and our father died of a heart attack at fifty-one which my brother believes was partly caused by the condition, and I am not going to argue with him about that. I am going to tell you what nobody will tell you, because Lucian cannot bring himself to tell you and our parents are both gone."

Elena waited.

"He will remember every time you have ever been unkind to him." Isabel said it steadily, looking directly at Elena. "Every tone in your voice. Every sentence you've said in anger. Every face you've made when he disappointed you. Not because he wants to, and not because he holds it against you — he doesn't, I promise you he does not hold grudges, he has never in his life held a grudge, I don't know how he doesn't. But the memory is there. He can access it. He does access it. He cannot un-access it."

"I know," Elena said. "He told me."

"He told you the polite version. I am telling you the version that will matter." Isabel did not blink. "When you are having a good day, this will be a feature. He will remember the specific dress you wore on your second date and he will tell you that you look beautiful on your tenth anniversary and mean it in a way most husbands cannot mean it. When you are having a bad day, this will be a problem. You will say something in anger that you regret before you finish saying it. You will apologize. He will mean it when he says he has forgiven you. And the sentence you said will still be in him, sharp and specific, for the rest of his life. He will not bring it up. But it will be in him."

Elena found that she had stopped breathing. She made herself start again.

"So what you have to learn," Isabel said, "is to be gentle with him in a way you did not know you were going to have to be gentle. Not all the time. Not in a way that keeps you small. You will fight with him; you should fight with him; couples fight and that's not the problem. The problem is that most of us get to be casually cruel occasionally and have it wash away. You don't get that with him. You have to mean what you say. You have to not say what you don't mean. You have to be the kind of woman who, on a bad day, is still responsible for her own tongue."

"That sounds exhausting."

"It's a discipline." Isabel's mouth twitched toward something like a smile. "It turned our mother into a very precise woman. Our father did his best. Our father was, I want you to know, adored by her. What I am telling you is not a warning. It is a training."

Elena was quiet for a long moment. Outside the kitchen window the harbor was turning the slate color it turned when the wind came up from the northeast.

"You're telling me this because you want me to leave," she said, testing.

"No." Isabel shook her head, calmly. "I am telling you this because you are not going to leave and I want you to be prepared. I have watched women meet my brother and decide they could not stay with him. Two of them I liked very much. One of them I was glad to see go. None of them were wrong to go; the requirements of loving him are real. I am telling you because I looked at your face when I walked in and I recognized something in it and I do not want you to break my brother's heart by making promises you did not know you were making. Do you understand what I am saying?"

"Yes."

"Good." Isabel sat back. "Now tell me about the hotel. Lucian says you have done something remarkable with the silk panels."

They talked about the hotel for half an hour. Then they talked about Isabel's son, who was nineteen and studying music in Montreal. Then Lucian came downstairs and made them lunch, because cooking for people was one of the ways he had learned to feel at home in a body that did not always forget things cleanly, and Isabel watched him move around his kitchen with an expression that Elena could not read at first. Eventually, watching Isabel watch Lucian, Elena recognized it.

It was the expression of a woman who had spent her life protecting someone she loved, and who was now, cautiously, being invited to consider that someone else might be willing to help.

That evening, when Isabel hugged her goodbye at the train station, Isabel held her a beat longer than strangers usually hold each other.

"Thank you," Isabel said into her ear, quietly. "For being careful with him."

"Thank you," Elena said back, "for warning me."

She watched Isabel's train pull away. Lucian stood beside her on the platform with his hands in his coat pockets. She leaned against his arm and he let her, and for a long moment neither of them said anything at all.

"She told you," Lucian said finally.

"Yes."

"I was going to."

"I know."

He was quiet. The lighthouse beam was already starting its evening sweep, even though the sun had only just set. "And?"

"And I'm still here." She took his hand and laced her fingers through his. "You'll notice that."

"I've noticed."

"Good," she said. "Take me home."

He did.

CHAPTER THIRTEEN

LUCIAN

LUCIAN HAD NEVER WANTED to hurt someone as badly as he wanted to hurt Adam Blackwell. When he thought about what Adam had done to Elena — the years of manipulation, the slow erosion of her confidence, the way she still flinched when her phone buzzed — something dark and dangerous stirred in his chest. He wanted to find Adam Blackwell and make him understand what he had done. He wanted to make him understand, in visceral and unmistakable terms, what it felt like to be afraid. Instead, he did what he always did when confronted with a problem: he researched.

The unwanted memory arrived, as they always did, without warning. He was making breakfast — scrambling eggs, a task so mundane it should have been immune to ambush — when the smell of butter in the pan pulled him backward twenty-three years, to a kitchen in Connecticut, to a Tuesday morning when he was nine years old and his father was making eggs and his mother was standing in the doorway with a suitcase and his father said, without turning around, "So you're really doing this." Every detail.

The pattern on the kitchen wallpaper — blue cornflowers on a cream background. The sound of butter sizzling. The way his mother's hand tightened on the suitcase handle. The way his father's shoulders didn't move, didn't react, as if he'd known this was coming and had already grieved it in advance.

"I'll be back for the children's things next week," his mother had said, and she had not been back next week, or the week after, or the week after that.

She had come back eventually — three months later, contrite and overwhelmed and full of explanations that a nine-year-old couldn't evaluate — but those three months lived in Lucian's memory at the same resolution as this morning's eggs. He couldn't dim them. Couldn't soften the edges. Couldn't let time do what time was supposed to do — blur the details, round the corners, transform a wound into a scar. For Lucian, every wound was still a wound. Always fresh. Always nine years old. Always standing in a kitchen watching his world come apart over scrambled eggs. He set down the spatula. Breathed. Keats padded over and pressed his nose against Lucian's hand — the dog's version of checking in.

"I'm fine," Lucian told the dog.

"Just remembering." Keats looked at him with the unconvinced expression of a creature who had spent eleven years observing human behavior and found most of it suspect.

"I'm fine," Lucian repeated, and went back to the eggs.

This was what people didn't understand about HSAM. They thought it was about Elena — about the romantic devotion, the beautiful obsession, the fairy-tale premise that sold books and inspired articles. And it was, partly. But it was also about every cruel thing a classmate had said in fourth grade, preserved at full volume. Every argument with Isabel, word for word. Every patient he'd failed to help during a brief and disastrous stint volunteering at a crisis hotline in graduate school. Every loss, every embarrassment, every moment of cowardice or unkindness — his own or others' — stored forever, accessible at the slightest sensory trigger. Butter in a pan. Cornflowers on wallpaper. A Tuesday morning. The gift and the curse. Mostly the curse, on mornings like this. But he finished the eggs. Fed the dog. Got dressed. Went to work. That was the other thing people didn't understand: you learned to live with it. Not by forgetting — never by forgetting — but by choosing which memories to attend to and which to let pass through like weather. The unwanted ones still arrived. They always would. But they didn't have to be the ones that defined the day. He chose Elena. He chose the morning she'd brought the boxes back, the wine cork on the AFTER shelf, the look on her face when she said "ours." He chose that memory, and the eggs tasted fine, and the day began.

Adam Blackwell was not hard to find online. He was a partner at a prestigious consulting firm in Boston, specializing in corporate restructuring. His LinkedIn profile was immaculate — Harvard MBA, impressive client list, dozens of connections singing his praises. His company website featured a professional headshot: blond, chiseled, the kind of handsome that looked like it had been manufactured in a laboratory. Lucian studied the photograph with the intensity he usually reserved for primary sources. This was the man who had controlled Elena for four years. This was the man who had diminished her light, made her doubt herself, convinced her she was worthless without him. This was the man Lucian had watched lead her out of a Brooklyn café with a proprietary hand on her back, and done nothing to stop. The guilt of that memory still burned. He had been right there, close enough to intervene, and he had let his fear of overstepping paralyze him. He had watched her walk away with a man who was slowly destroying her, and he had told himself it wasn't his place to interfere. Never again. He dug deeper. Court records, property filings, social media — anything that might give him insight into who Adam Blackwell really was beneath the polished exterior. What he found was both reassuring and troubling. Reassuring: there were no criminal records, no restraining orders, no public evidence of violence. Adam was careful. He knew how to maintain appearances. Troubling: there were whispers. A pattern, if you knew how to look for it. An ex-girlfriend's cryptic post about "surviving" a relationship. A former colleague's vague reference to Adam's "intensity." A woman in a support forum for emotional abuse survivors who described her ex with details that sounded eerily familiar — the charm, the control, the way he made you feel like you were going crazy.

Elena wasn't the first. She probably wouldn't be the last. Lucian saved everything. Screenshots, links, notes. He created a file on his computer, organized and thorough, how he would approach any historical research project. If Adam escalated, when Adam escalated, they would have evidence. A pattern. Something to take to the police, or a lawyer, or whoever else might be able to help. It wasn't enough. But it was something.

Isabel called that afternoon, as if sensing his turmoil from two hundred miles away.

"You sound terrible," she said without preamble.

"What's wrong?"

"Elena's ex found her." The words came out flat, controlled.

"He sent a text. 'I know where you are.' Classic intimidation tactic." A long pause.

"The abusive one?"

"There's only one."

"Shit." Isabel's voice sharpened.

"What are you doing about it?"

"We reported it to the local police. Elena's moved in with me. I've been researching him — building a file on his history, looking for patterns."

"That's all good. Practical." Another pause.

"But that's not why you sound like you're about to commit a felony." Lucian closed his laptop, leaning back in his chair.

"I want to hurt him, Isabel. Not metaphorically. I want to find him and make him feel what he made Elena feel. The fear, the helplessness, all of it." He exhaled.

"I've never felt like this before. It's... disturbing."

"It's human," Isabel said quietly.

"You love her. Someone is threatening her. The protective instinct is primal — it bypasses all our civilized conditioning and goes straight to the lizard brain." She paused.

"The question is what you do with it."

"I'm not going to actually hurt him."

"I know you're not. You're too smart for that. But the feelings are there, and you need to acknowledge them or they'll come out sideways." Isabel's voice took on the gentle authority she used with patients.

"Are you talking to Elena about how you're feeling?"

"She has enough to deal with. I don't want to add my emotional baggage to the pile."

"Lucian." His name was a reprimand.

"That's exactly the kind of thinking that gets couples into trouble. You're supposed to be partners. That means sharing the load, not protecting her from your feelings."

"She's scared. She's dealing with trauma being triggered all over again. The last thing she needs is to know that I'm fantasizing about violence."

"Or she needs to know that you're scared too. That this situation is affecting you, not just her." Isabel sighed.

"You spent years watching her from a distance, unable to help. Now you're finally in her life, and the first real challenge you face together, and your instinct is to go back to protecting her from afar? To handling everything yourself?" The words landed like stones.

Lucian stared out the window at the harbor, where the afternoon light was painting the water in shades of gold and gray.

"I don't know how to do this," he admitted.

"I know how to love her from a distance. I know how to wait and hope and catalog every moment we share. But being in an actual relationship — dealing with problems together, being vulnerable together — I don't have a template for that."

"Welcome to adulthood." Isabel's voice was gentle now, the sharpness fading.

"None of us have a template. We're all just making it up as we go along, trying to learn from our mistakes before they destroy us." She paused.

"Talk to her, Lucian. Tell her you're scared. Tell her you're angry. Tell her you don't know what you're doing but you want to figure it out together. That's what partnership looks like."

"And if she thinks I'm weak? If she needs me to be strong right now?"

"Then she'll tell you. And you'll adjust. That's what partnership looks like too." He could hear the smile in her voice.

"You've waited all this time for this woman. Don't blow it by trying to be something you're not."

He saw Adam Blackwell for the first time three days later. Lucian was at the coffee shop, picking up lattes for himself and Elena, when the man sitting at the corner table. Blond. Chiseled. Expensive suit that looked out of place in Camden's Rise, where flannel and fleece were the dominant fashion choices. The face from the LinkedIn photo. The same manufactured handsomeness. The same practiced smile. Adam wasn't looking at him. He was looking at his phone, scrolling with casual indifference, as if he were just another customer enjoying his morning coffee. But Lucian knew better. There was nothing casual about Adam Blackwell's presence in this town. The barista called his name, and Lucian collected the drinks with hands that wanted to shake but didn't. He could feel Adam's eyes on him now — a prickle at the back of his neck, the predator's awareness of being watched. He should leave. He should take the coffees and go, report Adam's presence to Chief Patterson, let the authorities handle it. Instead, he walked to Adam's table.

"Adam Blackwell." His voice was steady, calm.

The voice he used when lecturing to large audiences or defending his research before skeptical academics.

"I thought I recognized you." Adam looked up, and his smile was everything Lucian had expected: charming, practiced, hollow.

"I'm sorry, have we met?"

"No. But I know who you are." Lucian set the coffees on the table, freeing his hands, though he had no intention of using them for violence.

"And I know what you're doing here."

"I'm having coffee." Adam gestured to his cup.

"Is that a crime in this charming little town?"

"Harassment is. Stalking is. Intimidation is." Lucian kept his voice low, aware of the other customers around them.

"Elena doesn't want to see you. She doesn't want to hear from you. She's built a new life here, and you're not part of it." Adam's smile didn't waver, but something shifted in his eyes — a hardening, a calculation.

"Ah. You must be the new boyfriend." He leaned back in his chair, studying Lucian with undisguised contempt.

"She always did have a type. Intense. Obsessive. The kind of man who thinks he can save her."

"She doesn't need saving. She saved herself when she left you."

"Did she?" Adam's voice was silky, dangerous. "Is that what she told you? That she's fine? That she's moved on?"

He laughed softly.

"Elena is broken, friend. I know because I broke her. And broken people don't heal — they just find new ways to fall apart."

The rage was back, hot and immediate, clawing at Lucian's self-control.

He wanted to wipe that smug smile off Adam's face. He wanted to make him understand, in no uncertain terms, that he had chosen the wrong woman to terrorize. But that was what Adam wanted. He wanted a reaction. He wanted Lucian to lose control, to do something that could be used against him, to prove that he was just as unstable as Adam probably claimed Elena's past partners were. Lucian took a breath. Let it out slowly. Picked up the coffees.

"You're going to leave this town," he said quietly.

"Today. If I see you again, if you contact Elena again, if you so much as look in her direction, I will make sure the authorities know about every woman you've done this to. Every pattern. Every victim. I've already started building the file." He leaned in slightly.

"I'm a historian, Adam. Research is what I do. And I'm very, very good at it." For the first time, something flickered in Adam's expression.

Not fear, exactly — men like Adam didn't feel fear the way normal people did. But wariness. The recognition that he might have underestimated this particular obstacle.

"Are you threatening me?"

"I'm informing you of consequences." Lucian straightened. "There's a difference."

He turned and walked out of the coffee shop without looking back.

His hands were shaking by the time he reached his car. The lattes were lukewarm, and he would have to go back for fresh ones, but he sat in the driver's seat for a long moment, letting the adrenaline work its way through his system. He had done it. He had faced the man who had haunted Elena's nightmares, and he had held his ground, and he had not given Adam the satisfaction of a violent reaction. It wasn't enough. Adam was still here, still a threat, still capable of destroying everything they were building. But it was something. He pulled out his phone and called Chief Patterson.

Elena was waiting for him when he got home. She was sitting at the kitchen table, her laptop open in front of her, but she looked up the moment he walked in. Her eyes scanned his face, reading him with the same intensity he usually directed at her.

"What happened?" He set down the fresh coffees — he had stopped at the bakery on the other side of town, unwilling to risk another encounter — and took the chair across from her.

"Adam is in town." The color drained from her face.

"You saw him?"

"At the coffee shop. He was sitting there like he owned the place." Lucian reached across the table, taking her hands in his.

"I talked to him."

"You —" Her grip tightened.

"Lucian, that was dangerous. You don't know what he's capable of —"

"I needed him to know that you're not alone. That he can't just waltz into town and intimidate you without consequences." He met her eyes.

"I didn't threaten him. I didn't touch him. I just... let him know that I know who he is. What he's done. And that I'm watching." Elena was quiet for a long moment.

He could see her processing, weighing his words against her knowledge of Adam, calculating risks.

"What did he say?" Lucian hesitated.

"He said... things. About you. About us. Things designed to provoke me." He squeezed her hands.

"I didn't take the bait."

"Tell me." Her voice was steady, stronger than he expected.

"I need to know what he said." So he told her.

The manufactured charm. The contempt. The ugly claim about breaking her. Elena listened without interrupting. When he finished, she exhaled slowly, like she was releasing something she had been holding for a long time.

"He said that to you," she said.

"That I'm broken. That broken people don't heal."

"It's not true, Elena —"

"I know." She cut him off, and there was something fierce in her eyes. "I know it's not true. I spent years believing it was. I don't anymore."

She was quiet for a moment, holding his hands across the table, looking down at them.

"I'm not broken. I was hurt. I was damaged. Those are different words, and I know the difference now." She looked

177

up. "I'm still healing. I'm going to be healing for a long time. That's what this looks like." He held her close, breathing in the scent of her hair.

"I wanted to hurt him," he confessed.

"When he said those things, I wanted to make him pay. I've never felt like that before."

"But you didn't."

"No. I didn't."

"That's the difference." Elena pulled back to look at him.

"Adam would have hurt you. He would have done whatever it took to win, to dominate, to prove he was in control. But you walked away. You controlled yourself." She touched his face.

"That's strength, Lucian. Real strength."

"It doesn't feel like strength. It feels like cowardice."

"That's how you know it's strength." She kissed him, soft and certain.

"The brave thing is rarely the satisfying thing. You did the right thing, even when it was hard. That's all anyone can ask." He held her tighter, this woman who had survived things he could barely imagine and emerged not broken, but stronger.

This woman who saw his flaws and loved him anyway. This woman who, after everything she had been through, still believed in the power of doing the right thing.

"I love you," he said.

"I love you too." She rested her forehead against his.

"And we're going to get through this. Together. The way we should have been doing things from the start." Together.

It was a small word for such a large promise. But as Lucian held Elena in the quiet kitchen of the home they now shared, the afternoon light spilling through the windows and the lighthouse standing sentinel in the distance, he thought it was the only word that mattered. Whatever Adam did next, they would face it together. That would have to be enough. He thought, for once, it might be.

Isabel arrived the following weekend, as promised. She swept into Lucian's house with three bottles of wine, a care package from their mother, and enough energy to power a small city. Elena was already there — they had been spending most evenings together now, cooking dinner, reading in comfortable silence, learning the rhythms of each other's lives.

"So," Isabel said, settling into the armchair like a queen taking her throne, "I hear you've seen the Archive." Elena glanced at Lucian, who was trying to look innocent and failing completely.

"He told you?"

"He tells me everything. It's one of the perks and drawbacks of having a brother with extraordinary memory — he can't even pretend to keep secrets because he knows I'll remember that he's lying." Isabel poured herself a generous glass of wine.

"So. What did you think?"

"Honestly?"

"I don't deal in any other currency." Elena considered her words carefully.

She had been thinking about the Archive a lot since that afternoon — about what it meant, what it represented, how it made her feel.

"I think it's the most romantic thing anyone has ever done for me," she said finally. "And also the saddest." Isabel's eyebrows rose.

"Sad?"

"He built it because he didn't think he'd ever have me in real life. Every object in that room is a consolation prize — a piece of something he couldn't have, kept because the piece was better than nothing." Elena looked at Lucian, who was watching her with an unreadable expression.

"I don't want to be a consolation prize anymore. I want to be real."

"You are real," Lucian said quietly.

"You've always been real. The Archive was never about replacing you — it was about remembering that you existed.

That what I felt was based on something actual, not something I imagined."

"I know." Elena reached for his hand.

"I'm not criticizing it. I'm just saying — I'm here now. You don't need to collect pieces of me anymore. You can have the whole thing." The moment stretched, warm and weighted.

Isabel cleared her throat.

"Well," she said, her voice suspiciously bright, "I'm going to go inspect your refrigerator and judge your food choices. You two clearly need a moment." She disappeared into the kitchen with her wine glass, leaving Elena and Lucian alone.

"The whole thing," Lucian repeated.

"You mean that?"

"I mean it." Elena squeezed his hand.

"No more watching from a distance. No more hoping without acting. We're in this together now." He pulled her close, and she went willingly, fitting against him like they had been designed for each other.

From the kitchen, Isabel's voice carried: "You have three kinds of mustard and no vegetables. This is a cry for help." Elena laughed against Lucian's chest.

"I like her."

"Everyone does. It's her superpower." He pressed a kiss to the top of her head.

"Thank you. For seeing the Archive. For understanding."

"Thank you for showing me. For trusting me with it."

"I've trusted you with it since the day I started building it. I just didn't know it yet." They stood there, wrapped in each other, while Isabel made pointed comments about the state of the cheese drawer and the beacon swept its eternal path across the harbor.

And Elena thought: This is it. This is what I was looking for. Not perfection. Not fairy tales. Just this — two people choosing each other, day after day, building something new out of everything that came before. It was enough. It was more than enough. It was enough.

❖ ❖ ❖

Later that week, Elena found June sitting alone in the library, Theodore's letters spread across the desk.

"He never stopped loving her," June said without looking up.

"Twenty years of letters. Even after he knew she never would come back." Elena sat down across from her.

"That kind of devotion is rare."

"Robert was like that." June's voice was soft.

"My husband. He loved me for forty-seven years. Little things — coffee brought to my desk, flowers for no reason, the way he'd reach for my hand when we walked." She touched one of Theodore's letters.

"When he died, I thought that kind of love was over for me."

"And now?" June finally looked up, tears in her eyes — but also hope.

"Now I'm not so sure. Marcus asked me to dinner. At that little Italian place on the harbor."

"And you said yes?"

"I said yes." June smiled — bright and brave.

"I'm terrified and excited and I haven't felt this way in two years." Elena took her hand.

"That's exactly how you know it matters."

CHAPTER FOURTEEN

ELENA

THE MORNING HAD BEEN good.

That was what she would remember afterward — how ordinary it had been, how safe it had felt.

She had been in the east wing since seven, overseeing the installation of the restored silk panels. The crew had gotten the tension right on the third try, and Elena had stood back and watched the fabric settle into place with the particular quiet satisfaction of a design problem solved correctly. The room looked the way she had promised June it would look: the panels catching the morning light in the way Clara had intended them to catch it, the brass picture rail gleaming against the soft green, the new chandelier bar ready for when the electricians finished the next phase.

June had brought her coffee at eight-thirty and left it on the sawhorse without interrupting. That was one of the things Elena had come to love about working for June — the way she managed a project by trusting the people she had hired to do the work. Adam had managed projects, when he was still a consultant before he made partner, by announcing his presence every twenty minutes. June managed by leaving coffee and walking away.

By ten Elena had moved on to the service hallway, checking the plaster work where a crack had opened along the ceiling in a pattern she did not like. She was standing on a step-ladder with a flashlight in her teeth and a putty knife in her hand when she heard the front door open and close in the lobby beyond, and a man's voice she had not heard in almost two years say, *Hello?*

She knew the voice before her mind knew it. The body knew it. Her hand on the putty knife went numb.

Hello? Is anyone here?

She did not answer. For a long second she could not have answered. The step-ladder wobbled beneath her and she made herself put both hands on the top rail and lower herself, slowly, like a woman descending a cliff face. She put the putty knife down on the drop cloth. She pulled the flashlight out of her teeth.

The voice again, closer now: *Elena? Elena, are you here?*

Her mouth was dry. Her skin had gone cold in a way that felt borrowed from someone else's body. She had not heard that voice in twenty-two months. She had rehearsed, with Dr. Keane, with Marla, with her own reflection in the bathroom mirror at three in the morning, what she would say if she ever heard it again. She had rehearsed two dozen variations. She had been careful to make sure the rehearsed version was not a question, was not a plea, was not an apology; was, instead, a clean refusal. She had been proud of the version she had settled on.

She discovered now that she did not remember a word of it.

She walked into the lobby.

Adam was standing by the front desk with his coat open and his hair expensively disordered, the kind of disorder that requires a stylist. He looked exactly the way he had always looked. He looked exactly the way he had looked the morning she left him, when he had stood in the doorway of their apartment in his Harvard sweatshirt and said, in the reasonable voice he used when he was preparing to be unreasonable, *Elena, if you walk out that door, you are making a mistake you will spend the rest of your life correcting.*

He looked up. His face opened into the smile she had once, a very long time ago, believed meant something good.

"There you are," he said.

"Get out."

The smile did not waver. The smile was a project. It had been designed, over years, not to waver. "Is that any way to greet an old friend?"

"We are not friends. Get out."

"Four years of marriage, and we don't have anything to discuss?"

"Three years of abuse."

The word landed between them. *Abuse.* She had said it to Dr. Keane, to Marla, to the empty walls of her apartment at three in the morning. She had never said it to his face.

Adam's composure flickered — a tightening around the eyes, a muscle jumping in his jaw. Then the mask resettled, smooth as glass. "That's a strong word, Elena."

"It's an accurate one."

Her heart was pounding. Her palms were slick with sudden sweat. Every instinct she had developed during those four years was screaming at her to run, to hide, to make herself small and agreeable and safe. She ignored all of them. She was not sixteen years old in a prep-school parking lot. She was not twenty-four and newly married and learning, too late, that her husband had a temper he kept locked away for special occasions. She was thirty-three years old and she had done two years of work with a woman named Dr. Keane specifically so that on the day Adam showed up again she would know, in her body, that she did not have to manage him.

"This is private property," she said. Her voice came out steadier than she felt. "You are trespassing."

"The door was open. I'm just a tourist, admiring the restoration." He stepped into the room, and every cell in Elena's body tensed — the old, wired-in response, the years of practice at reading the weather of him for the first change. But he was only walking. He was only moving farther into the lobby the way he used to move farther into any room, expanding to fill whatever space he was in. He ran his fingers along the restored wainscoting, examined the silk panels, turned to look at the ceiling where the new chandelier hung waiting for its wiring. "It really is beautiful work. You always did have an eye for this sort of thing."

"Leave."

"I came all this way just to talk. To clear the air. We didn't exactly part on good terms, and I've always regretted that."

"You regretted losing control of me. That's not the same thing."

Something flickered in his eyes — surprise, maybe, or the beginning of anger. In the old days she would have apologized by now. She would have made excuses. She would have found a way to de-escalate before his temper could build. She would have said, *I'm sorry, I didn't mean it like that, you know I didn't mean it like that.*

She had said those words a thousand times in four years. She had said them so often they had lost their shape.

"You've changed," Adam said. The charm was fading now, replaced by something harder. "Your new boyfriend's influence, I suppose. The historian with the memory problem."

"Lucian doesn't have a problem. He has a gift."

Elena kept her voice level, though her hands wanted to shake. "And I changed because I finally got away from you. Because I finally saw what you were doing to me."

"What *I* was doing?" Adam laughed, the sound carrying an edge of genuine disbelief. "I loved you, Elena. I took care of you. I gave you everything —"

"You gave me nothing except fear." The words came out sharp, honed by two years of therapy and self-reflection. "You monitored my phone. You isolated me from my friends. You criticized everything I did until I couldn't trust my own judgment. You waited up for me when I worked late, not because you were worried, but because you wanted me to know I had been watched. That is not love, Adam. That is abuse."

The word hung in the air between them.

Adam's expression hardened into something ugly. "You're being dramatic. You always were too sensitive —"

"No." Elena cut him off, and the power of that single syllable shocked them both. "I am not going to listen to you rewrite history. I am not going to let you gaslight me again. I know what happened. I know what you did. And I know that nothing you say now will change it."

She pulled out her phone, her movements deliberate. "I am calling the police. Chief Patterson is expecting to hear from me if you showed up. She takes harassment very seriously."

"Harassment?" Adam's laugh was incredulous, but she could see the calculation behind his eyes. "I haven't done anything illegal. I'm just talking to you."

"You're on private property without permission, after I explicitly told you to leave, following weeks of intimidating messages." She kept her voice calm as she dialed. Her thumb missed the first time. She dialed again. "I think Chief Patterson will have plenty to discuss with you."

For a long moment, Adam did not move.

She could see him weighing his options, calculating risks, trying to find an angle that would give him back control of the situation. This was the face she knew best, actually — not the charm face, not the temper face, but the face he wore when he was figuring out what to do next. The strategist's face. The face of a man who had made his career in corporate restructuring and knew, at a cellular level, how to identify the lever that would move the largest weight with the least effort.

She waited for him to find his lever. She had lived with him for four years. She knew he would find one.

Then something happened to Adam's face. It was small — a flicker, faint, lasting perhaps two seconds before the mask reassembled. But Elena had spent four years studying that face, mapping its moods the way a sailor maps storms, and she saw it.

Fear.

Not fear of her. Not fear of the police. Something older — a flash of the expression she had seen once, early in their relationship, when she had come home late and found him sitting in the dark. Not angry. Just sitting. And when she had turned on the light, he had looked at her with eyes that were young and lost, and he had said: *I thought you weren't coming back.*

It did not excuse anything. Understanding the wound doesn't forgive the weapon. But it changed something in Elena. Looking at Adam across the half-restored lobby, the old fear — the one that made her smaller — loosened and shifted into something unexpected.

Pity.

"You need help, Adam," she said. Without anger, without contempt. "Real help. Not from me. But from someone."

His jaw tightened. The mask came back — smooth, impenetrable.

"I'm not afraid of anything," he said.

"I know you believe that. That's the saddest part."

He moved toward the door. An officer had arrived — she could see the uniform through the lobby entrance, Chief Patterson's deputy Ray, a man she had met exactly once and who had, unbelievably, remembered her name. Adam straightened his coat, smoothed his hair. Became, in a breath, the reasonable man who had simply come to check on an old friend.

At the door, the officer's hand on his elbow, he turned back.

"Your historian," he said. His voice was even. Casual. "The one with the condition. He remembers everything about you, right? Every time he's seen you. What you were wearing, where you were, who you were with. All catalogued somewhere."

Elena kept her face still.

"Interesting, isn't it? That level of attention. That much detail about a woman who didn't know she was being watched." He tilted his head — the gesture that preceded his cruelest observations. "I hope it's different. I really do. But you might want to ask yourself: when a man knows everything about you before you've told him — does it matter whether he calls it love or something else?"

The officer guided him through the door.

His footsteps receded.

The front door opened and closed.

Elena stood in the half-finished lobby, surrounded by restored silk and plaster dust, and felt something cold settle into the space deep inside her. He was wrong. He was manipulating her. This was what he did — he found the fault line and pressed.

But fault lines only hurt when they are real.

Her knees gave out, and she sank into the nearest chair.

She sat for a long time without moving. The silk panels caught the late-morning light the way Clara had intended them to catch it. The new chandelier hung above her, waiting for its wiring. Somewhere outside the lobby windows a gull was making the long, laughing sound gulls make when they are telling each other about food. The world was going on being the world. She had survived. She had done the thing she had rehearsed doing, and she had done it well, and Adam was gone now, in a patrol car, with a man in a uniform, and by tonight he would be on a plane back to Boston.

She should feel triumphant.

She felt, instead, a small, steady fracture opening somewhere under her sternum, at a point she could not quite locate.

Interesting, isn't it? That level of attention.

She made herself breathe.

When a man knows everything about you before you've told him —

She made herself breathe again.

She was not going to think about this now. She would think about it later, when she had the strength for it. She would talk to Marla. She would talk to Dr. Keane. She would not, she promised herself, let Adam's voice be the voice inside her head on the subject of the man she had been waking up next to for three weeks.

She sat in the chair in the half-finished lobby until her legs stopped trembling, and then she got up, and went to find June.

June found her there, actually — ten minutes later, on the chair, the phone still open in her lap. June sat down on the arm of the chair without asking and took Elena's hands in both of hers. June's hands were warm and dry. They smelled faintly of lavender hand cream.

They sat in silence while Elena's breathing steadied.

"Adam," Elena said finally. "He came."

"I know. Marcus told me." June's voice was low and unsurprised, the voice of a woman who had seen a great many things in seventy-odd years and was not, at this point, available to be shocked.

"I stood up to him. Told him to leave. Called the police."

"Good."

"He said something on the way out. Something I can't stop thinking about."

June waited, the way Marla would have waited. The two women in Elena's life who understood that waiting was a form of attention.

"Nothing." Elena shook her head. "It doesn't matter. He was just trying to get inside my head. That's what he does."

"And did he?"

Elena looked at June — this woman who always seemed to know the right question to ask.

"I don't know yet," she said honestly. "Ask me tomorrow."

Lucian arrived twenty minutes later, worry etched into every line of his face. He crossed the lobby in three strides and pulled her into his arms, and she let him, and it felt safe, and she told herself that was all that mattered.

189

But that night, lying in his bed, listening to him breathe, she could not sleep.

Adam's words circled in the dark.

When a man knows everything about you before you've told him — does it matter whether he calls it love or something else?

She pressed closer to Lucian and told herself it was different. Of course it was different. She had been over this — Marla had been over this — the difference between Adam's knowledge as weapon and Lucian's knowledge as witness was the whole point.

She told herself that.

She told herself that for a long time in the dark.

Lucian's breathing was steady and even against her ear. His hand had found hers in his sleep — it always did, that was one of the things she had come to love about him, the way his body kept reaching for her even in dreams — and his thumb moved once, in his sleep, across her knuckles. A small, unconscious tenderness.

She loved him. She loved him with a clarity and a depth she had not known she was capable of. She did not doubt that.

She doubted, for the first time, whether love was the only question.

The lighthouse beam swept across the ceiling, then away. Swept across, then away. Steady. Patient. The rhythm she had fallen asleep to every night for three weeks.

She did not fall asleep.

LUCIAN

He had been in the Archive when Marcus called him about Adam.

He had been standing in the Archive, in fact, looking at the photograph — the Rhode Island photograph, August 2019, a woman reading on a beach with her face turned away from the camera and her dark hair blowing in the wind. He had been standing there thinking about it the way he had been thinking about it intermittently since Elena had seen it on her first tour of the room: thinking about how he had pulled out his phone that day on the beach, and framed the shot carefully to make sure her face was not in it, and pressed the shutter, and told himself the whole time that he was not doing what he was doing.

He had been thinking, in other words, that Elena was right to have looked at that photograph the way she had looked at it, even though she had not said anything. And he had been thinking about what a man does with an object like that when it can no longer be justified.

Then his phone rang. Marcus. Adam was in Camden's Rise.

Everything else fell away. He was in his car before he had finished the conversation. He was at the Rowan in four minutes — a drive that took seven at legal speeds. He was not thinking about photographs. He was thinking, with a cold clarity he had not felt since his mother's diagnosis, about the precise location of Adam Blackwell in space, and about what he was going to do to him if Adam had put one hand on her.

He did not have to do anything. The deputy had already come. Adam was already gone.

But Lucian did not know that when he walked into the lobby and saw her in the chair, with June beside her, with the drop cloths and the dust and the installed silk panels watching over both of them like witnesses. He did not know anything yet. He only saw Elena, and crossed the room to her, and took her in his arms and held her without speaking, because there was nothing he could say that would not arrive later.

The photograph in the Archive could wait.

It could wait, it turned out, for almost exactly a week.

CHAPTER FIFTEEN

ELENA

SHE COULDN'T STOP THINKING about what Adam had said. Not the threats; those she could dismiss. Not the entitlement or the familiar condescension or the way he'd stood in the hotel as if he still owned every room she walked into. She'd handled all of that. She'd called the police, watched his face go slack with surprise, and felt something she hadn't felt in years: the weight of her own power. No. What she couldn't stop thinking about was the last thing he'd said. Tossed over his shoulder as the officer escorted him out, casual as a coin flipped into a fountain.

"He knows everything about you. Doesn't he? Your little historian. All the details. What you were wearing, where you were, who you were with." A smile — not cruel, not even angry.

Almost sympathetic.

"Ask yourself how that's different from what I did, Elena. Really ask." She'd said nothing.

Watched the door close behind him. Told herself it was just Adam being Adam; finding the crack and driving a wedge into it, because that was what he'd always been best at. But it was two in the morning now, and she was lying in Lucian's bed, listening to him breathe beside her, and she could not make the thought go away. She got up carefully, easing out from under his arm. He stirred but didn't wake. She stood in the dark bedroom and looked at him — the shape of him under the white sheets, his face soft and unguarded in sleep, one hand still reaching toward the warm spot where she'd been. She loved him. She was sure of that. As sure as she'd been of anything in her life. But certainty had failed her before. She pulled on his sweater — it hung past her thighs, smelling of him, of wool and soap and the particular warmth of his skin — and went downstairs. The house was quiet. The kind of deep coastal quiet where you could hear the ocean if you held still enough. She made tea and sat at the kitchen table in the dark, her hands wrapped around the mug, and let herself think the thing she'd been refusing to think since Adam said it. Lucian had been watching her for fifteen years. All that time. She'd been seventeen the first time. A girl in a library, reading poetry her dead grandmother had given her. And a man she didn't know had looked at her across the room and begun a project of observation that had lasted half her life. He'd watched her on a hiking trail and helped her down a mountain and never said: I've seen you before. He'd watched her in a café while Adam pulled her out the door and never said: I can see what he's doing to you. He'd watched her in a gallery, on a train platform, at a farmer's market, on a beach. He'd watched her from distances she never knew he crossed, collecting details she never consented to share. He'd kept objects. A book she'd left behind. A napkin. A ticket stub. He'd built a room in his basement, a room with a name, and filled it with evidence of her existence. And he'd called it love. Elena's hands tightened on the mug until the heat was painful. Adam had called it love too. Adam had memorized her schedule. Known her coffee order, her habits, her friends, her fears. He'd tracked her phone. Showed up at places she hadn't told him she'd be. Made her account for her time, her conversations, her thoughts. And when she'd tried to name it — tried to say this isn't normal, this isn't what love looks like — he'd looked at her with wounded eyes and said: I pay attention because I love you. Most women would kill for a man who pays this much attention. The parallels spread across her mind like cracks in glass. Adam collected information to control her. Lucian collected objects and memories. Adam knew where she was before she told him. Lucian knew things about her she'd never shared; the book she'd been reading, the painting she'd loved, she tilted her head. Adam's attention had been a cage. Lucian's attention — was what? A cathedral, she'd told herself. A shrine. Something beautiful built around her. But she hadn't consented to either. No one had asked her. Not Adam, who'd surveilled her openly and called it devotion. And not Lucian, who'd surveilled her invisibly and called it memory. The tea went cold. Elena didn't drink it. She sat in Lucian's kitchen, wearing Lucian's sweater, in Lucian's house, surrounded by Lucian's books and Lucian's piano and Lucian's Archive beneath her feet, and felt the walls close in. Calling Marla. Marla, who had said — back at the beginning, when Elena first told her about HSAM — "That's a lot, Elena. A man who can't forget you. That's a lot for anyone to carry, and it's a lot for anyone to have carried about them." She hadn't listened then.

She'd been too swept up. The romance of it — the cosmic, predestined, fairy-tale quality of a man who'd loved her across time and distance and silence. It had felt like a story. Like something that happened to heroines in novels, not to women who'd spent three years being slowly dismantled by a man who smiled while he did it. That was the problem. She'd been so hungry for a love story that she'd missed the warning signs again. No. That wasn't fair. Lucian was nothing like Adam. But wasn't that exactly what she'd said about Adam in the beginning? Elena put down the mug and pressed her palms flat on the table. She could feel the wood grain under her fingers, the solid reality of it. Grounding herself the way her therapist had taught her. Present tense. Five things she could see, four she could touch, three she could hear. She could hear the ocean. She could hear the old house settling. She could hear Lucian breathing upstairs, steady and even, the breathing of a man who slept he lived; carefully, lightly, the world might shift while he wasn't watching. She loved him. She really did. But love had never been the part she had trouble with. Love had come easily, every time — quick and overwhelming, like stepping into a current. It was trust that cost her. Trust was the bone Adam had broken, and it had healed crooked. At four in the morning, she wrote Lucian a note. She left it on the kitchen counter, weighed down with a coffee mug: *Went back to my apartment. Need some space to think. Nothing is wrong — or everything is. I don't know yet. Please give me time. I don't know how long. — E* She let herself out quietly and walked through the sleeping town to her rental apartment above the bookshop. The streets were empty. The lighthouse swept its beam across the harbor in patient arcs, and she thought, irrationally, that it looked like a searchlight. Like something hunting for something lost.

She called Marla at seven, knowing her friend would be awake, knowing that whatever Marla said would hurt and be true.

"Tell me I'm not crazy," Elena said.

"You're not crazy." Marla's voice was careful.

The voice she used with authors whose manuscripts needed more than copyediting.

"Tell me what happened." Elena told her.

All of it; Adam's words, the two-a.m. spiral, the parallels she couldn't unsee. She talked for twenty minutes without stopping, and Marla listened without interrupting, which was how Elena knew it was serious. Marla always interrupted. Marla considered silence a waste of perfectly good airtime. When Elena finished, the line was quiet for a long time.

"I've been waiting for this call," Marla said finally.

"What?"

"Elena, I love you. I think Lucian is probably a good man. But I have been waiting, since the day you told me about the twelve encounters, for you to have this exact crisis." A pause.

"I said something in Camden's Rise, when I visited. When he showed me the Archive. Do you remember how quiet I got?" Elena did remember.

Marla had stood in the doorway of the Archive, looking at the shelves of carefully preserved objects, and her face had done something complicated; something Elena had interpreted as awe but which, she now realized, might have been alarm.

"Why didn't you say something?"

"Because you were happy. And because I wasn't sure I was right. And because —" Marla exhaled hard.

"Because I know what it's like to be the friend who ruins things by seeing problems that might not be there. I said something about Adam in the first year, remember? You didn't talk to me for three weeks."

"You were right about Adam."

"I was. But you weren't ready to hear it then, and if I'd pushed the Lucian thing before you were ready, you'd have shut me out again. I couldn't risk that. You're more important to me than being right." Elena pressed her forehead against the window.

The harbor was pale with early light. Fishing boats were heading out, their running lights blinking in the gray.

"So what do I do?"

"You figure out whether the thing that scares you is real or whether it's Adam's ghost talking."

"How?"

"I don't know. I wish I did. But here's what I think: the feeling you're having right now? The fear, the doubt, the pattern-matching? That's not weakness. That's your alarm system working. Adam broke it — no, Adam taught it to go off at the wrong times. But the system itself is good. It's trying to protect you."

"It protected me from Adam too late."

"Which is exactly why it's going off early with Lucian. It's overcorrecting. The question is whether it's right this time or whether it's flinching." Elena closed her eyes.

"I don't know how to tell the difference."

"Then take the time to figure it out. Don't let anyone rush you. Not Lucian, not me, not the voice in your head that says you owe him an answer because he waited more than a decade." Marla's voice hardened slightly.

"His patience is not your debt. You hear me? However long he waited — that was his choice. You don't owe him trust on a timeline." After they hung up, Elena sat on the floor of her apartment with her back against the wall and cried.

Not because she was sad. Because she was angry. Angry at Adam, for poisoning the well. For reaching into her new life with his long, clever fingers and planting doubt in the one place she'd felt safe. Angry at herself, for being susceptible. For still, after two years of therapy and seven hundred miles of distance, hearing his voice in her head when she tried to trust someone new. And angry, quietly, guiltily, at Lucian. For watching. For remembering. For building something beautiful out of her unknowing. For making it so easy to love him that she'd skipped the part where she decided whether it was safe. She stayed in her apartment for ten days. On the third day, Lucian had texted — the only text he sent during the entire ten days: *Keats misses you. He won't eat his dinner.* She'd driven to the house while Lucian was out, let herself in with the key she still had, and found Keats in his armchair, chin on the armrest, watching the door with the patient expectation of a creature who had been waiting for someone specific. His tail thumped once — slow, arthritic, but certain. He didn't get up. Getting up was a production at his age. But he shifted in the armchair, making room. She sat on the kitchen floor instead, and Keats slid off the chair with the dignified resignation of an old gentleman and put his head in her lap. They sat like that for half an hour. She didn't cry. She just breathed, and scratched behind his left ear — the magic ear, the one that made the back leg kick — and let herself be known by a creature who didn't care about Archives or HSAM or the difference between love and surveillance. Keats knew three things about Elena: she was warm, she scratched the right ear, and she smelled like the person his human loved. That was enough. That was his whole analysis. She came back the next day. And the day after. By the sixth day, she had a routine: let herself in at ten, sit with Keats for twenty minutes, fill his food bowl — he was eating again, but only when she was there — and leave before Lucian came home. On the seventh day, she arrived and found Lucian's jacket on its hook but the house otherwise empty. He'd gone out the back door. She was coming. He was giving her the space she'd asked for, even in his own house. She sat with Keats, and in a week, felt something loosen in her. Not resolution. Just the beginning of knowing what she was going to do. On the fourth day, she went back to work at the hotel. She couldn't afford not to; the restoration had a timeline, and wallowing wouldn't replace the water-damaged plaster in the east wing. She and Lucian developed a careful rhythm: polite nods in the hallways, professional exchanges about molding profiles and paint samples, the mutual pretense that nothing was wrong. It was excruciating. It was necessary. She threw herself into the east wing like a woman trying to outrun her own thoughts. She recalibrated the crown molding measurements twice, insisted the plasterer redo a section that was off by two millimeters — two millimeters that no human eye would ever detect — and spent an hour adjusting the height of a curtain rod by increments so small that Marcus finally said, very gently, "Elena. It's level."

"It's not."

"It is. I used a laser."

"The laser might be —"

"The laser is not wrong." He put a hand on her shoulder. "But something is. You want to talk about it?" She didn't.

She adjusted the curtain rod one more time, accepted that it was level, and moved on to the next thing that could be perfected. There were always more things that could be perfected. That was the gift, and the trap. On the sixth day, she went to the post office for her mail. Dorothy Hale looked at her over the counter — looked at the shadows under her eyes, the unwashed hair pulled back in a careless knot, the particular posture of a woman holding herself together through force of will — and said nothing for a long moment.

"You look like hell, Ward."

"Thank you, Dorothy."

"Whatever it is, it'll pass. Everything does in this town. Even the winters." Dorothy stamped a package with more force than necessary.

"There's soup from June in your box. And a note from Marcus. And something else I'm not asking about because it's none of my business."

"Since when is anything in this town not your business?" The faintest ghost of a smile crossed Dorothy's face.

"Since I decided I liked you enough to pretend." On the fifth night, she called Dr. Keane — her therapist in Boston, whom she still spoke to every two weeks by phone.

"I need to talk about Lucian," Elena said.

"I've been hoping you would," Dr. Keane said.

"Why?"

"Because you've told me a great deal about how he makes you feel, and very little about what you think. Those are different things, Elena. Feelings are weather. Thinking is navigation. You need both." They talked for an hour.

Dr. Keane didn't tell her what to do — she never did. But she asked questions that cut to the bone.

"When Adam monitored you, what was the purpose?"

"Control. He wanted to know where I was so he could manage me."

"When Lucian remembered you, what was the purpose?" Elena opened her mouth and closed it.

"I don't know. He said he did it anyway. The HSAM."

"That's his brain's mechanism. I'm asking about the rest of it. The objects. The Archive. The decision not to approach you all those years. Those were choices, not reflexes."

"He was afraid of scaring me."

"That's his stated reason. What do you think?" Elena pressed her fingers to her eyes.

"I think he was afraid of exactly this. Of me seeing him the way I'm seeing him right now."

"And how are you seeing him?" The question hung in the dark apartment.

"I don't know," Elena said.

"That's the problem. I'm looking at him and seeing two people at once. The man who waited for me — and the man who watched me. And I can't tell if those are the same thing or different things."

"What would help you decide?"

"If I could remember. If I had what he has — the ability to go back and see those moments. To know what it looked like from the outside. Was he watching me the way a bird-watcher watches birds? Or the way Adam watched me — cataloguing my movements so he could predict them?"

"You can't have his memories. So what else?" Elena thought for a long time.

"I need to look at the Archive again," she said.

"Alone. Without him there to explain it. Without the story he tells about it. I need to see it for myself and decide what I see."

"That sounds like a very clear, very brave plan."

"It doesn't feel brave. It feels like I'm about to find out something I can't un-find."

"Yes," Dr. Keane said. "That's usually what bravery feels like."

June brought food. Left it at the door. Didn't knock, didn't pry. Just a container of soup and a note that said: "The hotel will keep. So will we." Isabel texted once: "I'm here if you want to talk. No pressure. No agenda." Lucian sent nothing.

Left nothing. Respected the space she'd asked for with a discipline that was, depending on how she looked at it, either the most loving thing anyone had ever done for her or the most practiced form of patient observation she'd ever encountered. On the seventh day, Marla called again.

"How are you?"

"I'm working. I'm eating. I'm not crying anymore."

"That's not what I asked."

"I know. That's all I've got right now." On the ninth day, she found a box on her doorstep.

On the tenth morning, Elena put on her coat and walked to Lucian's house. He answered the door looking like he hadn't slept. There were shadows under his eyes that hadn't been there before, and his sweater was the same one he'd been wearing when she left — wrinkled now, lived in. He looked at her the way he always did — like she was the answer to a question he'd been asking his whole life. It broke her heart. It also, for the first time, made her afraid.

"I need to see the Archive," she said.

"Alone." He didn't argue.

Didn't explain. Didn't ask why or offer context or try to shape what she was about to see. He just stepped aside, the way he had the very first time she'd come to his door, and said: "You know where it is." She went downstairs.

The light switch was on the left. She flipped it, and the fluorescent tubes buzzed to life, filling the small basement room with their institutional glare. No candlelight this time. No warmth. Just a room, and its contents, and her. She looked. She looked at the shelves, the objects arranged with a curator's care. The Neruda book. The napkin from the Brooklyn café. A train ticket from Philadelphia. A tourist brochure from a New Hampshire hiking trail. A gallery catalog from the Hopper exhibition in D.C. Small things. Ordinary things. Things that meant nothing except to the person who had kept them. She picked up the Neruda. Opened it to the inscription. *For Elena, who feels things deeply. Love always, Grandma Rose.* Grandma Rose had died three months before that day in the library. Elena had been seventeen, hollowed out by grief, reading the poems her grandmother loved because it was the closest she could get to hearing her voice again. And Lucian had been three tables away. Twenty-two years old. A stranger. Watching a girl read poetry and falling into something he wouldn't be able to climb out of. He hadn't known about Grandma Rose. Hadn't known Elena was grieving. Hadn't known anything about her except what his eyes could tell him — a girl, a book, a smile she probably didn't remember giving. Elena held the book and tried to feel what Adam wanted her to feel: violated. Surveilled. Reduced to an object of someone else's obsession. She couldn't. What she felt instead was grief. For the girl who'd been sitting in that library, missing her grandmother so badly she could barely breathe, and not knowing that someone was paying attention. That someone had looked at her in her worst moment and thought: she matters. Not: she's mine. Not: I need to have her. Just: she matters. Elena put the book down and picked up the hiking trail brochure. Mount Washington, 2013. She'd twisted her ankle. A man had helped her. They'd talked for two hours. She'd felt — what? Safe. Seen. Interested in a way she hadn't felt interested in anyone since Adam had started turning her world small. And then Adam had called, and she'd lied about being alone, and she'd walked away. Lucian hadn't followed. Hadn't asked for her number. Hadn't tried to find her. He'd let her go, and then he'd kept the brochure, and he'd gone home and remembered all of it, because his brain wouldn't let him do anything else. That was the difference. Elena could see it now, standing in the Archive with its fluorescent glare and its careful shelves, without Lucian there to narrate or explain or put the best face on it. Adam's knowledge had been a tool. He'd learned her patterns so he could anticipate her. He'd tracked her schedule so he could ambush her with it. He'd memorized her weaknesses so he could exploit them in arguments. Every piece of information was ammunition. Every detail was leverage. Lucian's knowledge was something else. It was, she searched for the word, testimony. He hadn't used what he knew. Not once. Since the library. For years. He'd known she was in a bad relationship and he hadn't intervened. He'd known where she was and he hadn't shown up. He'd known her coffee order and her favorite paintings and how she tilted her head, and he had done nothing with any of it except keep it. Keep it and wait and hope that someday, maybe, she'd choose to know him back. Adam had used information like a fist. Lucian had held it like a candle. Elena sank into the desk chair and stared at the room — at the whole, strange, heartbreaking record of a man's devotion — and felt the fear that had been gripping her chest for more than a week begin, slowly, to loosen. Not disappear. She wasn't naive enough to think fear disappeared. Fear was her companion now, stitched into her nervous system by three years of survival. It would always be there — always checking, always pattern-matching, always asking: is this safe? Is this real? Am I making a mistake? But fear wasn't wisdom. Fear was a guard dog that barked at everything; intruders and mail carriers alike. Wisdom was knowing which bark to trust. She sat in the Archive for a long time. Then she went upstairs. Lucian was in the kitchen, not pretending to be busy. Just standing by the window, looking out at the harbor, waiting. He turned when he heard her on the stairs, and his face was so open, so terrified, so carefully prepared for the worst that she could barely speak.

"I need to tell you something," she said.

He nodded. Said nothing. Waited — because waiting, now, was the thing he was best at.

"For three days, I've been trying to figure out if you're Adam." She saw him flinch, saw the color drain from his face, and she pressed on because if she stopped she'd lose her nerve.

"Whether the watching, the remembering, the Archive — whether it's the same thing he did to me, dressed up in better clothes. Whether I fell for it again."

"Elena —"

"Let me finish." She held up her hand, and he went still.

"I went down there alone because I needed to see it without you. Without the story. Without the context you put

203

around it to make it beautiful. I needed to look at a room full of evidence that a man had watched me for fifteen years since he'd first seen me, and decide for myself what it meant." His jaw was tight.

His hands were at his sides, the knuckles white.

"And what did you decide?" His voice was barely audible.

"I decided you're not Adam." She took a breath.

"I decided that what you did is strange, and overwhelming, and not something I would have chosen — not something anyone would choose, to be the unknowing center of someone's inner life for over a decade. I decided that it raises questions I don't have answers to. I decided that some part of me will probably always flinch, because that's what happens when someone teaches you to be afraid of being known." She crossed the kitchen.

Stood in front of him. Close enough to see the lines around his eyes, the way his lashes were damp.

"But I also decided that the difference between you and Adam isn't complicated. He learned me so he could control me. You learned me because you couldn't help it, and then you did the hardest thing a person can do with that kind of knowledge."

"What's that?"

"Nothing." She took his hand.

His fingers closed around hers — carefully, like she was made of something that might shatter.

"For over a decade, you had everything you needed to find me, to push your way into my life, to make me see you. And instead you kept your distance and waited for me to choose. That's not surveillance, Lucian. That's —" She searched for the word.

"That's restraint. And restraint is the opposite of everything Adam ever was." He made a sound, not a word, something more animal than that, and pulled her against him.

She felt his chest heave, felt the shudder that ran through his entire body, and understood that he had been as afraid as

204

she had. Maybe more. Because he'd seen this coming from the beginning — had known, in the way that a man with extraordinary memory knows everything, that this reckoning would arrive. And he'd spent fifteen years dreading it.

"I should have told you sooner," he said into her hair.

"I should have told you all of it, from the first day, instead of letting you discover it in pieces."

"Maybe. But I don't think I could have heard it then." She pulled back to look at him.

"I needed to fall in love with you before I could be afraid of you. And I needed to be afraid of you before I could choose to trust you."

"Are you? Choosing to trust me?"

"I'm choosing to try." She touched his face, the stubble on his jaw, the wetness on his cheeks.

"That's the best I can do. Is that enough?"

"It's enough," he said.

"It's more than enough. It's everything." They stood in his kitchen, holding each other, while the morning light strengthened and the harbor turned from gray to silver to pale, shimmering gold.

Elena did not feel certain. She did not feel the swooning, uncomplicated happiness of a woman in a love story whose troubles were behind her. Better: she felt awake. Clear-eyed. Choosing. And for a woman who had spent three years asleep inside someone else's version of her life, that was enough. That was, in fact, extraordinary.

She made herself look at the photograph.

It was on the lowest shelf on the south wall, framed in a plain black wood frame, about the size of a paperback book. A woman on a beach, mid-afternoon light, her face turned away from the camera. Dark hair blowing. A paperback open in her lap. The edge of a striped beach towel. The hem of a blue linen dress.

The card under it said, in Lucian's careful handwriting: *Narragansett, RI. August 14, 2019. 2:47 p.m.*

She remembered the day. She had gone alone — she had told Adam she was at a work conference, she had driven three hours to Rhode Island and paid cash for a motel room and spent a Saturday reading on a beach by herself, and she had come home on Sunday with her skin warm and her shoulders loose for the first time in months, and Adam had met her at the door with a glass of wine and a smile and asked her, in the particular voice he used when he was checking her story, how the conference had been. She had lied convincingly. She had been getting better at lying.

She had not known, on that beach, that anyone was watching her. She had specifically chosen a beach where nobody was watching her.

She took the photograph off the shelf and held it in both hands.

The woman in the photograph — the woman who was Elena, who had been Elena on a particular Saturday in August, who had believed herself to be alone — looked like a woman at peace. You could not see her face. You could see her shoulders. Her shoulders looked loose. Her hands around the paperback looked easy. The composition of the photograph was lovely. Someone with a good eye had framed it carefully.

She put the photograph back on the shelf.

She took it off again.

She sat down on the floor of the Archive, with her back against the cold concrete wall, and she looked at the photograph for a long time.

It was not an ugly photograph. It was not a violation that looked like a violation. It looked like a stolen beat of peace — a small theft from a woman who had a great many small thefts committed against her, at that particular time in her life, by a great many people.

He took it to remember me, she thought.

He took it without asking me, she thought.

Both things were true. Dr. Keane's voice in her head: *Both things. Not one.*

She was still sitting on the floor when Lucian came down.

She had not heard him come down the stairs. He was there when she looked up — standing in the doorway, hands in his pockets, his face carefully composed in the way his face got composed when he had made up his mind to do something that was going to cost him.

"I was going to ask you about that one," she said. She did not bother to stand up.

"I know."

"It's not like the others."

"I know."

"You took a picture of a woman on a beach who didn't know you were there."

"Yes."

"Who didn't know you existed."

"Yes."

She turned the photograph over. On the back, in pencil, in handwriting she did not recognize at first as his — his handwriting was usually so careful; this was a scribble, a thing written fast, the way you write something you are afraid to write — was a single line. *She looked happy. I wanted her to be happy.*

She read the line twice.

"Lucian," she said.

"I know."

"Come sit down."

He sat down on the concrete floor across from her, his back against the opposite wall. He did not try to take the photograph from her. He did not try to explain. This, she had learned, was one of his gifts: he could hold silence for a very long time without mistaking it for hostility.

"I am not saying you are Adam," she said finally. "I am not going to accuse you of that. You know I don't believe that. I wouldn't be sitting on this floor if I believed that."

"I know."

"I am saying this photograph is different from the napkin and the brochure and the train ticket." She held it up between them. "The napkin you found on a table. I left it. I was done with it. The brochure was on a trail anyone could pick up. The train ticket you saved from your own pocket after I walked past you on a platform. I understand those. I do not love them, but I understand them."

"Yes."

"This one you took. You pointed a camera at a woman who had made a deliberate choice to be alone and you took her picture and you brought it home and you framed it. That is not the same thing."

"It isn't."

"Did you think it was, at the time?"

He was quiet for a long time. The overhead fluorescent made a low hum above them. Somewhere upstairs, the radiator ticked.

"I told myself it was," he said finally. "I told myself a lot of things in those years. The honest answer is that I didn't know what I was doing in any of the encounters after Brooklyn. Brooklyn scared me. I had watched him put his hand on you and I had done nothing. After that, every time I saw you, I was — I was trying to make sure you existed. I was trying to keep you existing, because it had started to feel, in those years, like if I looked away from you, something would happen. Like I was a — like my watching was holding you up, somehow. I knew that was not true. I knew I was making it about me. I took the picture anyway."

"And then you framed it."

"Yes."

"Why?"

He looked at her. His eyes in the fluorescent light were the color they always were. "Because I couldn't throw it away," he said. "I had already taken it. Throwing it away felt worse than keeping it. Keeping it meant I was going to have to answer for it, eventually, to somebody. Ideally to you. I think — I think I was already, in some part of my head, setting up the moment we are in right now."

"That's either the saddest thing you've ever said to me or the most honest."

"Both, probably."

She turned the photograph over and looked at it again. The woman on the beach. The loose shoulders. The paperback. The blue linen dress. The particular kind of peace she had almost forgotten she had ever had.

Then she held it out to him.

"Take it out of the frame," she said. "And give it to me."

He did. He took the back off the frame carefully, with the fingers of a man who had handled Theodore Rowan's letters in cotton gloves, and he slid the photograph out of its mat and handed it to her.

She took it.

She held it in both hands for a moment. Then, very deliberately, she folded it in half, and in half again, and in half again, until it was a small thick square. She put the square in her coat pocket.

"That one was mine," she said. "Not yours. Not ours. Mine. I get to decide what happens to it."

"Yes."

"I'll decide later. I'm not going to destroy it tonight. Maybe I'll keep it. Maybe I won't. But it is not going on this shelf. It is not going in the Archive. It is not yours to have kept."

"No."

"Are there others?"

He was quiet.

"Lucian, are there others?"

"One," he said. "A video. Four seconds long. From the farmer's market in Portland. I didn't — I wasn't filming, I was trying to text Isabel a picture of a pumpkin, and you walked through the frame, and I saw it later, and I kept it. It's on an old hard drive. I haven't looked at it in three years."

"Delete it."

"Tonight."

"And never do this again."

"Never."

"If you ever see me somewhere I don't know you're there," she said, "and you have a camera in your hand, and I am not looking at the camera, the camera goes in your pocket. Do you understand me?"

"Yes."

"Say it back."

"If I see you somewhere you don't know I'm there, and I have a camera, the camera goes in my pocket."

"Good." She stood up. Her knees hurt from the concrete. She brushed her hands off on her jeans. "Now let's talk about the rest of this room. Because there is a difference between what I accepted from you that first night and what I can still accept now that I have stood in here alone for an hour, and I want to walk through the shelves one more time with you, before we go upstairs, and I want to point at anything else that I did not know I was posing for. Is that okay?"

"Yes."

"And Lucian."

"Yes."

"Thank you for coming down here and not trying to explain it to me."

"I didn't think it could be explained."

"It can't. But most men would have tried."

They walked through the shelves together. She pointed at two more items. He removed them. One went into a box to be returned to her. One went into a box to be destroyed. They agreed, standing there on the concrete floor under the humming fluorescent, that the Archive was going to be a different kind of room after tonight.

She went upstairs first. He turned the light off behind them.

She called Dr. Keane at seven in the morning from the back porch of Lucian's house, wrapped in a blanket, watching the harbor turn silver under the rising sun.

Dr. Keane had, in the twenty-two months Elena had been seeing her, shifted her schedule to accommodate a number of unplanned early-morning calls. She did not charge for them. She said only, when Elena had once tried to apologize: *This is what I am for.*

"Talk to me," Dr. Keane said, when the call connected. Her voice was as steady as it always was. "What happened."

Elena told her. The lobby. The confrontation. The call to Chief Patterson. The parting sentence at the door. The long sleepless night afterward.

Dr. Keane listened without interrupting. When Elena finished, there was a small pause on the line. Elena had learned to recognize that pause. It was the pause of a woman writing a single word on a notepad, underlining it, and sitting back.

"Two questions," Dr. Keane said. "The first is easy. Are you safe?"

"Yes."

"Physically safe. Where is he."

"On a plane to Boston. Chief Patterson called me an hour ago to confirm."

"Good. Second question." Another small pause. "Whose voice is in your head right now?"

Elena closed her eyes. The blanket smelled of Lucian's laundry detergent, which smelled of cedar and something faintly medicinal. It was a good smell. She had come to love it. "Adam's."

"And what is Adam's voice saying?"

"That Lucian is just like him."

"Is Adam's voice the voice you want running the committee inside your head this morning?"

Elena almost laughed. *The committee* was Dr. Keane's shorthand for the set of internalized critics that lived inside her — a tactic Dr. Keane had introduced months ago, to give Elena some distance from the sentences that arrived in her own voice but had never actually belonged to her.

"No," Elena said.

"Then don't let him chair the meeting." Dr. Keane's voice was very dry. "You are permitted to hear what he said. You are permitted to take it seriously as a question. You are not obligated to take it seriously as his answer. He is not the authority on what love is. He is the authority on what he did."

"He said it was a question Lucian could not answer well."

"It is a question Lucian cannot answer well. It's also a question you can answer. You are the only person who can answer it, actually. Adam doesn't know Lucian. You do. What does the evidence in your own life tell you?"

Elena looked out at the harbor. A fishing boat was making its slow way out past the lighthouse, its running lights still on against the pale morning. She thought about the three weeks she had spent in Lucian's house. The way he made coffee. The way he did not flinch when she startled. The way he had, four days ago, reached past her for a book on a high shelf and then, without making a show of it, paused to ask her if she was comfortable with him moving that close to her while she was not looking — a small, specific question, asked by a man who had been paying attention to the small specific things that made her flinch. She had said yes. He had taken the book down. It had been a small thing. But the fact that he had asked was the whole thing.

"The evidence says he asks," she told Dr. Keane. "The evidence says he tells me what he knows and waits for me to say what I want to do with it."

"And Adam?"

"Adam used what he knew."

"So the difference is not in the knowing. The difference is in the asking."

"Yes."

"Say that sentence back to me."

"The difference is not in the knowing. The difference is in the asking."

"Good." Dr. Keane's voice softened, very slightly — the audible equivalent of her sitting forward in her chair, which she did at the same point in every session, whenever she was about to say something she wanted Elena to keep. "Listen to me. Adam is very good at one particular thing, which is finding the sentence that sounds like an insight and using it to hurt you. That sentence he gave you on his way out the door was designed. He rehearsed it. He had been holding it for a long time. He delivered it at the moment he was most likely to be remembered for delivering it. It landed because he is skilled at making things land. That does not make it true. It means Adam is good at his job, which we already knew."

"But the question is a real question."

"The question is a real question. Lucian should be able to answer it. If he cannot, that's information. If he can, that's information. Either way, you have a tool now — the question — and you can use it without being owned by the person who gave it to you. Do you hear the difference?"

"Yes."

"Are you going to ask him?"

"Yes."

"Good. You don't have to ask him today. It is also fine to ask him today."

Elena pulled the blanket tighter around her shoulders. The sun had come up enough now to turn the water from silver to pale gold. She could hear, distantly, Lucian moving around inside the house. The faint clink of a mug. Water running.

"Dr. Keane."

"Yes."

"I'm going to be okay. I want to say that out loud to you."

"I know you are."

"I wanted you to hear me say it."

"Thank you. Say it again in six months."

"I will."

"One more thing, Elena."

"Yes."

"This is not going to be linear. You know you will have moments for a long time. Every survivor has her own pace. Yours is yours. Slower and faster are not better and worse. Whatever pace you need to move, that's the correct pace."

"I know."

"Good."

They hung up. Elena sat on the porch for another minute, watching the fishing boat disappear around the headland. Then she folded the blanket and went inside. Lucian was at the stove, making eggs. He looked up when she came in and gave her the small private smile he only gave her, and did not ask who she had been talking to on the porch.

"Dr. Keane," she said anyway.

"How is she."

"Direct."

"That's what you pay her for."

"Yes." Elena crossed the kitchen and took the eggs out of his hand and set them on the counter. She put her arms around him. She stood against his chest for a moment, and he held her, and after a while she said, into his collarbone: "I have a question I need to ask you. Not this morning. But soon."

"Okay."

"Just so you know it's coming."

"Thank you for telling me."

214

"You're welcome." She stepped back. "Now finish the eggs. I'm starving."

He finished the eggs. She poured coffee. They ate at the kitchen table, in the soft morning light, with the harbor going gold outside the window, and for thirty minutes neither of them talked about anything important, and that was its own kind of gift.

CHAPTER SIXTEEN

LUCIAN

THE NOTE WAS ON the kitchen counter. He found it at six in the morning, after waking to a cold bed and an empty house and the specific silence that meant she was gone. *Went back to my apartment. Need some space to think. Nothing is wrong — or everything is. I don't know yet. Please give me a few days. — E* He read it three times. Then he set it down and made coffee with hands that were steady, because the worst thing he had ever feared was happening and his body, absurdly, had decided to be calm about it. He drank the coffee standing by the window. The harbor was dark. The lighthouse was still sweeping its beam, though dawn was beginning to bleach the sky at its eastern edge. He watched the light make its patient arc and thought about all the things he should not do. He should not call her. She had asked for space. He should not go to her apartment. She had asked for space. He should not text her an explanation, a justification, a carefully worded argument for why what he'd done was different from what Adam had done. She had not asked for his case. She had asked for room to build her own. He should not do any of the things that every nerve in his body was screaming at him to do, because doing them — reaching for her, closing the distance, making himself present when she needed him absent — was exactly the behavior that had brought them here. So he did nothing. He washed the coffee cup. He dried it and put it away. He went to his desk and opened Theodore Rowan's letters and tried to work. The words swam. Theodore's anguished Victorian handwriting, usually so absorbing, looked like marks on paper. Lucian's eyes moved over them without registering meaning, because his mind was in a kitchen that smelled of cold tea, reading a note on the counter, calculating the precise distance between his house and Elena's apartment (0.7 miles, eleven minutes on foot, he knew this, he had always known this, he knew the distance between himself and everything that mattered to him). He closed the letter box. Pushed it aside. Sat in his study and let himself think. Adam had said something to her. Lucian didn't know what ; Elena hadn't told him the details of their confrontation, only the broad strokes, only the parts that made her feel powerful. But Adam had said something that had worked its way under her skin, and Lucian didn't need a extraordinary memory to guess what it was. He'd been waiting for this. That was the ugly truth, the one he'd never told anyone, not even Isabel. For fifteen years, beneath the hope and the longing and the careful, practiced restraint, there had been a voice in his head saying: *She'll figure it out eventually. She'll see what you are. A man who watches. A man who keeps. A man who built a shrine to a woman who didn't know she was worshipped, and called it devotion.* The voice sounded different every year. Sometimes it sounded like his father, who'd left when Lucian was nine and never explained why. Sometimes it sounded like the researchers at UC Irvine, clinical and measured: "The subjects report difficulty with interpersonal boundaries." Sometimes it sounded like his own worst self, the part of him that looked at the Archive and saw not love but pathology.

Today it sounded like Adam Blackwell. *How is what you did any different from what I did?* The question had an answer. Lucian knew the answer. He could enumerate the differences with the same precision he brought to academic arguments — the absence of control, the absence of contact, the absence of any attempt to shape Elena's life or limit her choices. He had never tracked her. Never followed her. Never used what he knew to gain advantage. The encounters had been coincidental, and his response to each one had been the same: he had let her go. But knowing the answer and believing it were different things. And standing here, in the silence of a house she had left, Lucian found that his certainty, usually so reliable, so absolute, had a crack in it. Because the truth was: he had chosen to keep the book. He hadn't needed to. Elena had left it behind in the library, and any normal person would have turned it in to lost-and-found. Instead, he had taken it home. Put it on a shelf. Returned to it, again and again, touching the inscription like a talisman. He had chosen to build the Archive. No one had made him. HSAM stored the memories automatically, but the objects were deliberate. Each one a choice — to keep, to preserve, to build a physical monument to an attachment the other person didn't know existed. He had lived inside a love story that only he was writing. For half her life, Elena had been a character in his narrative — idealized, cherished, frozen in the amber of his recall. She'd had no say in the role. No vote. No voice. Was that love? Or was it something else — something that wore love's clothes but lived in a different house? At noon, Isabel called.

"How are you?" she asked, which meant she already knew.

"She left. Three days, she said."

"Good."

"Good?"

"Good that she's thinking about it, Lucian. Good that she's not just accepting everything at face value. Good that she's taking it seriously." A pause.

"I know that's not what you want to hear."

"I want to hear that she's coming back."

"I know. But what you need to hear is something else." Isabel's voice shifted — from sister to psychologist, the transition he'd learned to recognize over decades.

"Can I be honest with you? Really honest?"

"When have you ever not been?"

"I've held back. More than you know. Because you were hurting, and because the situation was already complicated enough, and because I didn't want to be the one to —" She stopped.

Started again.

"Lucian, I need to ask you something, and I need you to actually sit with it instead of deflecting with a self-deprecating joke." He sat down.

"Ask."

"For years of watching, you've been in love with a woman you didn't know."

"I knew her. I —"

"You knew what she looked like. You knew how she moved, what she read, where she went. You knew details. But you didn't know her, Lucian. You didn't know what made her laugh when she was alone. Didn't know her fears, her bad habits, her morning moods. You didn't know that she sings off-key in the shower or that she hates olives or that she cries at car commercials."

"I know all of those things now."

"Now, yes. But what you fell in love with — the Elena in your head, the one you built the Archive around — she wasn't real. She was a composite. A collage of moments you'd seen from a distance, assembled into a person by your memory and your longing." The words settled into him like cold water.

"I'm not saying your feelings aren't real," Isabel continued, more gently.

"I'm not saying you don't love the actual Elena — the one who's messy and complicated and afraid. I think you do. But I need you to be honest with yourself about the difference between loving someone and loving the idea of someone. Because if Elena is in her apartment right now asking herself whether you see her or whether you see a fantasy — she deserves a real answer." Lucian was quiet for a long time.

Through the window, he watched a fishing boat track a slow line across the harbor.

"You think I'm obsessed," he said.

"I think you're in love. And I think that for a person with HSAM, love and obsession share a border that other people don't have to navigate. You can't forget her, Lucian. Your brain literally won't let you. That's not your fault. But what you DO with that — the Archive, the preservation, the way you organized your entire emotional life around a woman who didn't know you existed — that's a choice. And choices can be questioned."

"What are you saying? That I should have — what? Thrown the book away? Forced myself to stop thinking about her?"

"I'm saying you should have tried. I'm saying that at some point in all those years, a healthy response might have been to go to therapy and say, 'I'm fixated on someone I can't have, and I need help letting go.' Instead, you leaned in. You built the Archive. You took the job with June partly because it brought you closer to the town where she was moving. Don't look at me like that — I know you did. You told me." He had.

He remembered the conversation — January, two years ago, his phone pressed to his ear while he paced his apartment in Portland. June had mentioned she'd hired a designer from Boston. He'd asked the name. June had said *Elena Ward*, and his heart had stopped, and he'd called Isabel and said, voice shaking, "She's going to be there. She's going to be at the hotel." And Isabel had said: "Then maybe it's time."

"You encouraged me," he said now.

"You said —"

"I know what I said. And I meant it. I believed — I still believe — that you two are good together. That the real Elena, the one you've gotten to know over these months, is someone worth loving. But that doesn't mean the path you took to get here was healthy. Both things can be true, Lucian. The outcome can be right and the process can be questionable." He leaned forward, elbows on his knees, and pressed his palms against his eyes.

"So what do I do?"

"You let her decide. Without helping. Without explaining. Without making your case." Isabel's voice was firm.

"If she comes back, it has to be because SHE looked at the evidence and decided what it meant. Not because you narrated it for her. Not because you told her the beautiful version. She needs to see it raw and choose."

"And if she doesn't come back?" Isabel was quiet for a moment.

"Then you grieve. And then you do the work you should have done years of watching ago. You talk to someone, a professional, not your sister, about what this pattern means, and whether there's a healthier way to carry what your brain gives you."

"You're saying I need therapy."

"Lucian, I've been saying you need therapy since 2011. You're just hearing it now because the stakes are high enough to listen." After they hung up, Lucian sat in his study for a long time.

Then he went to the Archive. He stood in the doorway and made himself look at it the way Elena must have looked at it. Not as a testament to love. Not as a cathedral. Just as a room. A small room in a basement, lined with shelves, filled with objects that belonged to someone who had never given them to him. A book she'd left behind. He'd kept it. A napkin she'd used and discarded. He'd kept it. A ticket stub she'd dropped on the floor of a gallery. He'd picked it up after she'd gone. He'd kept it. These were not gifts. They were artifacts of a life lived unaware that it was being documented. He loved Elena. He loved her genuinely, deeply, in the present tense — the real Elena, the one who argued with him about paint colors and stole his sweaters and fell asleep on his chest while reading. He loved her bad moods and her fears and her morning voice and she pronounced "croissant" with an accent that was neither French nor American but something uniquely, endearingly her own.

But he had also done something unusual. Something that, viewed from the outside, viewed from Elena's inside, might look less like love and more like something else. Isabel was right. The outcome could be right and the process could be questionable. He didn't have to be Adam to have crossed a line. There was territory between devotion and surveillance that most people never had to map, because most people's memories faded. Most people were given the mercy of forgetting. Lucian had never had that mercy. And in its absence, he had built something that looked, to the woman he loved, like the thing she feared most. He didn't go to the Archive to pack it up. He didn't go there to dismantle it or apologize for it or set it on fire. The Archive was what it was — a record. An honest one. The evidence of a man's heart, preserved without curation or apology. But he left the light on. And he left the door unlocked. Because if Elena came back, when Elena came back, if she came back, he wanted her to see it in plain light. No candles. No music. No narrative. Just the truth. All of it. And whatever she decided it meant.

On the fifth day, Lucian went to the Archive. He didn't go to sit. He didn't go to reflect. He went with two cardboard boxes and a roll of packing tape. He started with the napkin from the Brooklyn café. Folded it carefully, placed it in the box. The hiking trail brochure. The gallery catalog. The train ticket from Philadelphia. The conference program with Elena's question circled in red. One by one, he took the objects off the shelves and packed them away. Not because they were wrong. Not because he was ashamed. Because they weren't his to keep. They had never been his. Every object in this room had been collected without Elena's knowledge. The book she'd left behind, she hadn't given it to him. The napkin she'd used, she hadn't offered it. These were fragments of a life she'd been living without knowing she was being documented, and no matter how lovingly he'd preserved them, the preservation was a unilateral act. Isabel had said: "The difference between your Archive and Adam's surveillance is that you never used the information." But there was another difference.

One that mattered more. Adam would never have packed it up. Adam would never have voluntarily surrendered the evidence of his attention, because for Adam, attention was power, and power was never given away. Lucian was giving it away. He packed the last box, sealed it with tape, and carried both boxes upstairs. He set them on the kitchen table. Then he sat down and wrote a note — by hand, on a plain index card, because grand gestures were for men who needed to perform their love, and he was done performing. *Elena — These belong to you. They always did. I kept them because I couldn't help remembering, and I needed the remembering to be real — to exist outside my head, in objects I could touch. That was selfish. Not cruel, I think, but selfish. The memories are still mine. I can't give those back, and I wouldn't if I could. But the objects are yours. Do whatever you want with them — keep them, return them to the places they came from, throw them away. They're not my story anymore. They're yours. The Archive is empty now. Just a room with shelves. If you come back, I want you to come back to a man, not a museum. — L* He left the boxes on her apartment doorstep. Didn't knock. Didn't wait to see her face when she opened them. Just left them and walked home through the rain, feeling lighter and emptier and more afraid than he had ever been. Because the Archive had been his proof. His evidence that the love was real, that the years of watching had produced something tangible, that he hadn't imagined the connection. Without it, he had nothing but memory. But memory was what he'd always had. Memory was the whole point. And if the love was real, it didn't need evidence. It just needed her.

He went down to the Archive at eleven that morning.

He had told himself he would not. He had told himself, standing in the kitchen with Elena's note on the counter in front of him and a cup of coffee cooling in his hand, that he was going to give her the space she had asked for and not fill the empty house with the only activity that would feel like movement, which was rearranging a room that nobody had ever asked him to arrange in the first place. He had told himself that for about forty minutes. Then he had gone down to the Archive.

He did not turn on the overhead fluorescent. He turned on the small lamp in the corner — a reading lamp with a green glass shade that had belonged to his grandfather — and sat in the folding chair he had kept down there for the past ten years for no particular reason.

He looked at the shelves.

He had been looking at the shelves his whole life. He had not, he realized, ever looked at them through her eyes.

He made himself do it now. He made himself pretend he was Elena — Elena who had come down the steps for the first time in Chapter Six, Elena who had come down the steps alone in Chapter Fourteen, Elena who had walked through the room pointing at items and saying *that one* and *that one* and *not that one* — and he made himself see the shelves the way she would see them.

Some of what he saw he could live with.

The Neruda book. The Mount Washington brochure. The train ticket from Philadelphia she had dropped on the platform and he had picked up after her train pulled out. The conference program from the preservation symposium in D.C. where they had sat in the same panel and she had not seen him. These were objects he had kept for reasons he could defend — reasons that did not shrink when he tried to say them out loud to an imaginary version of the woman he loved.

Other things he could not live with.

The photograph from Rhode Island, which they had already addressed. He was glad they had. It was in her coat pocket now, and it was hers to decide about, and he was not going to think about it again until she told him what she had done with it.

The video clip from Portland, which he had deleted two weeks ago, the night Elena had asked him to, standing in his home office while she waited in the doorway so that she could see his screen and know it was gone.

But also: the receipt from a coffee shop in Cambridge, August 2018, a coffee shop he had never been in before or since, which he had saved because she had walked in, and he had followed her in, and she had ordered a latte and a scone, and he had ordered a latte and a scone, and she had left, and he had kept the receipt of the transaction on which he had followed her. That one was not a found object. That one was a document of a pursuit.

He stood up and took the receipt off the shelf. He held it between his fingers for a second. Then he put it in the small tin wastebasket by the door.

He went back to the shelves.

The printout of her professional website from 2020, archived two versions back, which he had kept because it had a photograph of her at a job site he did not recognize and he had wanted to know which site it was. That, too, went in the wastebasket. He could have asked her which site it was. He had not needed to archive a stranger's website.

A folded page from an old alumni magazine — BU, her class — with a brief update she had written about her career three years after graduation. This one he held for a longer time. It had been printed in a magazine. It had been sent to thousands of alumni. He had not stolen it. But he had cut it out with a box cutter, at his kitchen table, and slipped it into a manila folder, and kept it in the Archive alongside objects she had physically left behind, as if it were the same kind of thing, and it was not. It was a public document. It belonged, if anywhere, in a file, not in a shrine.

He put it in the wastebasket.

He kept working. He worked for almost three hours, without stopping, without eating, without taking his phone out of his pocket when it buzzed at twelve-forty with a message from Isabel he would read later. He worked the way he had worked on Theodore Rowan's letters for the past eight years — carefully, with attention, with the humility of a man who is handling material that does not entirely belong to him.

When he was finished, the shelves looked about two-thirds as full as they had before.

He stood in the center of the room and looked at what was left. Twelve physical objects, some small, some larger. Each one was an object Elena had physically left behind, or had shared an acknowledged experience with him, or had given him after the relationship had begun. Each one, if she walked into the room tomorrow morning, he could hand to her and say *this one, I can defend*. Each one, he could imagine her taking from his hands without needing to explain what she thought of him.

The rest of it was in a small tin wastebasket by the door.

He carried the wastebasket upstairs. He emptied it into the fireplace. He lit a match.

He watched the paper burn.

It did not feel noble, and it did not feel clean, and it did not feel, in any particular way, like the ending of anything. He had not been, he understood now, a man keeping a record. He had been a man accumulating evidence against his own desire to be left alone by a woman he was afraid to know and who was afraid, in those years, to be known by anyone. The difference between a record and an accumulation was not something you could see from inside it. You could only see it from outside. Elena had given him the outside view. She had handed him her own perspective on his Archive, and he had taken it, and he had come down here, and he had used it to do a thing that he should have done on his own, many years ago, without needing a woman to come back into his life to make him do it.

The fire took the paper and the paper burned.

He went back down to the Archive and opened the label book and wrote, on a fresh page, on the first line, the date, and *Archive reduced by owner's decision. Removed: receipt (Cambridge, 2018), alumni-magazine clipping (BU, 2015), three unlabeled items (farmer's-market handbill, hotel brochure, museum map) preserved without cause. Reason: these were not records. These were a pretext.*

He closed the book. He turned off the lamp. He went upstairs.

He sat at his kitchen table with the cold coffee and the note from Elena in front of him. He did not, it occurred to him, actually know what was going to happen next. Elena might come back. Elena might not come back. He had spent the morning doing work that was not contingent on her coming back. That was the first thing he had done in fifteen years on the subject of her that was not contingent on her. It was a small thing. It was also, he suspected, the only kind of thing that had any chance of mattering.

He made himself a sandwich. He ate half of it. He put the other half in the refrigerator, because wasting food was a thing he had stopped being able to do the year his mother died. He went into the study and opened the current box of Theodore Rowan's letters and put on his cotton gloves and began to read.

Theodore was writing to his sister, in 1889, about something unrelated. Lucian read for two hours. He took notes. He made a list of names to cross-reference with the town records. He did not think about Elena. That was a lie: he thought about her constantly, at a low persistent frequency, the way a man thinks about a tooth that aches. But he did not only think about her. He was, for the first time in a long time, a man doing something that was not a form of waiting.

At four o'clock his phone buzzed. A text from Elena. Three words: *How are you.*

He looked at the three words for a long time before he answered.

He wanted to write *I am not okay, I miss you, please come home.* All three sentences were true. None of them were what the moment wanted. He thought about Dr. Keane — whom he had never met, but whose voice Elena had quoted to him often enough that he had a sense of her cadence — and he thought about what Dr. Keane might say to him, if he were a client instead of a man who happened to love her client.

He typed: *I am working. I am doing some work on the Archive. I am not asking you to come back. I am telling you I am using this time the way you are using yours.*

He sent it.

She did not answer for forty-one minutes. Then:

Okay.

And then, two minutes later: *Thank you.*

He put the phone face down on the kitchen table and went back to Theodore's letters. He did not look at his phone again for two hours. When he looked at it, there were no new messages.

That was all right. He was using the time the way she was using hers.

CHAPTER SEVENTEEN

LUCIAN

SHE BROUGHT THE BOXES back on a Tuesday. No warning. No announcement. Just Elena on his doorstep at eight in the morning, the two cardboard boxes stacked in her arms, rain darkening the shoulders of her coat.

"These are yours," she said.

"I gave them to you."

"I know. And I'm giving them back." She pushed past him into the house and set the boxes on the kitchen table — the same table where he'd packed them, the same spot, as if she were rewinding a film.

"I spent ten days looking at these objects, Lucian. Holding them. Trying to decide what they meant."

"What did you decide?"

"That they're not yours and they're not mine. They're ours." She opened the first box and lifted out the Neruda book.

Held it in both hands, the way she might hold something living.

"My grandmother gave me this. I left it in a library when I was seventeen. You kept it safe for fifteen years. That's not your story or my story — it's the story of this book, and it belongs in a place where both of us can see it." He didn't speak.

He wasn't sure he could.

"So here's what I want," Elena said, her voice steady in the way it got when she'd made a decision and the decision was final.

"I want to put these back. Together. I want us to rebuild the Archive — not as your shrine to me, and not as evidence of anything. As the beginning. The record of how we started, kept by both of us, for both of us."

"Elena —"

"And I want to add to it. New objects. A wine cork from our first dinner. The napkin where you wrote your phone number — yes, I kept that. A photograph from the gala." She looked at him.

"I want the Archive to be alive. Not a museum. A living collection that grows with us." Lucian stood in his kitchen, in the gray morning light, and felt something he had carried for more than a decade — the weight of keeping, the burden of being the only one who remembered — begin, finally, to lift.

Not because the memories were gone. They never would be. But because he was no longer carrying them alone.

"Okay," he said.

"Let's go downstairs." They rebuilt the Archive that morning.

Elena placed each object with a designer's eye — the Neruda book at center height, the hiking brochure beside a framed photograph of Mount Washington she'd printed that morning, the Brooklyn café napkin in a shadow box. She rearranged the shelves, creating space for new additions. She labeled sections: BEFORE (their twelve encounters) and AFTER (everything that came next). When they were done, the room looked different. Still the Archive. Still the record. But shared now. Curated by two people instead of one. Elena stood back and surveyed her work.

"Better," she said.

"Better," he agreed.

She turned to him.

"One more thing."

"What?" She pulled a wine cork from her coat pocket — the cork from the bottle they'd shared at their first dinner with Isabel — and placed it on the shelf labeled AFTER.

"First entry," she said.

"Many more to come."

It was a Tuesday in February, nothing special, when Elena discovered that Lucian was wrong.

They had been together — in the strict post-reconciliation sense, the sense in which they had stopped going back and forth between apartments and she had unpacked the second box of books into his living-room shelves — for eight days. The snow had held off all winter and finally arrived overnight in a quiet two inches that made the harbor look like a black-and-white photograph of itself. They were at his kitchen table drinking the bakery's coffee and not talking, in the easy way that had begun to be possible between them, when Lucian looked up from his newspaper and said:

"The book was Neruda."

"What book?"

"In the library. When I saw you. *Twenty Love Poems and a Song of Despair.*"

"I know. You've told me."

"You were on page forty-three," he said. "I remember because you kept going back to it. You would read forward two pages and come back to that one. I always thought you were looking for a specific poem."

She went still for a second, with her coffee cup at her mouth. She put it down.

"Say that again?"

"You were on page forty-three, kept going back to it — what?"

"I wasn't reading Neruda." She said it carefully, the way you say a thing to a man who has, up to that second, been the authority on your own life. "I was reading *Twenty Love Poems*, yes. But not that day."

"I saw the book."

"I know you did. I had it with me every day that fall. I carried it around. It was my grandmother's; she had just died. I took it everywhere I went for about six months. I read it in bits." She was trying to remember now, actively, trying to see the specific afternoon in the specific light. "That day I think I was reading — I had an anthology I used for the literature class. A Norton, I think. I had Neruda sitting next to me on the table, but I was not reading Neruda. Not that day."

Lucian stared at her.

"I'm almost sure," she said. "I'm not a hundred percent sure. But I think you've — I think you've stitched it together. Because the Neruda was in your peripheral vision, it ended up being the book I was reading."

He did not answer for a long time.

He was not, she realized, upset. He was doing the thing his face did when he was conducting a kind of internal inventory — the slight narrowing of the eyes, the tilt of the head, the small pressure of his tongue against the inside of his cheek. He was going back. He was trying to find the file. He was trying to find out whether she was right.

"You're right," he said finally. Just that: you're right.

"Okay."

"I —" He stopped. He tried again. "I've been wrong about that for fifteen years. That is not a thing I thought was possible to be wrong about."

"Lucian."

"Yes."

"Are you okay."

He thought about it. He was a man who answered honestly about how he was, and she had come to love this about him, because it made the answer useful when it was good and useful when it was not.

"I don't know yet," he said. "Give me a minute."

She gave him a minute. She poured him more coffee. She sat across from him at the table and did not try to make it better. This was the kind of small crisis that her making-it-better would make worse.

After a while he said, "I want you to know something."

"Okay."

"I have always believed that what I had, what my mind does — I always believed it was the one thing I could trust. That everything else in the world might be wrong about you, but I wasn't. I had the facts. I had the record. That felt like — that felt like a gift, actually. Not a burden. I was the only person in the world who remembered you accurately, and that meant something to me. It meant I was being faithful to you, in a particular way, even when I could not be close to you."

"Yes."

"And I have just found out, at the age of forty-one, that I have been carrying a detail about you for fifteen years that was not correct." His voice was very calm. "Which means there are presumably other details. Which means the version of you I was faithful to, in those years, was — was ninety percent you, I think, and ten percent me. A composite. I was loving a woman who was mostly you and partly my imagination, and I did not know it."

She reached across the table and took his hand.

"Lucian."

"Yes."

"You know what you just did."

"What."

"You just described being in love with someone. Like everyone else is. That is how it works for the rest of us. We love a person who is partly a person and partly the person we have decided to see in them, and when we have been paying attention we find out, sometimes, that we were wrong about a small thing, and we adjust. Welcome."

He looked at her.

She watched his face change. She watched the tightness around his eyes release, slowly, like something that had been clenched for a very long time. He laughed once, softly — not a happy laugh, but the laugh of a man who had been braced against a fall and had discovered, at the bottom, that the ground was ordinary ground, and he had landed on it.

"Welcome," he said.

"It's nicer down here with the rest of us."

"I can see that."

They sat at the kitchen table for a long time in the quiet. The snow had not started again. The harbor was very still. Lucian's thumb moved, once, across her knuckles — the small unconscious tenderness, not even intended, that had always been one of the things that told her he would never be a man who had to perform for her.

"So what was I reading, really," he said finally. "In the library."

"I don't know. I'd have to look at the Norton anthology." She smiled at him, slowly. "It doesn't matter. Whatever it was, you remembered it with a book in the wrong hand. You remembered *me* with a face that was mine. That's the part that matters."

"Yes."

"Now drink your coffee."

He drank his coffee.

Outside the window the snow began again, thin and quiet, the light through it the color of the inside of a shell. They sat at the kitchen table. Neither of them said anything for a while. It was all right.

The Archive was quiet in the afternoon light — their Archive now, rebuilt together, the shelves rearranged by Elena's designer eye. She had been down here a dozen times since that first night, adding her own contributions to the shelves: a playbill from a show they'd seen in Portland, a dried flower from their first official date, a Polaroid Isabel had taken of them at Christmas. But today, something was different.

"You reorganized," Elena said, noticing immediately.

"The timeline's different. And there's —" She stopped.

Stared at the new display case in the center of the room.

"What is that?" Lucian's mouth was dry.

"Open it." She crossed to the case slowly, like she was approaching something that might startle.

Inside, on a bed of dark velvet, lay a ring. Platinum band, single diamond, elegant in its simplicity.

"Lucian." Her voice was barely a whisper.

"It was my grandmother's." The words came out in a rush, tumbling over each other.

"She left it to me when she died — said I should give it to someone who was worth waiting for. I've been carrying it around for over a decade, Elena. So many years, waiting for someone who was right." He moved to stand beside her, his reflection ghosting across the glass.

"And then I found you. Or you found me. Or we found each other. And I knew — I knew the moment you didn't run from this room — that you were the one she meant."

"Lucian —"

"I had speeches planned. Dozens of them. I was going to do this at sunset on the cliff overlooking the harbor. Or at the lighthouse, with the lighthouse sweeping overhead. Or in the ballroom where we first danced." He laughed, shakily.

"But this is where we really started, isn't it? This room. This collection of hope and madness and love that refused to die. This is where you saw everything I was and chose to stay anyway." He opened the case and took out the ring.

His hands were trembling.

"Elena Ward. I have loved you since before you knew my name. I will love you long after we're both dust and memory. Will you —"

"Yes." He blinked.

"I didn't finish."

"I don't need you to finish." She was crying — laughing and crying at once, tears streaming down her face even as her smile blazed like sunrise.

"Yes. Yes. A thousand times yes." He slid the ring onto her finger.

It fit perfectly. And then she was in his arms, and he was lifting her off her feet, spinning her around in the narrow space between the shelves, knocking against the collection of memories they had built together.

"You ridiculous man," she said against his mouth.

"You beautiful, impossible, ridiculous man."

"Is that a compliment?"

"It's a diagnosis." She kissed him, hard and joyful.

"I love you. I love our Archive and your obsessive organization and your inability to forget anything, including every embarrassing thing I've ever said in your presence."

"Including the time you told Marla that my eyes were 'oceanic' and she laughed for ten minutes?"

"You were eavesdropping!"

"I have exceptional hearing." He kissed her again.

"And oceanic is a perfectly reasonable description."

"I was drunk."

"You were honest." Another kiss, deeper this time.

"I'll take honest."

They didn't make it upstairs. Later, Elena would blame the champagne — the bottle Lucian had stashed in the Archive's small refrigerator, the one he'd been saving for exactly this moment. But the truth was simpler than that. The truth was that she looked at this man, this patient impossible man who had waited so long and built her a shrine and just promised her forever, and she wanted him. Here. Now. In the room where it all began.

"We should celebrate properly," she said, setting down her champagne flute on top of a filing cabinet labeled 2015-2017: The Portland Years.

"Upstairs. In a bed. Like civilized people."

"We should," Lucian agreed, but his eyes had gone dark, watching her movements as she reached for the hem of her sweater.

"We should call Isabel. Tell June and Marcus."

"All excellent ideas."

"So why aren't we moving?"

"Because you're taking off your sweater in my Archive, and I have suddenly lost the ability to think about anything else." She pulled the sweater over her head and dropped it on the floor.

Lucian made a sound, not quite a groan, not quite a laugh, and set down his own glass with exaggerated care.

"Elena. We cannot do this here. This room is climate-controlled. There are irreplaceable artifacts. There's a first-edition —" She reached behind her back and unclasped her bra.

He crossed to her in three strides, and then his mouth was on hers and his hands were everywhere, and she was laughing against his lips even as heat flooded through her.

"The desk," she gasped.

"Is the desk sturdy?"

"It survived a hurricane in 1987."

"Good enough." He lifted her onto it, scattering papers, and she wrapped her legs around him, pulling him close.

His hands slid up her thighs, and she shivered — not from cold, never from cold, not with he was looking at her.

"You're going to remember this forever," she said.

"I remember everything forever."

"No, I mean —" She pulled him down for a kiss, biting gently at his lower lip.

"I want you to remember this specific moment every single time you come down here. I want you to look at this desk and think about what we did on it. I want to become part of the Archive." He inhaled sharply.

"Elena —"

"Think about it." She was already working at his belt, fingers nimble and determined.

"A lifetime of memories on these shelves. And now, right here, we're making new ones. Better ones." She freed him, and he groaned.

"I want this room to remember us, Lucian. Not just you remembering me. Us. Together. Starting now." He looked at her — really looked, how he always did, like he was memorizing her for some future moment of need.

But this time, she looked back. This time, she saw him too.

"I love you," he said.

Simple. Certain.

"Prove it." He did.

They were enthusiastic. They were thorough. A stack of photographs slid off a shelf and scattered across the floor. A filing cabinet rattled ominously. At one point, Elena was fairly certain she heard something crack, but she was too far gone to care.

"The Neruda," Lucian panted against her neck, "is going to have opinions about this."

"The Neruda can write us a sonnet."

"It's a first edition."

"Then it's seen worse." She arched against him, gasping.

"Less talking. More — yes. That. Exactly that." It was nothing like their first time — nothing tender or careful or hesitant.

This was celebration. This was staking a claim. This was two people who had waited long enough and were done waiting. When she fell apart, she said his name like a prayer. When he followed, he said hers like an answer.

They lay on the Archive floor afterward — their Archive now, not just his — her head on his chest, both of them breathing hard. The carpet was industrial gray and desperately uncomfortable, but neither of them moved.

"We're getting married," Elena said wonderingly.

"We're getting married."

"In this town. Where we met. Where you built me a shrine."

"Please stop calling it a shrine."

"Never." She lifted her head to grin at him.

238

"I'm going to tell everyone. 'My husband proposed in his basement shrine. It was very romantic and also slightly concerning.'"

"Isabel is going to have a field day."

"Isabel is going to help me pick out my dress and also probably threaten you with bodily harm if you ever hurt me."

"She's already done that. Twice." Lucian traced the line of her spine, marveling at the fact that he was allowed to do this.

That she was here. That she was his.

"We should probably get up. Tell people. At least put on clothes before someone comes looking for us."

"In a minute." She pressed a kiss to his chest.

"First, I want to enjoy this. Being engaged. In your Archive. Surrounded by proof that we chose each other."

"I never had reason to give up. I had hope. That's different."

"That's enough." She looked around the room — at the scattered papers, the crooked shelves, the general evidence of enthusiastic celebration.

"We really did a number on this place."

"It'll recover. The Archive has survived worse than us."

"Has it though?" He considered.

"No. Actually. This is definitely the most action these walls have ever seen." She burst out laughing, and he laughed with her, and outside the small basement windows the afternoon faded into evening, and somewhere above them the Rowan Hotel continued its slow resurrection.

They would go upstairs eventually. They would tell June and Marcus, call Isabel and Marla, start planning a wedding that would bring Camden's Rise together. The gala was a month away, and little did they know, someone from Elena's past would appear uninvited, and Lucian would finally get the chance to fight for her instead of just waiting. But that was later. That was the future, already taking shape. For now, there was only this: two people in a basement full of memories, making new ones. The best ones yet.

Elena found them in the garden at sunset. She had come looking for June to discuss the final fabric selections for the ballroom drapes, but she stopped at the edge of the rose beds, held in place by a scene so intimate she felt like an intruder. June was sitting on the stone bench beneath the old oak tree, the one that had been planted by Theodore Rowan over a century ago. Marcus sat beside her — not quite touching, but close enough that the space between them hummed with possibility. They were looking out at the harbor, where the fishing boats were coming in with the day's catch, their running lights beginning to glow against the darkening sky. June said something Elena couldn't hear, and Marcus laughed — a low, warm sound that transformed his weathered face. He turned to look at her, and Elena saw something in his expression that made her stop mid-sentence. It was the way Lucian looked at her. Devotion. Tenderness. The quiet, patient hope of someone who had learned that good things were worth waiting for.

"She thinks no one notices," Lucian said quietly, appearing at Elena's elbow.

"She's wrong."

"How long?"

"He's been in love with her for two years. Since the day he showed up to give an estimate on the renovation and she argued with him for forty-five minutes about the historical accuracy of the proposed window replacements." Lucian's mouth quirked.

"She won the argument. He's been lost ever since."

"And June?"

"Slower. She loved Robert — loved him. Losing him broke something in her." He watched as June turned to Marcus, her silver hair catching the last of the daylight.

"But I think she's starting to realize that broken things can heal. That loving someone new doesn't mean forgetting someone old." In the garden, Marcus reached over and took June's hand.

Elena held her breath. June looked down at their intertwined fingers. For a long moment, she didn't move — and Elena could see the war playing out across her face. Grief and guilt and longing and hope, all tangled together in the fading light. Then, slowly, deliberately, June leaned her head against Marcus's shoulder. They sat there together, watching the boats come home, while the lighthouse began its nightly vigil and the first stars emerged above the harbor.

"That's what it looks like," Elena said.

"Choosing to live again."

"That's what it looks like," Lucian agreed.

"Choosing love over fear." He took her hand, and they stood there at the edge of the garden, watching two people find their way back to hope — and recognizing, in that quiet moment, the reflection of their own story.

Some loves came fast, like lightning. And some loves came slow, like the tide — patient and steady, wearing away resistance until there was nothing left but surrender. Both kinds were worth waiting for.

Six months passed like pages turning. The Rowan Hotel opened to the public on a warm evening in June, and half of Camden's Rise turned out to celebrate. The chandeliers blazed. The string quartet played Vivaldi. Elena's restoration work drew gasps from people who had watched the building decay for decades and were now seeing it reborn. The gala was everything June had dreamed it would be. Lucian stood at the edge of the ballroom, watching the celebration unfold like a scene from Theodore's own era. The chandeliers blazed overhead, throwing rainbows across the restored silk panels. String quartet music wove through the crowd of Camden's Rise's finest — the mayor and his wife, the historical society board, business owners and fishermen and families who had watched the Rowan Hotel decay for decades and were now witnessing its resurrection. And at the center of it all, Elena.

She wore the midnight blue gown, the one that made her look stunning. She was talking to June and Marcus, her hands moving expressively as she pointed out some detail of the restoration, her face bright with pride. The engagement ring caught the light every time she gestured — a small but visible reminder that she had chosen him, that she was his, that in just a few months she would be his wife. His fiancée. Three weeks since the proposal, and the word still felt like a miracle.

"You're staring." Isabel appeared at his elbow, elegant in deep green, a champagne flute in her hand and mischief in her eyes.

She had arrived from Portland that afternoon, refusing to miss what she called "the culmination of fifteen years of pining."

"I'm appreciating," Lucian corrected.

"You're mooning. There's a difference, and it mostly involves the degree to which your mouth is open." Isabel took a long sip of her champagne. "It's a good look on you, for the record. Tragic and unfamiliar, but good."

He didn't argue. She was right.

Across the room, Elena looked up, caught his eye, and smiled — the small, private smile he had loved longer than she had known he existed. He returned it, not caring who saw.

Let them look.

CHAPTER EIGHTEEN

ELENA

THE MORNING SHE REALIZED she was going to marry him was not a morning she had marked in advance for realization.

It was a Saturday in March. Four months since the Archive rebuild. Three months since the Neruda mistake. Twelve weeks since she had finally moved the last of her things out of the rental and handed the keys back to the landlord and carried the last box — mostly books, mostly her grandmother's — across the threshold of Lucian's house, which was now also her house, in the legal fiction of domestic life that takes time to become not-a-fiction.

They had been fighting.

Not seriously. Lucian and Elena did not fight seriously; neither of them had the stomach for it. But they had been disagreeing, with the low steady friction of two people learning the grain of each other's days, about something she could not now reconstruct the specific shape of. She thought it had started with a stack of mail and his insistence on opening it in a particular order. Maybe it had started with the fact that she had agreed, without asking him, to host a dinner for June and Marcus on a night he had set aside for a long-scheduled video call with a colleague. Maybe it had started earlier than that, the previous evening, when she had said something short to him about the way he loaded the dishwasher, and he had not said anything back, and she had felt, for a half-second, the old unease of a woman who had once, a long time ago, learned to treat silence as a weather system.

The point was: they had been disagreeing, and they had been careful about it, and she had watched him be careful about it, and she had been careful about it back. Isabel's voice had been in her ear the whole time. *You have to mean what you say. You have to not say what you don't mean.* Elena had been testing the shape of that all winter. She had been finding, to her quiet astonishment, that it was not as hard as Isabel had made it sound, because it was easier to mean what you said when the person you were saying it to was not going to use it against you later.

That morning — the Saturday, the morning of realization — she had come downstairs and found him already in the kitchen, making coffee. He was wearing the gray wool sweater she liked him in. He handed her a mug without looking at her. He said, "I have been up since five. I did not want to lie there being angry at you about last night because it was not really about last night. I think it was about the dinner. Which was about the phone call. Which was about the fact that I spent ten years not having anyone to rearrange my schedule for, and I am bad at it, and I was quiet with you at the sink because I was embarrassed that I was bad at it. I did not want you to think the quiet was the old kind. I want to say out loud that the quiet was me being embarrassed. I am sorry it looked like the other thing."

She took the mug. She looked at him.

She thought: *I am going to marry this man.*

It was not a dramatic thought. It was not accompanied by a soundtrack or a sunrise. It was, actually, the plainest thought she had had in her thirty-three years — plainer than *I love you*, plainer than any of the thoughts she had thought about Adam before she understood what Adam was. It was the thought of a woman who had just been told by a man why he had been quiet, before she had had to ask, in language that made the silence something small and human instead of something bigger than she was.

"Thank you," she said.

"For what."

"For the whole thing you just said." She took a sip of coffee. It was good coffee. She was going to marry a man who could not cook an egg without consulting a recipe, but who could make coffee the way she liked it because he had paid attention on the first morning, and not forgotten. "I was going to come downstairs and apologize for the dishwasher."

"I don't care about the dishwasher."

"I know you don't."

"I care about the fact that you got small at the sink." He said this very simply. "I want to know if that was me, or if it was an echo of somebody else, because if it was me, I have to stop doing it. And if it was an echo, I have to know it's there, so I can help you not hear it."

"It was an echo."

"Okay."

"Not a loud one."

"Still an echo."

"Yes."

He nodded. He kept making his coffee. He did not, she noticed, press. He did not ask her what had triggered it, what she had felt, how long it had lasted, whether it had happened before — all the questions she had been expecting to have to answer. He had learned, she saw, that an echo did not need to be dissected in the moment. It needed to be named out loud and then left alone, the way you name a storm and then let it pass over you.

She set her mug down. She crossed the kitchen. She put her arms around him from behind, and she stood there with her cheek against the gray wool of his sweater, and she said:

"I want to marry you."

He did not move for a second.

Then he said, without turning around: "You want to make sure you're hearing yourself before you say that again?"

"I've heard myself."

"Okay."

"Say it back to me."

"You want to marry me."

"Yes."

"Are you proposing to me, Elena."

"No. I'm telling you where I'm going to be in six months, and I want you to know, so you can plan your life accordingly."

He turned around inside her arms. He looked at her.

"I've been planning my life accordingly for fifteen years."

"I know you have."

"I'd like to do the proposing part, if that's all right."

"By all means."

"Not this morning."

"No, not this morning. I've ambushed you. You need time."

"You know me." He smiled, very slightly. The rare one. The private one. "I need a little time."

"Take it," she said. "I'll be here."

She stayed where she was, with her arms around him, and he stayed where he was, and after a while the coffee got cold, and neither of them cared. Outside the kitchen window, across the harbor, the lighthouse beam was doing its morning sweep — slower and further-spaced than at night, because the light had the patient self-importance of a light whose job was mostly done during other hours, and who was, in the daylight, a little bit superfluous, and enjoying it.

Elena had been going to make toast. She did not make toast.

They stood in the kitchen like that for a long time.

He proposed nine days later, in the Archive, on a Wednesday evening, with a ring that had belonged to his mother and a small speech he had been writing in his head for more than a decade. She said yes before he finished the speech. He made her let him finish it. She did. It was a good speech.

They did not tell anyone for a week. They wanted the thing to belong to them for a little while before it belonged to the town. When they did tell June, June put her apron over her face and cried in the hotel kitchen for two full minutes before she could speak, and Marcus handed her a dish towel without comment, and then Marcus shook Lucian's hand and held on longer than men usually hold on in New England, and said *good* in the particular low voice men use when they mean it.

Isabel cried on the phone. Marla, to Elena's surprise, did not cry. Marla said, "I knew three weeks in. I didn't want to tell you. You would have accused me of being a romantic. I am secretly a romantic. You heard it here first. This is embargoed."

"Embargoed."

"Until further notice."

"Noted."

"I love you, you ridiculous woman. Congratulations. I will see you in April."

"April?"

"For the planning. I am flying up. I have opinions about flowers."

"You have opinions about everything."

"That is a known fact."

Elena hung up smiling, and went downstairs to find Lucian sitting at the kitchen table reading a book about the history of lighthouses, which was the kind of book he read for fun, and she sat down across from him and did not say anything, and he looked up at her and smiled, and she smiled back, and they sat there for a long time in the evening light without saying a word.

She had been, at one point in her life, afraid that love would look like a man bringing her coffee on a tray. She had been very glad to find out that it did not have to. It could look like two people reading at a kitchen table. It could look like a sentence said plainly at a sink on a Saturday morning. It could look like the specific silence between two people who were not afraid of each other's silences.

This is what it is, she thought.

She had not known.
She knew now.

It was Elena who brought it up, which Lucian would remember.

They had been in the library of the hotel, her library, the room she had taken over as her workspace during the final months of restoration and was now using, officially, as her office. She was at her desk going through change orders from a cabinetmaker in Portland. He was in the armchair by the window reading a biography of a nineteenth-century lighthouse keeper, because he was the kind of man who read biographies of nineteenth-century lighthouse keepers for pleasure, and Elena had long since stopped pretending to be surprised.

She said, without looking up: "Lucian."

"Yes."

"Can I ask you something."

"Always."

"It's about the Archive."

He closed his book. He set it on the arm of the chair. He turned his full attention to her the way he turned his full attention to things, which was completely.

"All right."

"I'm not upset. I just — I've been thinking. For a while now. And I think I want to say it out loud to you, because I've been carrying it alone, and we don't carry things alone in this house if we can help it."

"No, we don't."

She put down her pen. She came around the desk. She sat across from him in the other armchair, her bare feet tucked up under her the way she sat when she was settling in for a conversation that mattered.

"When we sorted the Archive together," she said, "and you took out the photograph, and then you sorted it again on your own — I felt like we had done the work. I said so at the time. I meant it at the time."

"Yes."

"But I think what I meant was: we had done the work on the objects. We took care of the things. We agreed on what stayed and what went. That was real. I'm not going back on it."

"Okay."

"What I've been thinking about, lately — what I caught myself thinking about this week, specifically — is not the objects. It's the fifteen years. It's the — it's the part of what happened that we cannot, actually, take out of the room. Because it wasn't in the room. It was in your head. And some of it was in mine, and I didn't know it."

Lucian did not move. He was looking at her with the particular face he had when he was receiving something carefully, the face he had shown her the night she told him about the first time Adam had grabbed her wrist and she had told herself it had been an accident.

"Yes," he said. "That's true."

"I don't want an apology. I've had your apology. You gave it to me in the Archive that first night, and you have given it to me since, and I don't need another one."

"What do you want."

"I want you to name it." She was steady. "I have been loving you now for a long time. I want to love you without — without the part of me that is still, sometimes, catching up on what happened in those years. I want you to say out loud what you did, not what we sorted. Not the objects. The years. What you did in them."

He breathed out, once, slowly.

"You want me to take accounting."

"Yes. If you can."

"I can. Let me find the words."

He found them. It took him a minute. She waited. She was not in a hurry, and she had come to understand, over three years of knowing him, that one of the things his mind could do for him, when he gave it permission, was locate the exact sentence a situation required. He used the minute.

Then he said:

"For fifteen years I carried a version of you in my head that you had not given me. I watched you in twelve places. I remembered what you were wearing and what you were reading and what your face did when you thought nobody was looking. I filed those observations. I kept some of them as objects. I built, inside myself, a private relationship with a woman who did not know she was in a relationship with me. She was not consulted. She had no say. She was being, in some sense, used — not cruelly, not for power, but used nonetheless. Her image belonged to me because I had taken it, and she had no way to ask me to stop taking it because she did not know I was there."

He paused. He kept his eyes on hers.

"Removing the photograph did not undo that. Sorting the Archive did not undo that. Burning the receipts did not undo that. The watching happened. The version of you I built in those years is still, to this day, partly my invention — and even the part that was not my invention was gathered without your permission. You can ask me, now, to stop. I have stopped. But you did not get to ask me until you knew there was something to ask me about, and that was also a choice I made — the choice to wait, to let you find out, to let myself write the moment of disclosure on my own schedule rather than yours. That was another version of the same act. I took that from you too."

"Yes."

"I cannot give those fifteen years back. I can only tell you, out loud, that I know what I did, and that you were right to have been changed, for a time, by finding out what I did, and that if you had chosen, at any point, not to forgive me, you

250

would not have been wrong. It was not my choice to forgive. It was yours. You forgave me. I have tried to be worthy of it. I will keep trying. And I am going to try, going forward, to make sure that nothing I do without telling you first ever again adds up to the shape of what I did to you in those years by waiting."

She was quiet for a long moment.

Then she stood up. She came over and sat on the arm of his chair. She put her hand on the back of his neck, the way she did, and she said:

"Thank you."

"That was all I had."

"It was enough."

"It wasn't enough. Nothing would be."

"No, I mean — it was enough for me." She kissed the top of his head. "Not because it undoes the years. Because it names them. I needed them named. I've needed them named for longer than I realized. Some things are small enough that saying them out loud is what they require."

"Elena."

"Yes."

"Thank you for asking."

"You're welcome."

They stayed there for a while. She did not go back to the desk. He did not go back to his book. The afternoon light moved across the library floor in its slow late-winter way, and somewhere in the walls of the old hotel the radiator began to tick as the heat came up.

Afterward, in her memory of the rest of that year, Elena would mark this conversation as the real threshold. Not the engagement. Not the wedding, six months later. The afternoon in the library when she had named what needed naming, and he had named it with her, and the room had held them both without either of them pretending the thing had not happened.

That was the marriage, actually. Not the ceremony. The willingness, of two people who could have looked away, to look at what was there.

The first real fight they had as an engaged couple was about a dinner party, which was, Elena thought afterward, exactly the stupid kind of thing couples fought about, and was actually about none of the things it appeared to be about on the surface.

It was a Thursday in April. Marcus and June were coming over — they had finally, in their quiet careful way, started calling what they had a relationship, and Elena had invited them for dinner to celebrate. Nothing fancy. Just the four of them at the kitchen table, a chicken, a bottle of wine, the lemon tart Elena had been practicing because it reminded her of her grandmother. She had told Lucian about it on Monday. She had reminded him Wednesday. Thursday morning at breakfast she had said, cheerfully, *Don't forget tonight, Marcus and June, seven o'clock.*

He had said *of course, love, I'll be home by five to help.*

He had not been home by five. Or by six. Or by six-thirty.

Elena had tried his cell phone twice. It went to voicemail twice. By quarter to seven she had chopped every herb in the kitchen with the kind of rhythmic precision that she used when she was trying not to panic, and she had set the table, and she had put the chicken in the oven, and she had lit the candles, and Marcus and June had arrived on the dot of seven, and she had poured them wine and smiled and said Lucian was running late, he had gotten caught up at the library, he would be along soon.

He walked in at seven-thirty-two with a folder of papers under his arm and an expression of preoccupied distraction on his face that she had come to recognize from his worst Theodore-manuscript days — the face of a man who had been deep inside a document for six hours and had forgotten, in the particular way his mind sometimes forgot the present when the past had him, that there was any other place to be.

He stopped in the kitchen doorway. He saw Marcus. He saw June. He saw the candles. He saw Elena.

He said, "Oh."

She said, "Yes."

He said, "I'm so sorry, I —"

She said, "Take off your coat. Dinner's been on the table for twenty minutes. We're about to eat."

The dinner was fine. The chicken was a little dry. Marcus talked about the new commission he had taken, a barn renovation up the coast. June talked about the hotel's summer reservations. Lucian made conversation in the careful, attentive way of a man who knows he is in trouble and is trying very hard to pretend, for the sake of the guests, that he is not. Elena smiled. She laughed at the right moments. She served the lemon tart, which had turned out, actually, quite well.

At ten o'clock Marcus and June left. Elena walked them to the door and hugged June goodbye, and June held her a beat longer than usual and said, quietly, *You let me know if you need anything,* and Elena nodded, because she could not, just then, speak. She closed the door and stood with her forehead against it for a moment.

When she turned around, Lucian was standing in the hallway.

"Elena."

"Don't." She walked past him into the kitchen and started stacking plates. "I don't want to talk about it tonight. I'm too tired."

"I need to apologize."

"I know you do. Tomorrow."

"Please."

She stopped. She set the plates down. She turned to face him, and what came out of her mouth was not what she had planned to say, not what she had been rehearsing while she kept the table warm for him. What came out was:

"I made that lemon tart four times this week. Four. Because I wanted it to be right. Because June has been kind to me and Marcus has been kind to me and I wanted to give them something good. And I stood in this kitchen at six-forty-five and I thought — what if something's happened to him. What if he's in a ditch somewhere. What if he's hurt. And then at seven o'clock I thought — no, he's not hurt. He's with Theodore. He's in 1889. He forgot. And the thing that got to me, Lucian — the thing that I need you to hear — was not that you forgot. It was that I was standing there deciding whether to be worried or to be angry, and I realized I didn't know which one to be, because I didn't know you well enough yet to know which one you were going to be."

He did not say anything. He was listening. He was listening the way he listened, which was the one thing about him she had never wanted to give up.

"I used to know exactly which one to be," she said. Her voice was very even. "With Adam. Always. Always angry. Always waiting for the next thing. And I moved here and I met you and I have not had to be that woman in — in so long, and tonight, for twenty minutes, while the chicken was getting dry, I could feel her coming back. I could feel her sitting down in my chest and making herself comfortable. And I hate that. I hate that she gets to come back, ever, for a dinner party, because a man who loves me got caught up in a file."

"Elena —"

"I'm not done. I need you to hear the whole thing or I will have to say it again and I don't want to have to say it again. I am not saying you are Adam. I am telling you what happens in my body when I don't know where you are. I am telling you that the phone call, the 'hey I'm going to be late' phone call, is not a nice-to-have. It is a thing I am going to need, for a while, the way a person needs a railing on a staircase. Not forever. Not because I don't trust you. Because I need to not have to rehearse being angry at seven o'clock when my forks are getting cold. Do you understand?"

"Yes."

"Say it back to me."

"You need me to call you when I am going to be late." He said it carefully, the way he said the things he was working very hard not to get wrong. "Not because you don't trust me. Because if I don't call, you end up alone in a room with someone you worked a long time to leave behind, and I am the reason she is in the room. If I call, you stay in the room you are actually in."

"Yes."

"I can do that."

"Good."

"Elena."

"Yes."

"I am so sorry."

"I know you are. I'm going to bed. I love you. Don't follow me up for a little while. I need twenty minutes by myself."

She went upstairs. She brushed her teeth. She washed her face. She sat on the edge of the bed and looked at her hands in her lap and she waited for the old Elena — the one who would have apologized, by now, for overreacting; the one who would have gone downstairs and made it better; the one who was trained to repair a damage she had not caused — to arrive.

The old Elena did not arrive.

What arrived, instead, was the small hot quiet satisfaction of a woman who had said a true thing out loud to a man who had heard it. Who had asked to have it said back. Who had not made her apologize for her own railing.

When Lucian came up twenty-five minutes later, she was under the covers, reading. He sat on the edge of the bed. He did not touch her yet. He said, "May I lie down."

She said, "Yes."

He lay down. He did not reach for her. After a while his hand found hers, slowly, the way his hand always did, even in sleep — the small unconscious reach that she had come to understand was the truest thing about him.

"I called my assistant," he said. "The archives' voicemail system, I mean. I left myself a message. To remember to call you, if I'm going to be late, going forward. I'll hear it every morning."

"You set yourself a recurring reminder."

"I set myself a recurring reminder."

"For the next however many years."

"For however many years it takes. Indefinitely, I suppose."

She laughed, once, softly, into the dark. She put her head on his chest. His heart was beating steadily under her ear, the way it always was.

"You're going to be a good husband," she said. "It will cost you a little to get there. But you're going to be good."

"I'm trying to be."

"I know you are."

They slept. In the morning she made coffee and he made her toast and they did not mention the dinner again, because there was no need to. The thing had been said and heard. That, Elena was learning, was the difference. The thing had been said and heard, and neither of them had to carry it into the next day.

It happened on a Saturday, a month after the dinner party, for no reason Elena could afterward identify.

They had been at the farmer's market in town — Lucian had gone with her, which he had started doing on Saturdays, because he liked watching her choose things, he liked the way she touched a peach to know whether it was ready. She had gone ahead to get them coffee while he stopped at the bookstore's outdoor table. The line at the coffee truck was long. She had been standing in it for maybe five minutes, her reusable cup in her hand, not thinking about anything in particular, when a man behind her — a tourist, a stranger, a man she had never seen before in her life — leaned forward past her shoulder and said to the barista, *Two large black, please, for my wife and me.*

Just that. A perfectly polite sentence. Addressed to someone else. She was not even in the man's line of sight; he was speaking over her to the barista, the way tall people sometimes did without meaning anything by it.

But the voice — the pitch of it, or the cadence, or the timbre, or some combination of those things she could not now identify — was exactly the pitch and cadence and timbre of Adam's voice. Exactly.

She went still.

She did not know she had gone still. She was aware of herself only in the way you are aware of a room you have just walked into — the general shape of it, the light — and then she was aware that her hand was not holding the cup anymore, the cup was on the ground, rolling a little in a circle on the gravel, and her breathing had gone shallow and fast, and she was staring at the barista in the coffee truck, and the barista was looking at her with the particular careful expression of a person who had recognized a look on a customer's face and did not know what to do next.

The man behind her said, mildly, *Are you all right?*

It was not Adam. It had never been Adam. The voice was just a voice.

She tried to say yes. Her throat did not open.

Then Lucian was beside her. She had no memory of him walking over. He was simply there, the way he sometimes simply was. He picked up her cup. He did not ask her what had happened. He did not ask if she was okay. He put his hand on the small of her back — not pushing, just present, the flat warm weight of him telling her body where her body was — and he said, quietly, to the barista: *We'll come back in a little while.*

He walked her away from the line. They went around the corner of the market, past the stalls, to the small patch of grass by the fence where nobody was. He sat down on the grass. She sat down next to him. He did not speak.

She breathed.

It took her a few minutes. She had practiced the breathing enough that the shape of it was familiar. Four in, seven hold, eight out. Again. Again. The market was going on. A child was laughing somewhere. The harbor smelled of salt. The sky was the ordinary sky.

"I don't know what that was," she said finally.

"Okay."

"A man's voice sounded like Adam's. I don't even think it really did. I think my ear — I think my ear just heard it wrong for a second."

"Okay."

"I thought I was past this."

"You are past this. This is what past looks like sometimes."

She looked at him. His face was calm. Not pitying. Not worried. Just calm, the way his face was when he was waiting to see what she needed next.

"I didn't want to have this," she said. "I wanted to be — I wanted to be done. I'm getting married in six weeks. I wanted to be somebody who could stand in a coffee line."

"You were standing in a coffee line. For five minutes. Then your ear heard something. You're still the person who was standing in the coffee line. You're just also the person whose ear heard something."

"That's very philosophical for a man who has a recurring reminder."

"I contain multitudes."

She laughed. She did not know she was going to laugh. It came out watery, and then she was crying a little, in the discreet way she had come to allow herself to cry — the way a person cries who is not in danger of being punished for crying — and Lucian put his arm around her and she put her head on his shoulder and they sat on the grass by the fence for a while, and nobody came looking for them, and after a while she wiped her face with her sleeve and said:

"I don't think I want coffee anymore."

"We can skip it."

"I think I want to go home."

"Yes."

They went home. He walked beside her. He carried her cup and his books. He did not touch her again until they were inside the house. When they were inside, and the door was closed, he turned her around and took her face in both his hands and looked at her — the careful long look that was his — and he said: *Nothing is wrong with you.*

"I know."

"No, Elena. Say it back to me."

"Nothing is wrong with me."

"Again."

"Nothing is wrong with me."

"Good."

He kissed her forehead. He let her go. He went to the kitchen to make her tea, the way he did when he did not know what else to do, because tea was a thing a man could make with his hands when his words had run out, and she loved him for it.

Later, on the couch, her feet in his lap, she said, "Dr. Keane says these come in waves."

"Yes."

"She says they come smaller and smaller as time goes on. But they come. Sometimes for years. She says I shouldn't be surprised if I have one on my wedding day."

"All right."

"You're not scared."

"Of your wedding day."

"Of — of me still having these. Years from now."

"No."

"Why not."

He thought about it. He was always honest when he thought about it, because he did not know how to be any other way.

"Because the woman who has a wave on the grass at a farmer's market," he said, "is the woman I am marrying. She's not somebody else. The waves are part of you. They will get smaller, like Dr. Keane says. They might not go away. I don't need them to go away. I need to be the person who is there when one comes. I can be that person. I already am."

"All right."

"All right."

She drank her tea. He did not move his hand from her ankle. Outside the window, the afternoon was turning into early evening, the light going soft and slow the way it did in late spring. Somewhere on the harbor a boat was coming in. The lighthouse had started its nightly sweep an hour early, as it sometimes did when the sky was overcast.

She thought, with a clarity that surprised her: *I am not past this. I am in it. I am going to keep being in it, probably for a long time. And the thing I used to think was the finish line — "being past it" — is not actually the line. The line is here. The line is today. The line is a man making me tea because I cried on the grass.*

That was a line she could stay on.

She closed her eyes and slept a little, with her feet in his lap, and when she woke up an hour later, he was still there.

Six months flew by like pages turning in a book you never wanted to end. Elena stood in June's office at the hotel, surrounded by fabric swatches, seating charts, and enough flower catalogs to wallpaper a small house. The wedding was a month away, and she should have been stressed. Should have been overwhelmed by the endless decisions and logistics and details that seemed to multiply every time she thought she had them under control. Instead, she felt something she had forgotten was possible: joy. Pure, uncomplicated, bone-deep joy. The feeling still surprised her sometimes. She would catch herself humming while she worked, or smiling at nothing in particular, and have to stop and marvel at how different her life had become. A year ago, she had been a woman held together by caffeine and determination, flinching every time her phone buzzed, wondering if happiness was just something other people experienced. Now she was planning a wedding to a man who looked at her like she had personally hung the moon and stars.

"Earth to Elena." Marla's voice cut through her reverie.

"I asked you a question. Ivory or cream for the table linens?" Elena blinked, refocusing on her best friend.

Elena had reorganized the hotel's paint sample wall three times this week. The colors were arranged by period accuracy — Georgian through Victorian — and the first arrangement had been alphabetical within each era, which was logical but was wrong. The second had been by undertone (warm to cool), which was more intuitive but made the timeline illegible. The third — organized by the rooms they'd be used in, cross-referenced with the original paint analysis — was right. It was right. But she kept looking at it.

"You're staring at paint chips again," Marla said from the doorway.

"They're not chips. They're historically authenticated pigment samples."

"You're staring at historically authenticated pigment samples again. How long have you been standing here?"

"Twenty minutes."

"Elena."

"The Prussian Blue might be half a shade too warm for the library."

"Elena. It's paint."

"It's WRONG paint." Marla steered her away from the wall by the shoulders.

"This is what we in the professional world call 'displacement anxiety.' You're nervous about Lucian seeing the finished ballroom tomorrow, so you're fixating on paint."

"I'm not fixating. I'm quality-controlling."

"You've quality-controlled the same wall three times. That's fixating." But Marla's voice was gentle.

She'd seen Elena's perfectionism before — had watched it consume entire weekends during her design career in Boston, had listened to tearful phone calls about font spacing and grout color. It was Elena's way of imposing order when her inner world felt chaotic.

"The paint is fine. You are fine. Everything is going to be fine."

"The Prussian Blue —"

"Is fine." Marla had arrived three days ago with spreadsheets, color-coded binders, and opinions.

All three were extensive. She had taken over the planning with the same efficiency she brought to managing literary careers, and Elena had never been more grateful.

"Ivory," Elena said.

"It matches the silk panels better. The cream pulls too yellow in candlelight."

"Excellent choice. I was testing you." Marla made a note on her tablet with a satisfied nod.

"Your design instincts are still intact despite the wedding brain. Good to know."

"I don't have wedding brain."

"Honey, you've checked your phone four times in the last ten minutes to see if Lucian texted. You have industrial-strength wedding brain." Marla's expression softened with affection.

"It looks good on you." Elena felt her cheeks warm.

"He said he had a surprise. I'm curious."

"You're besotted. There's a difference." Marla scrolled through her tablet.

"Now, about the seating chart. I've put your aunt Margaret at table seven, as far from the bar as possible — we both remember what happened at your cousin's wedding. June's nephew is at table three with the other under-thirties. And I've strategically placed Lucian's colleague — the one who talks too much about maritime law — near the kitchen door so the serving staff can accidentally interrupt him."

"You're terrifying."

"I'm efficient. There's a difference." Marla looked up with a smile.

"How are you feeling? Really?"

June found her alone in the bridal suite that afternoon, staring at her reflection in the full-length mirror.

"Having second thoughts?" June asked from the doorway.

"No." Elena adjusted a strap that didn't need adjusting.

"Having twenty-second thoughts. And thirty-third thoughts. And thoughts about my thoughts." June came in and sat on the edge of the bed.

For a moment, she just watched Elena in the mirror — this young woman she'd come to love like a daughter she'd never had.

"I need to tell you something," June said.

"Something I should have said months ago." Elena turned.

"Henry — my husband — was a good man. I loved him. I want you to know that first." June smoothed the bedspread with hands that weren't entirely steady.

"But he was also controlling. Not cruel — not like your Adam. But controlling in the way that kind, intelligent men sometimes are. He had opinions about everything, and his opinions had a way of becoming the only opinions in the room." Elena stared.

"June —"

"I spent thirty-two years married to a man I loved, and for most of those years, I couldn't have told you where his preferences ended and mine began." June's voice was steady, but her eyes were bright.

"It took me five years after he died to realize I didn't know what kind of music I liked. He'd always chosen the records."

"Why are you telling me this? Now?"

"Because tomorrow you're marrying a man who loves you deeply. And I want you to marry him with your eyes open — not because an old woman who's projecting her own regrets told you it was romantic." June reached for Elena's hand.

"The hotel taught me something. You can restore a building to what it was, or you can restore it to what it should have been. The second is harder. But it's better."

"Lucian isn't Henry."

"No. He's not." June smiled.

"But every marriage is a building. And every building needs maintenance. Don't ever stop checking the foundations, Elena. Even when the walls look perfect." Elena hugged her; this fierce, complicated, imperfect woman who had given her so much more than a job.

"Thank you," she whispered.

"For being honest."

"It only took me seventy-three years to learn how." June pulled back, straightened her shoulders, and became herself again — brisk, capable, in charge.

"Now. Marla tells me there's a crisis with the table linens. Ivory or cream?"

"Ivory."

"Good girl. I'll handle it." She swept out, and Elena turned back to the mirror, and saw, in a long time, a woman who was choosing with her eyes wide open.

The rehearsal dinner had ended three hours ago. It had been perfect — intimate, warm, full of laughter and stories and the particular joy of people who loved each other gathering to celebrate. They had held it at the Italian restaurant in town, the one with the red-checked tablecloths and the family recipes that went back four generations. June had insisted on paying, claiming it was her gift as the woman who had brought them together.

"My hotel, my matchmaking, my treat," she had said, brooking no argument.

Isabel had given a speech that made everyone cry. She had started with stories of Lucian as a child — the boy who remembered all of it, the brother who could recite their mother's shopping lists from ten years ago, the teenager who had once corrected a history teacher so thoroughly that the man had retired early.

"But here's what I never told anyone," Isabel had said, her voice growing soft.

"My brother wasn't just remembering. He was waiting. All those years, cataloging moments and preserving details, he was waiting for someone worth sharing them with." She had turned to Elena, eyes shining.

"Thank you for being that person. Thank you for seeing him — really seeing him — and choosing to stay." Elena had cried.

Lucian had cried. Even Marcus, stoic Marcus who had faced down Atlantic storms without flinching, had dabbed at his eyes with his napkin. Marla had followed with a speech designed to lighten the mood — tales of Elena's college disasters, her disastrous attempt at cooking for a boyfriend that had resulted in a fire department visit, the time she had gotten lost in a parking garage for four hours because she was too stubborn to ask for directions.

"What I'm saying," Marla had concluded, grinning, "is that my best friend is brilliant and talented and hopeless at certain basic life skills. Lucian, you are now responsible for making sure she doesn't burn down your house or wander into the ocean. Good luck. You're going to need it." The table had erupted in laughter.

Elena had thrown a roll at Marla's head, which Marla had caught with the ease of long practice. And then June had risen, glass in hand, and the room had gone quiet.

"To second chances," she had said simply.

"To love that waits, and love that heals, and love that was worth the waiting and the healing." She had looked at Marcus beside her, then at Elena and Lucian across the table.

"Theodore built the Rowan Hotel as a monument to hope. Tonight, I think he would be pleased to know that hope has finally been rewarded." Marcus had raised his glass.

"To hope," he had echoed.

"To hope," everyone had repeated.

Elena had been radiant throughout. She had worn a simple blue dress — not because it matched her eyes (which it didn't) but because she had said, that morning, that she felt blue, and Marla had laughed and said *then dress for the weather.* Lucian had cataloged the line in his memory because he loved that she had said it. She had smiled at him across the table like he was the only person in the room, like the dozen other guests had faded into background noise.

"Tomorrow," she had whispered to him as they said goodnight in the hotel lobby, tradition demanding they sleep apart.

"Tomorrow I get to marry you."

"Tomorrow," he had agreed, kissing her forehead, her cheeks, the corner of her mouth.

"Tomorrow I finally get to keep you." And now it was tomorrow, and he still couldn't find the words.

A knock at the door interrupted his spiral.

"Come in." Isabel entered, still in her rehearsal dinner dress, a deep green that brought out the copper in her hair, carrying two glasses of whiskey.

Her feet were bare, her heels abandoned somewhere between the front door and his study.

"I thought you might be doing exactly this," she said, eyeing the crumpled paper scattered across the floor.

"Doing what?"

"Overthinking." She handed him a glass and settled into the armchair across from his desk, tucking her legs beneath her like a cat.

"You've been staring at that paper for hours. I could see the light from my window across the street."

"The vows won't come." He took a sip of whiskey, letting the burn ground him in the present moment.

"I have fifteen years of memories, Isabel. All those years of loving her. Every detail preserved in vivid clarity. And I can't find a single sentence that feels adequate."

"That's because you're trying to say everything." Isabel swirled her whiskey, watching the amber liquid catch the lamplight.

"You can't. It's impossible. Even for a man who remembers everything, some things are too big for words."

"Then what do I say?"

"The truth. The simple truth." She studied him with that knowing gaze she'd had since they were children, the one that said she could see through all his carefully constructed defenses.

"Why do you love her, Lucian? Not the memories, not the encounters, not the Archive. Why do you love her?" The question cut through all his careful constructions, all his attempts at eloquence.

He set down his glass and closed his eyes, searching for the core of it. The essential truth buried beneath more than a decade of accumulated detail.

"Because she sees me," he said finally, the words coming from somewhere deeper than thought.

"Not the HSAM. Not the oddity, the walking encyclopedia, the man who can't forget. Just... me. Lucian. A person. And she chose to stay anyway." Isabel smiled — a soft, proud smile that reminded him suddenly of their mother.

"There you go," she said.

"Start there." She finished her whiskey, set the glass on his desk, and rose to leave.

At the door, she paused.

"Mom would have loved her, you know. Elena. She would have adored her." Lucian's throat tightened.

"I know."

"Good. Remember that tomorrow." Isabel blew him a kiss.

"Get some sleep, brother. Big day ahead." She closed the door behind her, leaving him alone with his memories and his blank page.

After Isabel left, Lucian descended to the Archive. The basement was cool and quiet, the only sound the soft hum of the dehumidifier that kept the air at the precise level required for paper preservation. The room had changed over the past months, Elena's touch everywhere now — new shelves installed along the far wall, the lighting softened from harsh overhead fluorescents to warm sconces that made the space feel less like a museum and more like a sanctuary. A comfortable reading chair sat in the corner, upholstered in a deep blue that Elena had chosen because it reminded her of the sea. She came down here sometimes, curling up with a book while he worked, keeping him company in the space that had once been his alone. The objects from his years of waiting were still there, carefully preserved on the original shelves: the Neruda book with its worn spine and marginal notes, the café napkin in its protective sleeve, the trail map with its careful creases, the gallery postcard faded to soft pastels. Each one a breadcrumb on the trail that had led him to her. But they shared space now with newer additions. A program from the hotel's grand reopening, where Elena had unveiled her restoration work to thunderous applause. A pressed flower from the garden where they'd had their first official date, when he'd finally summoned the courage to ask her to dinner. A photo of Elena laughing at something Isabel had said, her head thrown back, her joy unguarded. The beginning of a new collection. Their collection. Evidence of a shared life. Lucian ran his fingers along the spine of the Neruda book — the one Elena's grandmother had given her, the one he had kept safe for eight years without knowing why. Tomorrow, it would witness their wedding. Elena had insisted on displaying it at the ceremony, a tribute to the grandmother who had shaped her love of beauty and the strange providence that had brought the book back to her hands. He pulled the book from its shelf and opened it to a page marked with a faded ribbon. Elena's grandmother had underlined one passage in pencil: I love you as certain dark things are to be loved, in secret, between the shadow and the soul. He had loved her like that for over a decade. In secret, between the shadow and the soul. But tomorrow, everything would change. Tomorrow, the secret would become a vow. The shadow would become light. The first time he had seen Elena. Really seen her.

October 15, 2009. Boston University Library. She was crying over a book. Lucian had noticed her the moment she walked in — it was impossible not to, how she moved through the stacks like she belonged there, her fingers trailing along the spines with reverent familiarity. She wore a green sweater that made her hair look like burnished copper, and she carried herself with the particular grace of someone who had spent a lifetime in libraries, who understood their rhythms and their silences. But it was the tears that stopped him. She had settled into his favorite corner — the one by the tall window where the October light fell just right, making dust motes dance like tiny stars — and her lips were moving with the words. Not reading aloud — whispering them, like a conversation with someone who wasn't there anymore. The book in her hands was Neruda. Twenty Love Poems and a Song of Despair. Even from ten feet away, Lucian could see how worn it was, how loved. The spine was cracked, the pages soft with handling. This was not a new book. This was a companion. He should have looked away. Should have given her the privacy that grief demanded. But something in her sorrow felt familiar, like an echo of his own loneliness, and he found himself rooted to the spot. She looked up suddenly, as if feeling his gaze, and she found his eyes across the stacks. Hazel eyes, surprised and a little embarrassed. For a moment, neither of them moved.

"Sorry," she said, wiping her face quickly with the back of her hand.

"I'm having a moment. My grandmother just —" She stopped, swallowed hard.

"This was her favorite book. She gave it to me when I was sixteen. Told me it would teach me about love better than any boy ever could." A sad smile flickered across her face.

"She was right, mostly. And now she's gone, and I can't stop reading the poems she marked, and —"

"You don't have to apologize." The words came out before he could stop them, before he could analyze and second-guess.

"Grief deserves space. Even in libraries. Especially in libraries, maybe." She laughed — a small, surprised sound, like a bird startled into flight.

"That's... very understanding."

"I lost my mother when I was twelve." He didn't know why he told her that.

He never told anyone that — never offered up his grief to strangers, never used it as a conversation starter. But something about this woman's solitude made him want to show her she wasn't alone.

"Libraries are good places to be alone without being lonely." Her expression softened, the embarrassment giving way to something warmer.

"I'm sorry. About your mother."

"It was a long time ago." But not for him.

Never for him. For him, it was yesterday and every day, preserved in vivid detail — the way she had smiled at him that last morning, the way she had smelled of lavender and coffee, the exact pitch of her voice when she said, I love you, sweetheart. Have a good day at school.

"Would you like some company?" he heard himself ask.

"Sometimes it helps, having someone nearby who understands. You don't have to talk. You don't have to do anything. Just... not be alone." She considered him for a long moment — really looked at him, as if trying to determine whether he was safe, whether his offer was genuine.

Then she nodded and gestured to the chair across from her. They sat together in the October light, not speaking, just existing in the same space. She read her grandmother's poems, turning the pages slowly, pausing sometimes to trace words that must have held special meaning. He pretended to read his research notes while memorizing every detail of her face — the way her eyebrows drew together when she was sad, the small mole above her left ear, the delicate movement of her throat when she swallowed. He wasn't falling in love. He had already fallen. Somewhere in the space between her tears and his confession about his mother, he had tumbled headfirst into something vast and terrifying and wonderful. After an hour — an hour he would remember in vivid detail for the rest of his life — she closed the book and stood. The October light had shifted, grown golden with the approach of evening. The library was emptying as students headed to dinner, to dorms, to lives he knew nothing about.

"Thank you," she said, clutching the Neruda book to her chest like a talisman.

"For letting me grieve. For staying."

"Anytime," he said.

She smiled — the first real smile he'd seen from her, transforming her tearstained face into something luminous — and walked away. He never got her name. He didn't think he'd ever see her again. But he was already in love.

The memory settled over him like a familiar blanket, worn soft with years of handling. That moment in the library — that was when it all began. Not with a grand romantic gesture, not with fireworks or destiny or love at first sight in the way movies portrayed it. But with shared grief and quiet company. Two lonely people finding a moment of connection in a sun-drenched corner of a library, united by loss and Neruda and the particular solace that books could offer. He had spent those years wondering what would have happened if he'd asked her name. If he'd been braver. If he'd said something more than "anytime" as she walked away.

But that wasn't the point. Maybe the point was that they had found each other anyway. Despite the missed connections and the years apart, despite Adam and the distance and the thousand ways the universe could have kept them separate — they had found each other. And tomorrow, they would make it permanent. Lucian picked up a pen and began to write. The words came easily now. Not perfectly — he still crossed out lines, still searched for the right phrase. But the core of it was there, rising up from somewhere deeper than memory, deeper than the Archive, deeper than half a lifetime of waiting, welling up from his heart. Elena, I fell in love with you in a library, on an October afternoon, while you cried over your grandmother's book. I didn't know your name. I didn't think I'd ever see you again. But I remembered. I remembered every time we met after, and all the times between. I thought for a long time that my memory was the truest thing I had of you. I know now it wasn't. The truest thing is you choosing me. I promise to show up — every morning, every difficult night, every ordinary Tuesday — and choose you back. For as long as memory lasts. Which, for me, is forever. Lucian set down his pen and read the words back. They weren't perfect. They weren't poetry. But they were true. And that was enough. That was everything. He folded the paper carefully and slipped it into his jacket pocket, next to his heart. Tomorrow, he would stand in front of everyone he loved and read these words to the woman who had transformed his life. Tomorrow, Elena Ward would become Elena Calder. And the man who remembered all of it would finally have memories worth keeping. He placed the Neruda book back on its shelf, turned off the lights, and climbed the stairs to bed. Tomorrow was coming. Tomorrow was finally here. And for the first time in all that time, Lucian Calder fell asleep without dreaming of the woman he loved. Because tomorrow, he would wake up and marry her.

CHAPTER NINETEEN

ELENA

THE MORNING OF HER wedding, Elena woke to sunlight and the smell of roses. Someone had filled the bridal suite with flowers overnight — cascades of white and blush pink blooms arranged on every surface, their petals catching the early light like scattered silk. Roses on the dresser, roses on the windowsill, roses in tall crystal vases that threw prisms across the walls. The effect was overwhelming, like waking up inside a dream she had been afraid to want. She lay still for a moment, letting the reality wash over her like warm water. The sheets were soft against her skin. The morning air carried the salt tang of the sea through the open window. Somewhere in the distance, a seagull cried its plaintive call. Today was her wedding day. Today, she would marry Lucian Calder. The thought sent a shiver through her — not of fear, but of anticipation. Of joy so sharp it was painful. A year ago, she had driven into Camden's Rise with nothing but three suitcases and a desperate hope that she could outrun her past. Now she was about to bind her future to a man who had loved her since before she knew his name. The door burst open, and Marla swept in carrying a tray laden with champagne, strawberries, and an elaborate breakfast spread — croissants and fruit and some kind of quiche that smelled divine. Behind her came Isabel, already dressed in her bridesmaid gown of soft gold that made her look like a sunset personified, and June, resplendent in silver with her silver hair pinned up in an elegant twist.

"No bride of mine is getting married on an empty stomach," Marla announced, setting the tray on the bed with the authority of a general deploying troops.

"Eat. Drink. And then we're going to make you the most beautiful woman Camden's Rise has ever seen."

"She already is," Isabel said, perching on the edge of the bed and stealing a strawberry.

"But we're going to gild the lily anyway. It's our sacred duty." Elena laughed, pushing herself u

LUCIAN

His wife.

The word echoed through Lucian's mind like a bell ringing in a cathedral, resonant and strange and true. His wife. Elena Calder. The woman he had loved for over a decade, through chance encounters and missed opportunities and one desperate, hopeful Archive in a basement, was finally, legally his. He led her from the ballroom into the garden for the reception, her hand warm in his, and felt the reality of it settle into his bones. Her ring caught the evening light — the simple band of white gold he had placed on her finger not an hour ago. Her ring. His wife. This was real. The garden had been transformed into a wonderland of light and bloom. String lights wove through the old oak trees like strands of captured stars, their glow soft and golden against the deepening blue of the evening sky. Candles flickered on every table — dozens of them, perhaps hundreds, their flames dancing in the gentle summer breeze. The roses that Marcus had tended for thirty years perfumed the air, their scent mixing with the salt tang of the nearby sea. A band was setting up near the dance floor, their instruments catching the light as they tuned. Waiters circulated through the gathering crowd with trays of champagne and hors d'oeuvres — tiny crab cakes, bruschetta with fresh tomatoes from Marcus's garden, delicate pastries filled with local cheese. The guests milled about, their laughter and conversation creating a warm hum of celebration. But Lucian barely noticed any of it. He couldn't stop looking at Elena. The flowers in her hair had begun to loosen, and she hadn't noticed, and she was the most beautiful thing he had ever seen. She laughed at something Marla said, throwing her head back, her joy unguarded and complete, and the sound washed over him like everything good he had ever imagined but never quite believed he could have. He was memorizing everything, of course. He couldn't help it. The exact shade of the sunset behind the trees — salmon and rose and the deep purple of approaching night. The way Elena's eyes crinkled at their corners when she smiled. The particular warmth of the summer evening, the soft murmur of conversation from the gathered guests, the distant cry of a gull wheeling over the harbor. But for once, memorizing didn't feel like a compulsion. It felt like a gift. A way of honoring the moment, preserving it not out of fear or obsession but out of gratitude. Out of love.

"Mr. Calder?" He turned to find Marcus standing beside him, looking uncomfortable in his formal suit but beaming with genuine warmth.

Marcus had cleaned up remarkably well — his weathered face shaved smooth, his silver hair neatly combed — though his hands still bore the calluses of decades spent in the garden.

"Marcus." Lucian clasped his hand.

"Thank you for everything. The garden looks incredible."

"June's vision," Marcus said, ducking his head with characteristic modesty.

"I just did the heavy lifting. She told me where to put things, and I put them there." He glanced toward the dance floor, where June was directing the band with characteristic authority, her silver dress catching the light as she moved.

His expression softened into something tender and private.

"She's something, isn't she?"

"She is," Lucian agreed.

"You're a lucky man."

"So are you." Marcus looked at Elena, then back at Lucian.

"I've been in this town for ten years, and I've never seen anything like what you two have. The way you look at her..." He paused, searching for words.

"It's like she's the only person in the world. Like the rest just... fades away."

"She is," Lucian said simply.

"She always has been." Marcus nodded slowly, seeming to understand.

"I know what that's like," he said quietly.

"To wait for someone. To hope." His eyes found June again across the garden.

"Sometimes the waiting is worth it."

"It is," Lucian agreed.

"It always is."

Elena spotted them during the band's second set, when the dance floor was full and no one was paying attention to the edges of the garden. Marcus and June were sitting on the stone bench beneath the old oak — the one with the carved initials that predated even Theodore. June's silver dress caught the string lights, and Marcus was in his borrowed suit, and they were talking with the particular intensity of two people who had been circling each other for months and had finally run out of reasons to keep circling. Elena watched Marcus say something that made June laugh — really laugh, not the composed, gracious laugh she used at events but the real one, the one that made her look thirty years younger. And then Marcus reached over and took her hand, and June looked down at their joined fingers with an expression Elena recognized. Surprise. Not that it was happening. Surprise that it had taken this long. Elena turned away before they could notice her watching. Some moments weren't meant to be observed. Some moments just needed to happen, quietly, between two people who had earned them. She found Lucian by the dessert table, eating cake with the focused attention of a man cataloging every crumb.

"Marcus and June," she said.

"I know." He didn't look up from the cake.

"I've been watching them not-watch each other for six months. It was getting painful."

"You're one to talk about watching people for extended periods." He looked at her.

She looked at him. And they both started laughing — the helpless, giddy laughter of two people who knew their own story was absurd and loved it anyway.

Later, Marla found Lucian alone by the dessert table, studying the cake with the focused attention of a man cataloging every crumb.

"Can I steal you for a minute?" He looked up.

Marla was holding two glasses of champagne, her gold dress catching the string lights. Her expression was uncharacteristically serious.

"I owe you something," she said, handing him a glass.

"And I've been putting it off because I'm not great at being wrong."

"About what?"

"About you." She took a breath.

"When Elena first told me about you — the memory, the twelve encounters, the Archive — I was scared for her. I thought you were another version of what she'd already survived. Another man who watched too closely, who knew too much, who'd built a world around her without asking permission."

"You weren't entirely wrong."

"No. But I wasn't right, either. And the difference matters." Marla looked at him steadily.

"You packed up your Archive and left it at her door. You gave up the only physical proof of fifteen years of love because she needed you to. Adam would have burned the world down before he surrendered that kind of control."

"I'm not Adam."

"I know that now. I should have known it sooner." She raised her glass.

"I'm not sorry I was suspicious. That's my job — Elena's had enough people who failed to be suspicious on her behalf. But I am sorry I didn't see who you were faster. You're a good man, Lucian. A strange one, but good."

"Strange is fair."

"Strange is the nicest thing I've ever called a man my best friend is marrying." She clinked her glass against his.

"Welcome to the family. Officially."

The first dance was approaching, and A flutter of nerves that had nothing to do with the ceremony. He had practiced, of course. Spent hours with a YouTube tutorial and Isabel's patient instruction, trying to master the basic steps of a waltz. He could remember every lesson in vivid detail — his sister's exasperated sighs, the way his feet had refused to cooperate, the increasingly creative insults she had deployed when he stepped on her toes for the fifteenth time. But this was different. This was real. And everyone would be watching. Every misstep, every stumble, every moment of graceless fumbling would be witnessed and remembered. Though, he supposed, only by him. Elena appeared at his side, her hand slipping into his as naturally as breathing. Her dress rustled softly as she moved, and he caught a whiff of her perfume — something floral and warm that made him want to bury his face in her neck and never leave.

"Ready?" she asked.

"No," he admitted.

"I'm going to step on your feet. Probably multiple times. Possibly enough times to require medical attention."

"Probably." She grinned, that impish smile that had undone him from the very beginning.

"But I don't care. I didn't marry you for your dancing skills."

"What did you marry me for?" She pretended to think, tapping a finger against her chin.

"The house with seventeen rooms. And the extraordinary memory — very useful for remembering anniversaries. You can never pretend you forgot."

"I see. Purely practical considerations."

"Exactly." She rose on her toes to kiss his cheek, her lips warm against his skin.

"Also, I love you desperately. That might have factored in."

"Might have?"

"A minor consideration. Tertiary at best." The band struck up the opening notes of their song —"The Way You Look Tonight," because Elena had insisted on something classic — and Lucian led his wife onto the dance floor.

The guests parted to let them through, forming a loose circle around the polished wooden platform that had been laid over the grass. The first few steps were awkward. He was too aware of his feet, too aware of the watching crowd, too aware of the hundred ways he could embarrass himself and his new bride. His shoulders were tense, his movements stiff, his counting audible even to himself: one-two-three, one-two-three... But then Elena moved closer. She rested her head against his shoulder, her body relaxing into his, and suddenly the steps didn't matter. The watching crowd didn't matter. Nothing mattered except the woman in his arms and the music flowing around them like warm water. They swayed together in the candlelight, and the world fell away.

"I can't believe this is real," Elena murmured against his jacket.

"I keep waiting to wake up. To discover it was all a dream and I'm still in Boston, still with Adam, still..."

"It's real." He held her tighter.

"I've pinched myself approximately seventeen times today to make sure."

"You counted?"

"I count everything. You knew this when you married me."

"I did." She pressed closer. "And I don't regret a single count."

They danced until the song ended, and then they danced through another, and another. Elena lost track, eventually, of how many songs had passed. She knew only that the chandeliers above them were blazing — the ones June had pointed out on her first morning in Camden's Rise, the ones Theodore had hung for Clara more than a century ago — and that her husband's hand was warm against her back, and that somewhere in the room her best friend and her sister-in-law and her adopted grandmother were dancing with men they loved, and the Rowan Hotel was doing what Theodore had built it to do.

She thought, without quite meaning to, of Clara. Of the ballroom standing empty for decades because Theodore could not bring himself to host a dance here without her. Of the letters hidden in a wall, each one a small act of faith that someone, someday, would find them and know that this room had been built out of hope and the stubborn refusal to give up on love. Somewhere, she liked to think, Theodore was smiling. His ballroom was full of love again. And this time, the story would have a happy ending.

The bridal suite was quiet after the chaos of the reception. Elena stood at the window, still in her wedding dress, watching the moon trace a silver path across the harbor. The sounds of celebration had finally faded — the last guests departing, the caterers packing up, June's exhausted but happy voice calling final instructions. Now there was only the whisper of waves and the distant cry of a gull, and the soft click of the door as Lucian entered behind her. She didn't turn around. Not yet.

"Mrs. Calder." The name sent a shiver through her.

Not from cold — the room was warm with candlelight, dozens of votives flickering on every surface — but from the weight of what that name meant. The permanence of it. The promise.

"It doesn't feel real," she said.

"I keep waiting to wake up."

"You're not dreaming." His footsteps crossed the room. A warmth of him behind her, close but not touching.

Waiting, as he always did, for her to set the pace.

"I'd know. I remember all my dreams. None of them were ever this good." She turned then.

He had removed his jacket somewhere between the ballroom and here, loosened his tie. His hair was slightly disheveled from hours of dancing, his eyes tired but bright. He looked exactly like a man who had just married the love of his life. Her husband. The thought was a bell ringing in her chest.

"I was thinking about Clara," she said.

His expression shifted — soft understanding replacing joy.

"On your wedding night?"

"On my wedding night." She reached out, traced the line of his jaw.

He leaned into her touch like he couldn't help it.

"She never had this. All those letters, all that love, and she never got to stand with Theodore in a room like this. She never got to call him her husband. She never got to —" Her voice broke.

"I know."

"It seems unfair. That we get this and they didn't. That we're standing in the hotel he built for her, celebrating the life they should have had." Lucian took her hands in his, raised them to his lips.

Kissed each knuckle, slowly, reverently.

"Do you know what I think?" he said against her fingers.

"I think they're here. Not in any ghostly sense — I don't believe in that. But in the way people live on through the things they create. Through the love they leave behind." He turned her hand over, pressed a kiss to her palm.

"Theodore built this hotel as a monument to hope. And tonight, we're proving that hope was justified. We're the ending they never got to have." Elena felt tears prick her eyes.

"That's beautiful."

"It's true." He stepped closer, cupped her face in his hands.

"We carry them with us, Elena. Every time we walk through that ballroom, every time we see Clara's paintings, every time we read his letters — they're with us. And tonight, when I love you how he never got to love her, they'll be with us then too." She kissed him.

It was different from every kiss that had come before. Not the desperate hunger of their first time, not the playful passion of their engagement night. This was something else entirely. This was a vow made physical. A promise sealed. This is what marriage is, . Not the ceremony. Not the rings. This.

"I want to do this properly," she whispered against his mouth.

"Properly?"

"Slowly. Deliberately. The way they would have, if they'd had the chance." She stepped back, turned so he could reach the long row of buttons down her spine.

"Undress me, Lucian. Like you have all the time in the world. Because you do. We do. We have forever." His fingers found the first button.

He had never undone so many buttons in his life. Each one was a small surrender. Each one revealed another inch of her skin, luminous in the candlelight. He could have rushed — God knew part of him wanted to, the part that had spent the entire reception watching her dance and smile and be beautiful, the part that had been counting the minutes until they could be alone. But she had asked for slow. For deliberate. For the wedding night she had always imagined. So he went slowly.

"The first time I saw you," he said, freeing the fifth button, "you were crying over a book in a library. You had no idea I existed. And I stood there, barely breathing, watching you, thinking: this is the woman I'm going to love for the rest of my life." Button six.

Seven. Eight.

"I didn't know what love was, not really. I was twenty-two and arrogant and certain I understood everything. But I knew, somehow, that what I was feeling wasn't small. Wasn't temporary." Nine.

Ten. Eleven. The dress began to loosen around her shoulders.

"I spent those years waiting for you. Some people would call that obsessive. Some people would call it sad. But I never felt sad. I felt..." He paused, searching for the word.

"Certain. Like you were a fixed point in my universe. Like as long as you existed somewhere, the world made sense." The last button fell free.

He pushed the dress from her shoulders, and it pooled at her feet like spilled moonlight. Elena turned to face him. She was crying — quiet and full of something too large for words. He understood. He felt it too.

"I'm going to spend the rest of my life making you glad you waited," she said.

"You already have." He pulled her close, skin against skin, heartbeat against heartbeat.

"Every single day since you walked into my life, you've made me glad."

"Even when I'm difficult? When I steal the covers? When I leave my shoes everywhere and forget to replace the coffee filters?"

"Especially then." He kissed her forehead, her cheek, the corner of her mouth.

"I've memorized all of your imperfections, Elena. Every single one. And I love them. I love you. I'm going to love you until memory fails me, and since memory never fails me —"

"Forever," she finished.

"Forever."

He carried her to the bed. Not because she couldn't walk — because she wanted him to. Because there was something about being held in his arms that made her feel cherished in a way she had never known before. The sheets were cool against her back. He settled beside her, propped on one elbow, and — His elbow slipped. He caught himself awkwardly, half-sprawled across her, and for a moment they just looked at each other with wide eyes. Then Elena started laughing.

"Smooth," she said.

"Very smooth. Very romantic wedding night energy."

"I was going for 'devastatingly suave.' Did I miss?"

"By a mile." But she was grinning, pulling him back down.

"Try again. And maybe don't put your elbow on the silk pillow this time."

"Noted." He settled beside her properly this time, propped on one arm, and just looked at her.

Not rushing. Not demanding. Just seeing.

"Better?" he asked.

"Much."

"What are you thinking?" she asked.

"I'm thinking that I want to remember this exactly as it is. The candlelight on your skin. The way you're looking at me. The fact that an hour ago, I made vows to you in front of everyone we love, and now we're here, and it's just us, and you're my wife."

"Say it again."

"My wife." He bent to kiss her collarbone.

"My wife." Her shoulder.

"My wife." The curve of her neck.

She pulled him down to her. What followed was nothing like any time before. It was unhurried. Reverent. Every touch a statement, every kiss a promise. He learned her body all over again — not with the desperate curiosity of their first time, not with the gleeful abandon of the Archive floor, but with the patient attention of a man who knew he had forever to explore.

"Still counting?" she asked, breathless.

"Always," he said.

"That's from the ceremony." Her voice was breathless.

"I know. But I meant it then, and I mean it now." He moved lower, and she gasped.

"With my body, I thee worship."

"Lucian —"

"That's what this is. Worship. That's what you deserve." She wanted to argue — wanted to say she didn't deserve worship, that she was just a woman, just human, just flawed.

But the words dissolved as his mouth found her, and all she could do was feel. It built slowly. Inexorably. Like a tide coming in, like the sun rising, like all the inevitable things that couldn't be stopped. She clutched at the sheets, at his shoulders, at anything solid, while the world narrowed to sensation and the sound of his voice against her skin.

"Let go," he said.

She did. And before she could catch her breath, he was there, sliding home, and the feeling of it, of him, of belonging, of finally, drew a sound from her throat that was a sob.

"I love you," she said.

"I know." He began to move, slow and deep.

"I've always known. Even before you did."

"That's arrogant."

"That's memory." He kissed her.

"I remember the exact moment you fell in love with me. July fourteenth, 11:23 in the morning."

"You're making that up."

"I am not. You were looking at me across the ballroom, and your face changed, and I knew."

"What did my face do?"

"It got very soft. And then you tried to hide it behind your wine glass, and missed your mouth slightly." He was laughing now, even as his breathing went ragged.

"It was the most beautiful thing I've ever seen."

"I did not miss my mouth."

"You absolutely did. This is documented." She pulled him closer.

"I love you."

"I know."

"Even when you're insufferable."

"Especially then." His voice broke.

"Elena —"

"I know," she said.

"Together." They fell together — like arriving somewhere she'd been heading all along.

The candles burned low. They lay in a tangle of limbs and sheets, her back against his chest, his arms wrapped around her. Through the window, she could see the lighthouse beam sweeping past, steady and sure.

"I used to think love like this only existed in old letters," she said quietly.

"No."

"He never got to feel her fall asleep in his arms. Never got to wake up next to her. Never got to know what she looked like in the morning, before coffee, with pillow marks on her face."

"No. He didn't."

"But we do." She turned in his arms to face him.

In the dim light, his eyes were soft, unguarded, full of a peace she had rarely seen.

"We get all of it. The mornings and the evenings and the ordinary days in between. We get to grow old together, Lucian. We get the ending they never had."

"We get to live the life they dreamed about."

"For them." She kissed him softly.

"And for us."

"For all of us." He pulled her closer, tucking her against his chest.

"Go to sleep, Elena. We have the rest of our lives to figure out what comes next." She closed her eyes.

The lighthouse swept past. And in the bridal suite of the Rowan Hotel, in the building that Theodore Rowan had built for a love he lost too soon, Elena Calder fell asleep in her husband's arms and dreamed of nothing at all. She didn't need dreams anymore. She had finally woken up.

CHAPTER TWENTY

ELENA

Three years later

The Archive is a smaller room than it used to be.

That was the thing Elena noticed first, on the rare afternoons when she went down the basement steps alone — which was not often anymore, since the room had become a part of the house the way a study or a pantry was part of a house, a room that belonged to both of them and therefore belonged, in the particular way of shared rooms, to neither of them specifically. She had started going down more, lately, because she had taken on her first solo restoration commission since the hotel, a small Federal-style townhouse in Portland that needed its library put back together. She kept some of her research notes in the Archive because it was quiet, and because the climate control was good for papers, and because Lucian did not mind.

Tonight she was down there looking for a book. A specific one — a manual on nineteenth-century Portland cabinetmakers that Lucian had bought for her two Christmases ago. She found it on the third shelf, next to a sheaf of her own sketches from the Rowan project, and she was pulling it off the shelf when her eye caught on the lowest shelf, the one nearest the floor, where the original objects still lived — the ones they had kept, the ones they had agreed to keep — in a single straight row.

The Neruda book. The Mount Washington brochure. The napkin from the Brooklyn café, flat now under a pane of museum glass. The conference program. The train ticket from Philadelphia.

Five objects. That was all there was now. The twelve had become eight had become five, by slow attrition, as Lucian had gone on, over the years, removing items that on second and third look could not quite be defended. He had told her each time. He had shown her what he was taking out. She had not, usually, had an opinion. She trusted him, now, to keep the ones that belonged there and to let go of the ones that did not. The trust had not come all at once. It had come the way trust comes — a Tuesday at a time.

She crouched down in front of the shelf and looked at the five.

Then she reached into her cardigan pocket and took out the photograph.

She had kept it, in the end. She had not known she was going to. For the first year after she took it from the Archive, she had moved it from drawer to drawer, never quite throwing it out, never quite displaying it. For the second year it had lived in the bottom of her jewelry box, face down, under an envelope of her grandmother's letters. Sometime in the third year she had taken it out and flattened it between two sheets of acid-free paper, and she had put it in the top drawer of her desk in the study upstairs, because she had come to understand, slowly, that the photograph was hers, and being hers meant that she did not have to choose between keeping it and destroying it. She could simply have it. It was a thing that had happened. It was a woman on a beach, on a Saturday, when she had been alone for the first time in a long time, and she had been at peace, and someone had loved her enough to take a picture of her peace, even though he had loved her wrongly, that afternoon, in the way he had taken it.

Both things, not one.

Tonight, for the first time, she had brought it down to the Archive with her. She did not quite know why. She looked at it now in the green lamplight — the dark hair blowing, the shoulders loose, the paperback, the blue linen dress — and she thought: *She was a woman who had a Saturday.*

Then she put the photograph back in her pocket. She would not leave it here. The Archive was not the right place for it. The Archive was for the objects that belonged to both of them. The photograph belonged only to her. It was all right that it belonged only to her. Some things a marriage did not need to hold.

She turned off the lamp and went upstairs.

Lucian was in the kitchen making dinner. Badly, but he had gotten better — he could produce a pasta and a salad without looking at a recipe most nights now, which had been, for him, a project of several years. The kitchen smelled of garlic and something burning slightly at the edges.

"I can hear you smiling," he said without turning around.

"I wasn't smiling."

"You were."

"I was walking up the stairs. You can't hear a person smile on the stairs."

"I can hear you smile anywhere. I'm a gifted listener."

"You're burning the garlic."

"I am not."

"Lucian."

"Oh."

He moved the pan off the heat. She crossed the kitchen and put her arms around him from behind, and she stood there with her cheek against his shoulder blade for a moment, the way she had started doing, in the habit that had become, over three years, one of the shapes their life was made out of.

"What were you doing downstairs?" he said.

"Looking for the cabinetmakers' book. Found it."

"Good."

"I brought something else down. For a minute. Then I brought it back up."

"Okay."

She did not explain. He did not ask. One of the things about being married to a man who remembered everything was that you did not have to tell him every thought you had,

290

because he was already holding enough thoughts for both of you. One of the things about being married to this particular man was that he had learned, over years, to wait for what was yours to become yours before he asked about it.

"Theodore," she said.

"Mm."

"Did you finish the second volume."

"Today. The last letter went to the copy editor this afternoon."

"Lucian."

"I know."

"Is it good."

"I think so. I'll know in six months when the reviews come in. Right now I'm too close to it."

"It's good." She said it into his shoulder. "I read it last week. The last section. It's good, Lucian. It's the best thing you've ever written."

He put his hand over hers, on his stomach. He did not say anything for a while. She felt him take a long breath and let it out.

"I didn't know you read the last section."

"I know you didn't. I didn't want you to know. I wanted to know what I thought before you knew what I thought. I wanted to be a reader, not a wife, for one evening."

"And."

"And you are very good, Lucian Calder."

"Thank you."

"You're welcome. Now turn the heat back on. Your pasta water is cooling."

He turned the heat back on. They made dinner together, badly, and ate it at the kitchen table, the way they did almost every night unless June and Marcus had them over, which had been happening more lately, and might happen more still, because June had lately started talking about taking on a full-time cook for the hotel and spending more evenings at home, and Elena had an idea this had to do with Marcus having begun, the previous November, to leave a toothbrush at June's house overnight.

That was one of the things too. The life you built with someone turned out to be, among other things, the lives other people were building alongside you, the quiet domestic seasons of other households becoming the weather you lived in. Marla had called three days ago to say that she and the agent at her firm, a man named Nathan whom Elena had met exactly twice, were looking at apartments together. Isabel had come down from Portland for Elena's birthday in February and stayed for three days and shown Elena pictures of a woman she had been seeing — a potter in Montreal, soft-eyed, a widow, someone Isabel had described, carefully, as *somebody I'd like you to meet, if it goes on.* The world kept pairing up around them.

After dinner they did the dishes together. Elena washed. Lucian dried.

"What made you go down for the book tonight," Lucian said.

"The Portland townhouse. I have a meeting with the owners on Monday."

"You're nervous."

"A little."

"You're going to be good."

"I know I'm going to be good." She handed him a plate. "I'm nervous because I'm going to be good. That's a different kind of nervous."

"A better kind."

"Yes."

He dried the plate. He put it in the cupboard. The cupboard was on his side of the kitchen, because his arms were longer, and they had divided the cupboards that way by unspoken agreement sometime in the first year, the way couples divide every small task by a thousand tiny arrangements neither of them ever articulates.

"Elena."

"Yes."

"I want to tell you something."

"All right."

"I threw out a thing today. Out of the Archive. I was going to tell you about it before dinner and then I got distracted."

"Which thing."

"The receipt from the bookshop in Cambridge. The one I kept from the day I followed you in. The one I told you about, back when we sorted the first time."

"I thought that was gone. I thought you burned that."

"I thought I did too. I found it today, in a folder of other papers, in a box I hadn't opened in a long time. It must have gotten put aside. I threw it away."

"Okay."

"I wanted you to know."

"Thank you."

"I also wanted you to know that I have not, in three years, added anything to the Archive. Nothing. Not one thing. The five objects on the shelf are the five objects that will be there."

She set the dish in the rack. She wiped her hands on the dish towel. She turned to look at him.

"Lucian."

"Yes."

"Why are you telling me this tonight."

He dried his hands. He set the towel down. He looked at her with the particular face he had, the one that was only for her, and he said:

"Because I wanted you to know that the Archive is closed. The collecting part, I mean. Whatever I remember of you going forward, I remember. I don't keep evidence of it anymore. I don't need to. You're here. I don't have to preserve you. I get to have you."

"Oh."

"I thought about that sentence for a long time. I wanted to say it out loud. To the person it was about."

"Lucian."

"Yes."

"Come here."

He came over. She put her hands on either side of his face. She kissed him — not the way she had kissed him at the altar three years ago, with everybody watching, but the way she had learned to kiss him across three years of ordinary Thursdays, the kind of kiss that said *yes, still, here, all of it* without saying any of those words out loud. She stepped back. She looked at his face. She said:

"You are the best man I know."

"I'm not."

"You are. It is unfair of me to have known this many good men and then to still say it. But it's true. You are the best man I know."

"All right."

"Now go get the book you were reading. I want us to sit on the porch. It's warm enough tonight. I'm going to bring the cabinetmakers down and we're going to read for a little while."

They went out on the porch. The porch swing creaked, a familiar sound that had become as natural as breathing. The lighthouse beam was already starting its nightly sweep. A fishing boat was coming in, the last one. The harbor was quiet.

Elena opened her book. Lucian opened his. They did not read, at first. They sat with their shoulders touching and watched the boat come in. After a while Lucian said, without looking up from the book he was not reading —

"Theodore wrote something in the last letter. In 1911. A few months before he died. It's the last thing he wrote in the box. I didn't include it in the volume because it didn't fit the scholarly frame. I kept thinking I'd show it to you sometime."

"Show me now."

"I memorized it. It's short." He was quiet for a moment, finding the words. "He wrote: *I have come, at last, to understand that the record I have kept of her is only a record, and that she is out there in the world, alive or dead, as she is, regardless of what I have preserved. If she is dead, she was loved, and my loving her did not reach her. If she is alive, she is loved, and my loving her did not reach her. The one and the other, and I must be content, because they are the only two possibilities, and both of them are outside the reach of my attention."*

She was quiet for a long time.

"That's very sad," she said finally.

"Yes."

"It's also, maybe, the most peaceful thing he ever wrote."

"Yes."

"I'm glad he got there."

"Me too."

"Lucian."

"Yes."

"I'm glad you got here."

"Me too."

They sat. The boat came in. The lighthouse kept its watch. She rested her head against his shoulder, and he put his arm around her, and after a while they did, finally, start reading — she the cabinetmakers, he his lighthouses — and they stayed on the porch until it got dark, and neither of them said anything else for a long time.

Inside the house, the kitchen was clean. The dishes were dry. The Archive was closed. The town of Camden's Rise was doing what it did every night at this hour, which was the ordinary quiet business of shutting down. And the two of them were on the porch swing, with the harbor in front of them and a hundred and forty-two years of lighthouse behind them, the way two people sit on a porch together after a day like any day, when what they are doing, by sitting there, is the whole thing — the entire thing — the only thing any love ever has to do in the end, which is keep going.

The End

The End

About the Author

Scarlett Vale writes contemporary romance with literary ambition. She is drawn to the quiet machinery of long love — memory, patience, restraint, and the courage it takes to let someone stay. *The Memory of Us* is her debut novel. She lives in Florida with her husband and son.

www.ingramcontent.com/pod-product-compliance
Lightning Source LLC
Chambersburg PA
CBHW070556260626
47161CB00002B/624